T0367563

INHERITED

Victoria Beer

authorHOUSE®

AuthorHouse™
1663 Liberty Drive
Bloomington, IN 47403
www.authorhouse.com
Phone: 833-262-8899

Published by AuthorHouse 07/28/2023

ISBN: 979-8-8230-1198-3 (sc)
ISBN: 979-8-8230-1199-0 (e)

Print information available on the last page.

PROLOGUE

Smoke billowed up from the valley rising above the treetops, almost blocking out the distant mountains.

"Izzy!"

Isabelle Hampton sat curled up on the floor with her back against the wall and her face buried in her lap. She raised her head at the sound of someone shouting her name. Curls of hair hung over her eyes as she blinked back the tears stinging her eyes from the choking black smoke. Above the sounds of the crackling fire, she heard the pounding of footfalls. Strong hands gripped her shoulders pulling her to her feet.

"Isabelle, you must get out of here!" Col. Hampton shouted above the roar of the blaze, the cracking of beams. Taking a firm hold of her arm, he shoved his daughter towards the stairway.

"Where's mother?" she asked, jerking free of his grasp, refusing to move any further, and turning to face him.

Ash creased the lines in his face as he stared hard at her. "You need not worry. I will get her!" the Col. shouted taking her by the wrist, he dragged her to the window.

"No, no!" she protested. "I won't leave you!"

Tears filled her eyes as she trembled with fear. Her father ignored her pleas and plunged on through the smoke and ash towards the stairs. Isabelle's long skirt caught on a jagged board. She stumbled as it halted her. She screamed as the skirt dragged her to her knees. Her father crouched down as a chunk of ceiling fell, missing them by inches. Col. Hampton crawled to her and pulled her into his arms. In a giant step, he lifted them both to their feet. The snagged skirt tore and remained clinging to the board as it released Isabelle from its grasp. He hurried away from the flaming carpet before the stairs and pressed their backs against the wall. Cupping her face in his dirty hands Col. Hampton gazed into his daughter's frightened face.

"Don't be afraid."

Isabelle's chin quavered as she stared at her father; tears spilled down her cheeks.

"I will get you out of this." He touched his forehead to hers for but a second. His gaze shot to the roof, which gave an ominous rumble as it sagged. Isabelle trembled and clung to his chest. Looking at his daughter, Col. Hampton gave her a squeeze. He placed his massive hands on her shoulders and stepped away from her. As he held her at arm's length, his eyes brimmed with tears. Isabelle grasped for him, not wanting him to let her go.

"We can't go that way. How will we escape?" Isabelle began to sob.

The Col. pulled her further along the wall. The floor swayed beneath their feet. They looked at each other.

"The fire is downstairs," Isabelle murmured.

He looked down at the floor which was the ceiling of the drawing room.

"Hannah…"

Isabelle grabbed his charred sleeve. "No, father, no."

The color drained form his face. With a sad shake of his head, he propelled them both forward. "I promised to get you out. I will."

The floor cracked open under his feet and one of his legs fell through. Isabelle clung to his sleeve and fell as the Col. lost his footing. The Col. bellowed as the jagged wood tore through trouser and flesh.

He gripped her tight to balance himself and keep her nearby. "I will not lose you too!" His eyes took on a wild expression. He hoisted himself from the hole and again hefted Isabelle to her feet. Isabelle stopped moving as his hands locked onto her waist. The Col. scooped her into his arms.

"I love you."

Isabelle looked into his streaked face. "Father."

He turned to the window, laid a kiss upon her cheek, and heaved with all his strength. His actions startled her so that she did not even scream. Glass shards spewed as she broke through the pane. Her tattered skirts fluttered as she took flight. A piece of the ceiling tore away from the from the roof and landed where she had been standing, crashing through to the lower level. Isabelle sat up trembling, but unhurt, in the shrubbery surrounding the house. She could feel the heat from the flames. Horrified, she looked on as the ranch house disappeared under a veil of flames. Her vision blurred and a half-chocked sob escaped her.

CHAPTER 1

Southampton, England. April 21, 1820,

The sun fought down through the gray mist off the sea and illuminated the ships waiting by the docks as their sails wafted in the breeze. Ship bells and gulls screeching echoed above the crashing of the waves on the harbor shoreline. Standing on the ship's deck, Isabelle looked out across the sea; her hair tossed about her cheeks. She studied the cliffs above her as the vessel pulled into port. For the past fourteen weeks, she had been bound to a boat crossing the ocean, destined for a country she had only heard of from her father. Standing by the ship's rail, she felt alone in the company of strangers. The past few months had done nothing but left her frightened and miserable. She bit her lip to keep it from quavering while pushing back loose strands of her long hair. She let it dangle and allowed it to dance in the breeze.

As the ship neared the port, she cast her eyes over the harbor: Southampton. Rows of squat buildings crowded tight to the water's edge above the coastline. The lack of sunshine made the dark buildings and landscape look even more dreary. The weather stained the docks a dull gray. The roads reflected gray stone. The buildings had gray roofs. Even the grass was gray. Isabelle's young heart nearly broke at the sight. This foreign land felt nothing like her America.

Her home was wild and bursting with life while this place seemed old and almost sad.

Excited chatter rose around her as people bustled around deck. A crew of leathery men managed the rigging and railings as the gangway swung into place, connecting the ship to the dock. Soon people were clamoring down it and crowding onto the dock. Hugs and cheers celebrated the meetings of relatives and friends. The crewmen shouted and a whistle sounded. Strange accents accosted her ears from the dock workers who hollered at one another across the pier. Strange smells hung in the air and made her feel ill. Isabelle glanced about as she picked her way down the wooden gangplank. Every step saw her bumped and jostled by the confusion around her.

Setting her suitcase down beside her, she worried they might not come for her. She grew faint at the idea. Isabelle fought back the tears stinging her eyes. After all, she had never met this Sara Dawson who had sent for her. The woman could have changed her mind. Lots could happen in fourteen weeks. She stood away from the rest of the passengers looking as pitiful as she felt.

If her parents had not died, she never would have gone to a stranger in a country halfway around the world. England. She left her beautiful America for this. *A chance at a new life*, the letter had said. Isabelle read it so many times the words had nearly faded off the page. Isabelle doubted anything could be new in a town as old as Southampton.

"Who would want to live here?" the bitter words escaped her lips before she knew what she was saying.

A man brushing past her stopped and looked at her; Isabelle

could feel the heat rise in her cheeks. She looked away from him. He cleared his throat.

"Miss Isabelle Hampton, I presume?"

Isabelle shifted under his gaze.

"Your aunt is expecting you."

Isabelle frowned. "And who are you?"

The older gentleman gave a weary sigh. "I am the butler, madame. Your aunt sent me to collect you."

An image of a doddering old woman flashed through Isabelle's mind. "She didn't come?"

"She sends her regrets. Now, where is your luggage?"

She looked down at her lone suitcase. It looked a bit abused. "This is everything I have."

He muttered something under his breath while picking up the suitcase. They made their way through the crowd to a fine carriage, which sat at the edge of the dock. Two smartly matched bay horses stood waiting to convey her on the next phase of her journey.

As they approached the carriage, one of the attendants stepped forward and took the suitcase while the other helped Isabelle onto the carriage's cushioned seat. The butler muttered something to the attendant before climbing into the carriage, taking the seat across from Isabelle. At a whistle from the driver, the horses leapt forward. With a bit of clattering and a small lurch, the carriage was underway. Isabelle peeked out the window as they rolled along through Southampton. Before long, the sights of town turned to meadows and forests. The rolling English countryside slipped past as the bays moved along at a brisk trot. Isabelle looked across at the butler. He seemed asleep. She sighed, leaning back into the soft seats, and gazed out the carriage window. *What if Aunt Sara does not like me?* She raised her gloved fingers to her lips at the thought.

Before long, the green scenery included a low stone wall. Isabelle occupied herself with trying to see the house that belonged to it. She spotted a large mansion through the trees. Never in all her life had she seen a house that big. The carriage house alone looked like an average home where she lived.

A chuckle across from her turned Isabelle's attention to the butler. "That would be Lexington Estate home of Mister Edmond Walsh."

Isabelle looked again at the estate. "He must be very rich," she mused.

The butler rubbed his chin. "I would say he has a few thousand pounds to his name."

Isabelle sat back from the window while the butler kept an eager watch.

Suddenly, a contented smile crossed his face. "Ah, there it is. And this is your Brooklyn Manor, miss," he said, not a moment later.

Isabelle moved closer to the window and gazed upon her destination. The brick house stood tall with its many windows reflecting the morning sun. A large pond sat off to the right of the house and ran into the creek winding through the property. Nestled to the left, were the stable and carriage house. To the right of the house was an orchard of fruit trees. Isabelle held her breath as she tried to look at everything all at once. The carriage rolled up the drive and came to a halt in front of the mansion. The attendant opened the door and guided Isabelle to the ground; the butler retrieved her suitcase and led the way to the house.

Before they reached the bottom step, the door flew open, and a woman rushed out with her skirts streaming behind her. A tall dark-haired man dressed in a black tailcoat followed her. The woman glided down the stairs like a hummingbird floating on the breeze. She paused before Isabelle and took her hands in her own. Her bright eyes reflected kindness.

"My dear girl, how I worried about you making such a trip alone!" she spoke with a clear accent like her butler.

Isabelle ducked her head, feeling a touch ashamed about thinking Aunt Sara was a doddering old woman. Here stood a woman no older than her own mother. The man stepped forward offering her a friendly smile.

"Hello, Miss Hampton, it is good to finally have you safely in England. I am Phillip Dawson, and this is my wife, Sara."

Isabelle nodded politely, offering a small curtsy.

"It's a pleasure to meet you. There are no words to express how grateful I am to you for taking me in."

Tears swelled in her eyes as she thought about all that had happened in her life these last few months. Sara's expression grew soft.

"Dawson and I are quite pleased to have you here with us," she said gently. "Come. Let us show you to your room. Mansfield," she turned to the butler--"please bring Miss Hampton's things to her room."

Sara put her arm around Isabelle's shoulders. "My, such a fine young lady. How old are you, child?" she asked, leading the way up the stairs while her husband retired to the parlor.

"Eighteen, my lady," Isabelle replied, admiring the house as they walked.

Sara's smile lit her whole face. "Such a pretty girl."

Isabelle wiped away a stray tear with the back of her hand. Sara's sharp eyes noticed the movement. Her smile faded. They stopped in front of a door where Sara released the younger woman.

"This will be your room. If you are not comfortable, we can find you a more suitable space," Sara announced, opening the door, and stepping inside.

The room was large with a window facing east with a view of the fields and stables. A dressing table with a mirror above it stood along the north wall next to the bed and in the corner was an empty bookcase and chair.

Sara smiled as Isabelle ran her fingers along the scrolling of the bookcase. "I thought I would let you build your own collection from the library downstairs," she explained.

Isabelle looked up, wide-eyed. "You have a library?"

Sara nodded, noting the change in the girl's countenance. "Yes, of course, but if you don't find anything of interest, we can pick out some books on our next visit to Southampton."

"I'm sure I will find something I like. Thank you," Isabelle replied, glancing out the window. Her hair hung limp around her thin shoulders while the off-white dress made her look paler than she really was. Her gaze was forlorn as she stood soberly looking out the window.

Sara watched the girl drift off into another world. "Very well then. I will send in Heather. She is to be your maid. I feel confident she will be a good fit for you. You may want to rest, so I will take my leave now." She excused herself before she turned to go.

"Please wait!" There was a small plea in Isabelle's voice.

Sara stopped and faced the young woman expectantly. Isabelle moved away from the window and stood timidly before her aunt.

"What would you have me call you?" Isabelle's eyes showed concern and uncertainty.

Sara's shoulders softened. "Aunt Sara is fine, child." She offered a kind smile. "What shall I call you?"

Isabelle relaxed a little. "You may call me whatever you like." Sara tried to hide her smile. "My father used to call me Izzy," she finished softly; her eyes brimmed with tears as she bowed her head.

Sara's face took on a look of reverence. "Out of respect for your father, shall I call you Isabelle?" Sara asked tenderly.

Isabelle gave a tearful nod, willing the tears away. "Aunt Sara?" she asked tentatively.

"Yes, Isabelle?" "Thank you for welcoming me into your home."

"Not a problem, child. You are part of the family. Now get some rest."

CHAPTER 2

Lexington Estate,

The wooden door slammed, echoing through the house, narrowly missing Edmond Walsh's coat tails as he marched into his home. A servant rushed to his side.

"Master Walsh, I am terribly sorry for sending for you while you were out," the butler babbled, wringing his hands.

Walsh held up a gloved hand to cease the man. "Mr. Collins, I am not in the least upset by your request for me. There is obviously a matter of importance which requires my attention," he replied, in a rich tone.

Collins nodded. "Yes sir, the importance is in the library."

Walsh's brown eyes held merriment as he listened to the worried servant. "Very well Mr. Collins, I will take over now."

Collins nodded his agreement and went on his way.

Walsh chuckled, running his fingers through his dark hair before moving on to the library. The large double doors swung open to reveal an auburn-haired man facing the rows of books.

"Heavens, Weston! What on earth are you doing here?" Walsh

exclaimed as the man turned around, his eyes smiling but his expression blank, almost angry.

"Not much for greetings, are we?" he muttered, tossing a book on the sofa.

"Ought I greet the man who invaded my home? I received not so much as a whisper of your coming."

The guest straightened and cleared his throat. "Master Walsh, you should know by now I do not send word before dropping in for tea." The deep baritone sent a bewildered Walsh onto the arm of the sofa.

"Is that why you are here, cousin? Tea?"

"Yes, of course that's part of it, but my visit is not primarily a social call," Weston replied, lowering his six-foot three-inch frame into a tall, velvet wingback chair and stretching his long legs out before him. He crossed his polished tall black leather boots at the ankles.

"Well, are you going to tell me the other reason or leave it in suspense?" Walsh asked, annoyed by his cousin's silence.

"After you ring for tea."

Walsh held a look of disapproval while he rang for Collins. "Mr. Collins, it seems Mr. Weston will have tea. Please see to it," he announced when the butler appeared in the doorway. "Oh, and he will need a biscuit, I'm sure."

Collins nodded and departed.

Weston picked up the book he had tossed on the sofa and began flipping through it; Walsh gave a dry chuckle.

"Weston, must you be so odd?"

The bright eyes looked up quizzically. "Odd? Cousin, I have had many titles in my six and twenty years but never "odd.""

Walsh nodded absently. "I would believe people would refer to you by all sorts of names, although why not "odd" is beyond me for you certainly are. But it seems the last time I saw you, you actually smiled."

Collins arrived then and set before them a tray of tea and crumpets.

"Will that be all, sir?"

Walsh nodded. "Yes Mr. Collins, thank you."

The two men sat in silence for a few moments each with a teacup in hand.

"I see no reason to be jovial at this point," Weston finally replied breaking the silence.

"Is that the reason for your unexpected visit?"

Weston set his cup and saucer aside. "No, not exactly. My mother has not enjoyed my company in London lately. Honestly, she has grown wearisome as well."

Walsh frowned. "Goodness man! Henley being the size that it is and yet you still manage to get on poor Aunt Phoebe's nerves."

"The woman is impossible!" Weston retorted. "My point is, I find London dreadfully boring. Always the same old things happening, never anything new. The theatre, the parties, it is all so monotonous." He rubbed his jaw thoughtfully, his blue eyes studying the bookshelf. "I think a change of scenery would be welcome."

Walsh smiled, shifting his position on the couch's arm. "You never could stand to be idle."

Weston's eyes narrowed in annoyance. "Who could? Especially if one lives with an old woman who is constantly throwing any somewhat charming lady at you in the hopes that you will marry one of them! No, no, I could bear it no longer. Few could tolerate it for so long as I have."

Walsh cocked his head to one side. "Why would you come to me?" he asked, confused. "You couldn't possibly wish to stay at Lexington."

Weston leaned back into his chair folding his hands behind his head. "My dear cousin, you underestimate me. Country living may prove beneficial. That is if you could endure me for an unspecified length of time," he said smoothly.

Walsh's eyes grew large. "Certainly! Just think of the times we shall have! I invite you to stay for as long you wish."

Weston rubbed his chin. "Hmm, yes the times, as long as word of our pursuits never reaches Madame Weston's ears."

Brooklyn Manor

"Aunt Sara, you sent for me?"

Sara looked up from her writing desk to see Isabelle standing before her with her hands clasped behind her back.

"Yes dear, seeing how this is your second week at Brooklyn, I feel we should journey into Southampton and see about getting you some things."

"What sorts of things?" Isabelle inquired.

Sara pulled a fresh piece of paper from the stack on the desk and dipped her quill pen into the jar of ink. "You will need new clothing, gowns, hats, gloves. You shall have a lady's wardrobe. You are, after all, a Hampton, and you will be a proper young lady."

Isabelle gave a slight shudder as her aunt added more items to the list.

Sara set her pen aside and studied her niece: Isabelle wore her golden-brown hair twisted up and pulled back from her delicate cheeks, revealing her eyes hidden behind fragile lashes.

"Aunt Sara?" She stirred from her assessment at the sound of Isabelle's genteel voice. "When will we leave for Southampton?"

Sara folded the list and stood. "As soon as possible. I have rung for the carriage; it will be here shortly."

"Can I wait in the library?" Although it was her second week at Brooklyn, she was just beginning to snoop around.

Sara smiled. "Go ahead, dear, while I finish this letter."

Isabelle gave a slight curtsy before exiting the room.

Once in the hall, she hastened her way to the top of the stairs and fairly flew down them on her decent. The library doors swung open to her touch, and she found herself in a room edged with ceiling high shelves lined with books. She sighed and walked along one of the shelves, brushing her fingers along the spines. A fire crackled in the corner fireplace of the room as she removed a book of poems from the shelf and settled into a chair. Absently, she started reading.

"Miss Hampton?" Isabelle opened her eyes as Heather gently roused her.

"Heavens! Did I sleep long?" Isabelle asked, straightening up.

The book slid off her lap onto the floor. Heather bent down to pick it up, setting it on a side table.

"No Miss, Mrs. Dawson only just sent for you," Heather replied, fixing Isabelle's skirts as she stood and smoothed down her hair.

Sara and Isabelle seated themselves in the carriage and took seats across from each other. Isabelle stifled a yawn. As the carriage passed Lexington Estate, both women turned to the window. A wagon loaded with trunks stood in front of the mansion; servants bustled back and forth carrying them into the house.

"It seems Mr. Walsh has a guest," Sara commented as the house disappeared behind the trees.

Isabelle smiled leaning back into her seat. "Maybe he has also been out shopping."

Sara's bright laugh lightened the gray mood Isabelle found herself in this morning. "Mr. Walsh is an amusing gentleman; he often rides in the back fields of Brooklyn, and he calls on us whenever he is in the vicinity."

Isabelle was suddenly curious about their neighbor. "He is a horseman?"

Sara nodded. "Yes, and a fine one at that. He used to ride quite a bit more than has been lately; he very much enjoys it."

"Does he have family nearby?"

"None that I know personally. He has a sister who is married and lives in Brighton. Their parents died some time ago, leaving a large inheritance to Mr. Walsh."

Sara cocked her head to one side, her eyes narrowed. "I believe there is an aunt in London, but I know very little about her."

Isabelle nodded as understanding dawned on her. "Oh, then Mr. Walsh is an older man."

Sara's laugh startled Isabelle. "Heavens no, child! I do believe he is no more than five and twenty," she exclaimed with a twinkle in her eyes. "He wouldn't be much older than you."

That evening when the ladies returned to Brooklyn, Dawson met them at the door as the carriage attendant and Mansfield brought in the packages.

"Well, my dear, do all the shops in Southampton have empty shelves?" he asked with a smile as he surveyed the parlor heaped full of packages and parcels.

"Rubbish, Mr. Dawson. I assure you the shops in Southampton are fine. Our Isabelle had nothing when she arrived." Sara went on looking through the packages, unfazed by her husband's jest. Isabelle smiled as her aunt instructed a servant to put the packages in her room. "Heather will put your things away in their proper places." Sara rang for tea and settled herself into the sofa; she patted the seat next to her. "Come and sit."

Isabelle, who had begun to follow the servant upstairs, returned and sat beside her aunt on the sofa. Sara gave her a warm smile.

"I think it is time we discuss a few things," she began, as a tray of tea was set before them. Dawson sat within earshot reading a newspaper. "When you arrived, I had hopes of turning you into a lady, but I see now you have had an excellent upbringing, all you need is a little polish here and there."

Isabelle smile modestly.

Sara continued, "Also, you will soon be of marrying age. In the next few years, I expect we will find you a suitable husband."

Dawson's eyebrows rose above the paper.

A look of astonishment crossed Isabelle's face. "Aunt Sara, I..."

Dawson coughed, cutting off her response. The distraction ended her aunt's talk of marriage, for the time being.

"Aunt Sara, can I borrow a book of poems I found in your library?" Isabelle asked, changing the subject as she finished her tea.

Sara nodded. "Of course, you may." She looked at Dawson. "You might also want to go early to bed. You have had a busy day."

Isabelle stood and excused herself.

"One more thing, I would like it very much if you would wear the blue dress tomorrow; it looks so lovely on you." Sara flashed her a loving smile.

"Yes, I like it too. Thank you for all you have done today."

"Not a problem, dear."

Isabelle hugged her aunt around the neck.

"Goodnight."

"Goodnight, Isabelle." Sara watched as the girl quickly hugged Dawson before disappearing from the room. Sara smiled with joyful pride. "Phillip, she is a wonderful girl."

Dawson looked up from the newspaper. "Yes, she is." His eyes

_____

turned back to the page. "I am very glad she has come to Brooklyn," he added.

"So am I. She brings such life. Our home now feels complete."

Dawson reach over and squeezed his wife's hand, without looking away from his paper. "My darling, our family was never incomplete."

Sara bowed her head, her gaze falling on their intertwined fingers. "Of course." She grew quiet for a moment before rousing herself. "Now, Mr. Dawson, you won't spoil her, will you?"

Dawson looked indignant. "Why ever not? You have already had a head start on doing so." Sara looked ready to protest, but he continued. "Besides, what else is one to do with a girl?" He leaned in and gave his wife a quick kiss.

CHAPTER 3

The hoofbeats echoed across the courtyard of Lexington Estate as Walsh and Weston started off on a morning ride.

"That sunrise is spectacular. What a glorious day!" Walsh exclaimed moving his mount into a brisk trot. "Don't you think?"

"The weather is agreeable," Weston answered keeping the pace.

Walsh laughed. "Agreeable? Oh Weston, must you always be so obtuse?"

"You consider me obtuse?"

"Well, perhaps it's more like a higher level of propriety."

Weston's eyes held a mysterious twinkled as he tapped the heels of his boots into his mount's sides.

They cantered the horses through the backfields of hills and trees, jumping deadfall as they went along. They cut across the fields and jumped a pile of rocks running along the border.

"That is Brooklyn Manor." Walsh pointed to the mansion and slowed his horse to a walk. "Home of Mr. and Mrs. Phillip Dawson. They have invited me to ride in the fields whenever I wish and to call upon them as often as I can."

Weston looked over the well-kept grounds. "They sound like a couple of old busy bodies who have nothing better to do than manipulate your free time for they have not the ability nor inclination to leave the comforts of their own home."

Walsh laughed, appalled at the response his comment received. "Really, what a bitter old sap you are."

Weston shrugged but made no move to defend himself. "Perhaps they are perfectly charming."

Walsh smiled. "Indeed, they are. Shall we pay them a visit?"

"If you insist. I suppose I would enjoy meeting the couple who has seduced you into becoming their source of neighborhood gossip," Weston replied as they turned the horses in the direction of the mansion and continued at an easy trot.

"You certainly have venomous words against neighborhood gossips when you yourself were once the most well informed of all."

"That may be, but my information came from the soft lips of the frivolous girls, not the shrivelled vocal cords of an old woman."

Walsh laughed, none concerned with his cousin's banter.

While they were still a ways from the house, something in the orchard caught Weston's attention. It was a woman dressed in a blue gown surrounded by small bright green spring leaves and perched high up in the branches of one of the fruit trees.

He gave a slight chuckle. "And what is it you find amusing?" asked a puzzled Walsh.

Weston nodded in the direction of the orchard. "That would be Mrs. Dawson I, presume? She is younger than I anticipated."

Walsh frowned, squinting to get a better look at the figure in the tree. "Good heavens! I dare say that is not Mrs. Dawson. She is very much a lady, I assure you," Walsh stated.

Weston grinned wickedly. "When you say she is 'quite a lady' you confirm that she is old and too feeble to be climbing trees." Weston chuckled.

Walsh gave him an exasperated look. "Weston, you astonish me. Your behavior is tiresome indeed this morning. I am not the least bit surprised your mother grew ill of your company," Walsh said disapprovingly.

Weston sighed. "You are correct to rebuke me, cousin, I seem out of manners today. From this point on you shall find me a perfect gentleman."

They continued in silence until reaching the orchard where Walsh greeted the young woman in the fruit tree.

"Good morning, Miss."

Isabelle started with a small gasp. She dropped the book she had been reading and clung to a branch so as not to tumble out of the tree.

"I am terribly sorry for startling you," Walsh replied hastily, as Weston stepped down from his horse to retrieve the book from the grass below the tree.

"I shouldn't let myself get so engrossed in a book." Isabelle tried to conceal her embarrassment. She fluffed her skirts around herself.

Weston looked up at her while tucking the book under his arm; Isabelle wished there were enough leaves in the tree to conceal her. He offered her his hand. "Might I assist you down from your perch, my lady?"

"Oh my, I fear I might fall. I can come down once you've gone." Isabelle blushed and groped around the tree as if to steady herself among the branches.

"If you feel you may fall, then it is best to come down while there is aide. I will catch you. No harm will come to you."

Isabelle dared a look at the man beneath her. He stood tall and elegant. Although his expression was blank, she felt he looked amused. He gave his wrist a flick in his direction, beckoning her to climb towards him. Her body tingled with nervous energy. Having roamed the woods on her American estate, she considered herself nimble, although it was not the most ladylike trait. Now with these two Englishmen as onlookers, she really did fear she would fall. The thought of causing a scene filled her with dread. She already was a spectacle.

She took a determined breath and raised her chin. As delicately as she could she stepped towards a lower branch and accepted the offered hand. He wore riding gloves, and the leather felt soft against her skin. Her gaze flickered to the other man still on horseback. He tipped his head to the side and regarded her curiously. Isabelle looked back to her guide as he escorted her down the tree. His grip on her was firm, but gentle and his arm felt strong as he supported her when she hopped down. Pulling her to himself, he stabilized her on the ground. Isabelle flushed with humiliation as she brushed against his chest.

"Thank you, Mr.?" she said shyly as her eyes met his.

"Weston, Miss."

He stood rigid his expression unreadable, but his touch was soft, and his eyes searched hers before he stepped back from her.

Walsh dismounted and took hold of both horses' bridles. "Might we escort you to the house? We have come to pay a call on the Dawsons."

Isabelle's face lit up; she was eager to forget this incident. "Aunt Sara will be glad to see you." She turned and led the way to the house.

Weston looked at Walsh as he took his horse, hoping Walsh might know who she was. A perplexed Walsh shrugged. Isabelle hurried up the house steps followed by Weston while Walsh paused to hand the horses over to a groom.

Mansfield met them at the door. "Miss Hampton, your aunt has been looking for you," he said as she pushed open the door. He swept a small branch off her shoulder with a frown. Isabelle beamed at him. He squared his shoulders. "Do come inside at once. Ah, good morning to you, Mr. Walsh," he added with a curt nod towards Weston as the two men stepped into the entrance.

"Mansfield, where is Aunt Sara? These men have come to visit."

"She is in the parlor, miss," came Mansfield's reply. "But your aunt has instructed me to--"

"Thank you. Now don't worry. I will see the company to her myself. This way please." Isabelle guided the gentlemen down the hall, deftly circumventing the butler with the raised brow. He gave a small harrumph, rolling the twig between his fingers.

"Aunt Sara?" Isabelle called as she swung open the parlor door.

Sara raised her head from her needlepoint. "There you are child!" she said with a frown as her eyes landed on the girl. "Mansfield informed me you were climbing trees this morning! I dare say Isabelle I hope it is not true. We certainly cannot condone such--" Sara took pause as she noticed the two other people with Isabelle. Her frown disappeared as she rose to greet them, shoving her sewing aside. "Mr. Walsh, I didn't realize we had company. How good of you to call."

Walsh bowed at the waist. "Mrs. Dawson, the pleasure is ours. But we may have come at an inconvenient time."

"Not at all. Nothing pressing that cannot wait." She shot Isabelle a pointed look as she spoke.

Walsh put on a bright smile and laid his hand on Weston's shoulder. "Yes, then, I am glad of that. But first, I would like to introduce you to my cousin, Robert Weston; he will be staying at Lexington for a spell."

Weston bowed. "Pleasure to make your acquaintance, madame. You have a lovely home."

Sara's cheeks flushed as she met his gaze. Perhaps it was the man's striking features, or his piercing blue eyes that set a blush to her skin. "Mr. Weston, so good to meet a relation of Mr. Walsh. He has been our comfortable companion for many years. I feel confident you will enjoy your stay Lexington Estate. There is not a finer home nor better company for miles around." She diverted her gaze from the man and caught a pleased smile on the neighborly face of Mr. Walsh.

"Yes, indeed, Madame. Mr. Walsh is a fine host."

Sara smiled at the young men. "Mr. Walsh, I suppose you have heard our news by now. It seems there has been an addition to our household as well," Sara paused and indicated Isabelle take a step forward. "This is my niece, Isabelle Hampton."

Isabelle gave a shy curtsey while the two men bowed.

"She is the only daughter of my dearly departed nephew. He and his wife settled in America many years ago. Please, will you sit?" She gestured around the seating arrangement before continuing. "Quite surprised we were to receive the letter informing us of the dreadful fire at their home. The whole ordeal has been an event for poor Isabelle. Losing her parents, and then crossing the ocean to come here to live with my husband and I, well. None of it is easy." Sara looked upon the girl with a kind smile. Isabelle's complexion had grayed.

Walsh nodded. "That is a most horrid event. Miss Hampton, heaven only knows what you suffered." Walsh's expression was sympathetic, but Isabelle could not help feeling a bit perturbed. She flashed him a whisper of a smile. He continued: "What an experience you have had! I can only imagine what it is like to travel across the world. That would be trying enough. And to lose one's parents as well! My parents passed several years ago, a painful enough loss I assure you, but to relocate somewhere away from your home must make it unbearable."

Isabelle bit her lip, wishing the subject had never arisen. Now more than ever did she feel like crying, to run and lock herself in her room until she could never cry again. She looked down at her hands in her lap, willing herself not to cry.

She heard her aunt's response. "Great atrocity this has been. The poor girl has suffered a great deal. Dawson and I are trying our best to make the transition manageable for her. But despite our best efforts, it is challenging. So much adjusting on her part!"

Isabelle suddenly began drowning in emotions as memories flooded back to her in a rush that made her head swim. Images appeared in her mind with absolute clarity giving her the impression she could touch the scenes if only she were to reach out her hand.

Closing her eyes, she tried to focus on the conversation between Walsh and Aunt Sara. The tears would not halt, and they slipped down her cheeks. A handkerchief appeared before her. She accepted the handkerchief through the tearful blur. She glanced up in thanks but dared not trust herself to maintain her composure and so lowered her gaze again to her lap. She caught a fleeting glimpse of Mr. Weston's furrowed brow and outstretched fingers.

"You are unwell, Miss Hampton." Weston's voice, though deep, barely carried to her amid the conversation occurring around them.

Isabelle dabbed her eyes, aiming to avoid further attention. "I might be." Her words shook as she spoke. "I think I will go to my room."

"Do you require assistance?"

An image of her father came to mind. Such a simple question but tied to so many memories. Her chin trembled. How would this strange man ever know what she was thinking? She must certainly appear sensitive. She raised her head as much as she dared, uncomfortable to look at him. "Thank you, but I'll be fine." She took a quivering breath, trying to compose herself. As she offered back the handkerchief her eyes fluttered to his face. She paused. His eyes held such a look of compassion. Their gentle expression captivated her for a moment. There was no other emotion in his stony features.

"I hope you feel better, Miss Hampton."

The pressing weight of tears behind her eyes caused her to burn with a sense of urgency. "Thank you, Mr. Weston." She rose abruptly, ending the conversation.

Walsh looked surprised as the two men also got to their feet. Sara gave a slight start. "Isabelle, is everything alright?"

Isabelle opened her mouth, but the words felt strangled on her tongue.

"Miss Hampton has taken ill, madame. It may be best if she rests." Weston gave her the smallest nod, almost encouraging her to take her leave.

Isabelle would have smiled at him if she had not felt so dreadful.

"Oh, Isabelle. I will see you to your room." Sara moved as if to stand.

Isabelle found her voice. "Stay, please, Aunt Sara, I will be fine." Isabelle touched a hand to her cheek, drawing back from the group.

Reluctantly, Sara returned to her seat.

Another voice drew Isabelle's attention. Her insides quaked with the need to escape as she turned to face Mr. Walsh. "I am sorry you have taken ill, Miss Hampton. You have my sympathy and wishes for a full recovery." He looked so earnest that Isabelle felt guilty for feeling a bit irked with him for delaying her flight.

"That's very kind." The comment sounded flat, even to her. She added, "Perhaps we will see you again sometime soon." Lowering her eyes, Isabelle moved past them.

A shimmer of movement from Robert Weston halted her. He removed the book of poems from his waistcoat pocket. "Inopportune, but I believe this is yours." He looked a bit uncomfortable as he turned the book in his hand.

Isabelle extended her hand. "Yes, thank you. You've kept it for me. I'll take it now."

He relinquished the book and Isabelle noted the warmth of his hand. They paused, but she did not run. She got the impression he had more to say. He lingered a moment, appeared to debate within himself. Slowly, he spoke again. "Might I call upon you tomorrow?" His words were so quiet she doubted the others had heard the request.

She nodded, afraid of an emotional outpouring should she open her mouth again. He nodded once and bowed his head as she exited the room. Once in the hall, Isabelle fairly ran to her room. Throwing shut the door, she heaved herself face down onto her bed and sobbed. The pillows became wet in an instant. England. America. Ships. Ocean passages. Distant relatives. Strange men. It all felt too much for her in this moment. So many changes, so many hurts. She grieved for her parents and mourned for her life. She longed for the colonial house and the vast landscape. She wept for the people she would never see again. She cried for all that she left behind. She shook with fear over all the newness that lay ahead. The voyage across the ocean was only the beginning. Nothing had prepared her for what would come next: polite English society. Rules, and status, and etiquette she did not understand. New places, and people and expectations. Servants, and handmaids, and an old butler who would snitch on her if she stepped out of line. No, no, it was too much. Fresh tears flowed and sobs wracked her body.

CHAPTER 4

Isabelle did not know how long Sara had sat at her side. She looked over her shoulder when she became aware of a gentle touch on her head. Sara sat stroking her hair.

"Will it ever go away?" Isabelle spoke into the pillow between sobs.

Sara looked at Isabelle's quavering body. "No child the pain of loss never completely disappears." She laid her hands in her lap and her expression took on a distant look. "But it does become less."

"How many years will that take?" A hard edge wound itself around Isabelle's words.

Sara squeezed the girl's shoulder. "Isabelle, I know it is hard to do, but you cannot move on while holding onto the past. I know it feels impossible, but you must let go and begin to accept what has happened. I understand everything for you has changed. It must frighten you. Phillip and I are here to help you. Please, dear girl, we are your family, and this is your home. You must accept this while you grieve. Only then can you begin to heal."

Isabelle raised her tear reddened eyes to meet the compassion in Sara's. She bit her lip. "Everything I know is gone."

Sara nodded. "Yes, life has taken a sudden turn."

The answer was no more than a quavering whisper. "Everyone I ever loved is gone."

Sara swallowed, tears filling her own eyes. "Could you love me?" she asked opening her arms towards Isabelle.

Fresh tears traced down Isabelle's face. She looked at this woman who opened her home and her heart towards her. Inside, Isabelle trembled. Many changes, yes, but maybe this was a good change. So many things Isabelle could never get back, but she could have something new. The girl nodded and moved into her aunt's embrace.

Lexington Estate,

As the two cousins strode down the halls of Lexington Estate, Walsh shot Weston a lopsided smile. "I take it, Master Weston, you think highly of the Hampton girl?"

A deep chuckle sounded from Weston. "Really, Walsh, such an accusation."

"I will not be put off that easily! Now, out with it. You fancy her."

"Actually, far from it."

Walsh shot his cousin an odd look, cocking his head to one side. "You spoke to her and aided her."

Weston heaved a bored sigh. "Your attentions were engaged elsewhere."

"Rubbish. She is quite an attractive lady."

"Does Mr. Dawson know you say such things of his wife?"

"Oh really, Weston. You know I speak of Miss Hampton."

"I know not of what you speak. I rarely do."

Walsh grunted in exasperation. "You really are impossible. I say you took a fancy to Miss Hampton. She seems a keen girl and you cannot deny she is quite pretty."

"Whom we found in a tree," Weston murmured beneath his breath.

"Perhaps a bit eccentric, but that just adds to the exotic charm."

Weston stopped and gave his cousin a hard look. "Exotic? She is from America not the Indies."

"Despite your criticisms, you seemed rather taken with her. You even asked to call on her tomorrow."

Weston sighed lacing his fingers together and stretching his arms out before him. "It would be uncouth to show no concern for our young hostess. The girl was obviously distraught; the polite thing would be to return at a more appropriate time."

Walsh shook his head in mock amazement. "Weston, be careful what you do. The last thing that poor girl needs is to have her heart broken by an old impassive chap like you."

Weston stared blankly past Walsh. "I have no intention to harm her."

Walsh stopped and turned to face him. "You don't think she has anything to be desired?"

Weston plucked a horsehair from his coat. "Of course, she does. She appears rather charming, but she is a mere child; do you not agree?"

Walsh gazed into space a moment, a twinkle lighting his dark eyes. "I suppose she is young. I for one would like to know her better...much better." His voice trailed off into a dream state mutter.

Weston slapped him on the shoulder, perhaps a little harder than affection required. "Well then cousin, I shall not stand in your way." He turned down the hall towards his room. "Another thing, that poor girl doesn't need a Casanova such as yourself toying with her affections either."

Walsh cocked a brow. "I will behave myself."

Weston nodded with approval. "Good. I would take your word for it, but I will prefer to keep my sights on the situation. Keep me appraised." His long stride carried him from Walsh to his room. Closing the door behind him, he shook his head, retrieving a small leather case from a trunk in the corner. Again, he gave his head a slight shake before laying the case on the bed and opening it. The flickering candlelight reflected in the polished wood revealed inside. Gently, Weston lifted out the violin. Cradling it under his chin, he pulled the bow across the strings and a harmonious chord rang from the small instrument. Weston smiled sliding the bow along the strings making the violin sing as he continued to play his thoughts away.

Brooklyn Manor,

Isabelle had curled herself into the library's large wingback chair and sat engrossed in the book of poems.

Sara appeared in the doorway. "Isabelle? Are you here?"

Isabelle sat up and greeted her aunt. "Yes, ma'am."

Sara leaned against the doorframe.

"I spoke with Dawson last night about you."

Isabelle's face darkened with a wary look.

"Do not fret, my dear. He has a niece of about your age who lives but five miles from Brooklyn. He thinks you two would get on famously. I think having another young person in the house might help you adjust. Might I send a letter to ask if she would come for a visit?"

Isabelle's eyes lit up at the prospect of having a houseguest her own age. "Oh, Aunt Sara!" she exclaimed. "Yes, please do. I would like to meet her."

Sara chuckled. "There now, I shall write to her this morning."

Sara departed before Isabelle could bombard her with curiosity about the girl. Isabelle hoped she would agree to come, but she feared she might not want to come. Or worse, she might agree to come, but might not be interesting. Nothing could be worse than a boring houseguest! Isabelle would be miserable if the girl were not at all friendly or failed to provide any distraction. Isabelle decided to bury herself books until word came about what the niece wished to do. Into the world of fiction she flung herself and alone in the private of the library, she read aloud with dramatic affect:

"The bridegroom's doors are opened wide, and I am the next of kin; the guests are met, the feast is set: May'st hear the merry din."

"What a lovely ballad." The deep voice broke into her picture of the wedding feast described in the poem.

Isabelle looked up from the book. "Mr. Weston." Closing the book, she uncurled her legs from under her skirts and set her feet on the floor. He stood at the doorway, an unreadable expression on his face.

She cleared her throat. "You missed the beginning. That was the second stanza."

Like a cloud clearing away from the sun, a light smile broke across Weston's stoic lips. "Yes, I am familiar with the works of Coleridge."

"You're a fan of his?"

"No, I find his work depressed."

"Depressed? He creates beautiful images with words."

"A fanciful notion, Miss Hampton. If you prefer portraits of idyllic life, I suppose you would favour Wordsworth."

Isabelle blinked and looked down at the book in her hands. "I've not read any of his poems."

He strode into the room and approached the fireplace. He traced his fingers over the sconcing as he spoke. "No? I find this surprising as now both my encounters with you have involved you absorbed with poetry."

"Poetry yes, but none of his poetry. Maybe you could recommend some of his best works then, since you seem like a discerning man."

"Not I. I am not one for poetry, whatever my judgement may be. Walsh is more suited to the whimsy of rhyme and meter."

Isabelle cocked her head to one side. "You don't like poetry?" She watched as he stared into the flames lapping at the logs.

"Not dislike, simply put, I would rather engage my time

elsewhere," he replied turning to face her and leaning his shoulder into the mantle.

"Would you elaborate?"

He shrugged a shoulder. "I prefer music to the literary arts."

Isabelle's delicate eyebrows raised slightly. "You're a musician then."

"I suppose one could say that, yes."

"Do you play the piano?"

Weston gave a dry chuckle. The sound surprised Isabelle. He had a comfortable laugh that rang with genuine amusement. "The noises I have extracted from that tortured instrument could hardly qualify as 'playing music.'"

This brought a smile from Isabelle.

He regarded her with what she could only think to be kindness. "I hope I find you well today, Miss Hampton? Your spirits appear a bit lighter."

"Yes, I feel better, thank you. Will you sit?" She gestured to the chair across from her.

Weston pulled off his gloves and stuffed them into the hat he carried under his arm. He took the seat she indicated. Isabelle's thoughts tangled with the questions she wanted to ask of her guest, but she refrained in case her curiosity would be impolite. He appeared content to stare at the fire.

As the two sat listening to the crackle of the fire Isabelle would steal an occasional glance at her guest. His brow had a slight crease and she wondered what thoughts were playing through his mind.

While she studied his profile, Weston suddenly looked at his young hostess. She averted her gaze and turned away to hide the bright pink that rose in her cheeks. A sly smile flashed across his features but was gone in an instant.

He cleared his throat which drew her gaze to him, her eyes round with residual embarrassment. "Might we take a turn about the gardens?" He managed to refrain from smiling at her blank expression. He got to his feet and stood looking down at her. "Would you accompany me on a walk? I noticed your aunt's gardens were taking on a greenish look and they seemed welcoming enough."

"Oh, a walk. I never say no to being outside." Isabelle smiled.

"Come then, my lady. Spring awaits."

Weston took her hands in his and guided her to her feet. As Isabelle stood, she noticed she was still looking up him though she was now at her full height. He placed her hand in the crook of his arm. His warmth brought a twinge of shyness to Isabelle for she had never taken the arm of a man before, other than her father. She cast an appraising eye over him as he guided her through the house. Even in her embarrassment of yesterday's incident, she had correctly noted that he was indeed handsome. He moved in a manner that hinted at agility and his broad shoulders suggested strength. She at once thought back to him on horseback and assumed he must be a sportsman. Her father spoke about how popular the hunt was among the English gentlemen. This man fit the image in her mind. She stepped away from him long enough to collect her wrap and bonnet from their place by the door. He waited as she dressed for the outdoors. He put on his hat and gloves before returning her hand to the crook of his arm and guiding her into the fresh air.

Once outside he released her and folded his hands behind his back. "How have you enjoyed the English countryside, Miss Hampton?" he asked, glancing around at the scene before them with some fondness.

Isabelle gazed out across the land. "I like it. It's very pretty."

"You are fortunate to have relations in this part of the country. While other regions are pretty, few are as beautiful."

Isabelle gave a thoughtful nod. "I have not seen much of England yet."

"If you aunt is the woman, I believe her to be, you will soon be engaged in society and will see all the sights associated with it."

"I hope not. That sounds overwhelming."

"To a newcomer, it probably is overwhelming. As someone raised with a certain societal standing, I have had little opportunity to reflect, but I too have felt exhausted by the expectations."

"You sound like you don't enjoy your own society."

"Not all of society, just some of it, sometimes. Does this weather suit you?"

Isabelle paused in her step and looked at him, unsure how to respond. "The weather here is a little cooler than back home."

He continued walking along beside the stone wall. "In which part of America did your family settle?"

"How well do you know America?"

He stopped and looked at her. "I know it as well as the maps detail it."

"I lived in Virginia."

"Aren't there mountains in Virginia?"

Her heart swelled at his question. She had forgotten those majestic formations. "Yes, they were beautiful." She blinked as tears threatened. She began moving again. Weston fell into step with her as the pair strolled around the large gardens.

"Your father was an Englishman, am I correct?"

Isabelle smiled though memories tugged at her heart. "Yes, my father left England when he was twenty. He claimed he wanted adventure. He told me he wanted to build something new instead of just inheriting what others before him had created."

"A reasonable pursuit, undoubtedly. If everyone were content to rest in what already exists, there would be no advancement."

"He was creative, filled with ideas."

"What was your mother like? She was also English?"

Isabelle sank down onto a decorative stone bench. "No, she was American. Like him, she wanted adventure. They were creative together." She grew quiet, lost in her own reflections.

Weston studied the girl a moment. She seemed a fine young lady, American or no. She was sure to make an impression on society. Perhaps Walsh was not entirely wrong. "Possibly then, like your parents, you will enjoy the adventure of a new life in England."

Isabelle blushed. "Oh, I'm not sure. It still feels so foreign."

"In time, I am certain you will be happy here at Brooklyn. It is a fine manor and Walsh speaks highly of the Dawsons." Weston took a seat next to Isabelle on the bench.

She nodded, the ribbons on her bonnet slapping against the collar of her cloak. "It's a fine home, but it seems so large, so sad and almost lonesome." She gazed wistfully at the mansion rising into the gray overcast sky. "Something about it makes it seem as though it wishes to remain silent and brooding when what it really needs is life."

Weston's look was a puzzled one. "How so, Miss Hampton?"

Isabelle shook her head. "Oh, I don't know. Maybe it's just missing its soul."

Weston gave a low rumbling chuckle at her whimsical statement. "Well, whatever it is missing I am sure you be able to bring."

Isabelle frowned. "Do you think the things I say are silly?"

He shook his head, and the light breeze tousled his hair. "Not at all, Miss Hampton. I think you are young and inexperienced at life."

Isabelle's eyes flashed annoyance. "Inexperienced? Does that equate to 'young and foolish?'" There was a distinct edge in her voice.

Weston slung his arm over the back of the bench. "I meant no insult."

"No, of course. Because in polite English society insults are uncouth."

"Miss Hampton, if you feel slighted, I assure you that was not my intent."

"I do feel slighted. You make youth sound like a curse."

His expression took on a guarded look. "Some would argue that it is a curse."

"A drastic claim. Is experience all that important? Does it measure a person's worth?"

"Some would argue that it does."

She sucked in her breath. "I see how it is. And you sir, have experience at life?"

His mouth twitched. "Yes, I would say that. I have seen and done things you could not have even imagined doing in your few years."

Isabelle's anger flared. "Mr. Weston, I may be young, even younger than you, but I am no fool to the ways of this world. I know a great deal about life and about people and about other places in the world."

Weston shot her a smirk that seemed taunting to her. "An interesting assertion, Miss Hampton. While I do not agree entirely, wisdom, unfortunately, comes only with experience. Experience takes time."

Isabelle frowned. "Therefore, no young person could ever hope to have any sort of insight into life?"

Weston shrugged. "I know of many young people who cannot comprehend the premise of life. Perhaps they will in time, but their youth blinds them to wisdom. As they age, most people will learn to reflect on their experiences, which provides them insight into just how much they have learned."

"Do you believe that no life circumstances can expedite the learning process? But that when a person has simply had enough life experience, he will wake up one day with wisdom?" The pace of Isabelle's speech increased as her frustration grew.

Weston looked unmoved and replied in an unhurried manner. "Life dictates what sort of experience a person has. Some circumstances are unavoidable and do result in learning. But learning does not equate to wisdom nor does every experience result in learning."

Isabelle gripped her wrap in her fists in an effort to restrain her irritation. "Oh, trust me, some circumstances are unavoidable. My life has shown me that experience can happen in an instant. You don't think I've learned that I've grown as a person in the months that my entire existence has changed?"

"Yours is a unique situation. No doubt it will shape your future as you continue to adapt. It does not add years to your life though."

"I feel like I have aged a decade. I don't know who I am anymore."

"Yes, that makes sense. You may feel that way now, but in time you will see how much more there is to learn though now you feel burdened with the struggle to adjust to the changes."

"More to learn? You seem intent on discounting my experience. What then gives someone the precious experience you consider so important? Simply living? Growing old? Many people live their whole lives without the benefit of the experiences you think are so important but may only be subjectively so. Maybe other people consider those same experiences completely pointless," she replied coolly sitting rigid keeping herself away from his dangling fingers lingering on the back of the bench.

"True the wealthy often engage themselves in bizarre pursuits in the name of entertainment, but what I mean is that the knowledge of young people is limited simply because maturity comes only with age."

"Oh, now we are getting somewhere. Your argument is not at all about experience, but maturity."

"If you prefer to see it that way."

"In light of that, then being 'inexperienced at life' is your polite way of calling me childish."

A new level of hurt fell upon her, although she was unsure why. This man meant nothing to her, so his opinion should be irrelevant. She grew uneasy as she looked at the fine cut of his waistcoat. He appeared the sort of man that people would regard his opinion. Stranger or not, she did not want him thinking ill of her. However, he had just insulted her, in a way. She gave an indignant sniff.

Weston sighed running his thumb and forefinger over his chin. "I mean you no offense. You asked my thoughts on a subject, and I gave them."

"That you did, in an upper-handed sort of way. Since I can't age, and you've already discounted my ocean voyage and immersion into a new society, how else can I gain this 'life experience' you speak of if it is so important?"

"If you sincerely ask my opinion, know that I will give it honestly." He looked at her sharply.

She quailed a little inside, but her curiosity bested her. "Speak your mind."

"It would benefit you to rely on the experience of others, especially as you embark on a new life in a new country."

"I intend to learn what I can from those around me."

"Fine. You would also do best to put aside fantastical whimsy."

Isabelle frowned. "Fantastical whimsy? What do you mean by that?" As soon as she spoke the words, she regret them, and feared his candid response.

"Those romantic notions young girls get. They are unbecoming of a lady. If you will permit me, I advise you to keep your comments about such things, like a house having a soul, to yourself," he replied in a bored tone.

"Romantic notions do not mark a person's value! Nor are they childish or whatever else you might call them. Greater men than you, like Coleridge or your Wordsworth, engage these ideas and I think those men would surpass even your ridiculous standard of experienced at life. My father loved art, and literature, and he would never call them romantic whimsy or look down on a person for being expressive. My father was a gentleman, but he still had room for imagination. Why else would he start a life in a new land?" Annoyed to the limit she got to her feet. With a quick sweep or her cloak, she turned round to face him, as he rose awkwardly from his seat. "Maybe your bored and ancient standards need some flexibility. You hate all things pretty, and idealistic, and imaginative. No wonder you hate poetry. You have no feelings!"

"And you, my dear, seem to have plenty of feelings." He looked down at her with the same look he wore when he caught her in the tree, a mix of stern amusement. It angered her and made her bold.

"Sir, unlike you, I certainly know when I have said or heard enough." She spat the words at him. Her eyes snapped as she grabbed a handful of her skirt and spun away from him, returning to the house.

Weston made no attempt to stop or appease her. "I wasn't aware I had said anything offensive," he mused under his breath. Giving a careless shrug he began whistling as he plunked his hat on his head and gathered his gloves. He stared after Isabelle as she marched to the house. Her hair had come lose and strands swung into her face as she went. She batted at them as if they were flies on a summer's day. He gave his head a shake before going off to get his horse.

~

Sara stood peeking out through the sitting room window. She placed a hand on her forehead as if to pacify a headache as Isabelle hurried up the house steps. Isabelle raised her chin and refused to look at Mansfield when he opened the door for her. Sighing, Sara moved from the window to debrief her niece.

"What an arrogant man! Who does he think he is?" Isabelle grumbled, fighting with the ribbons on her bonnet managing to tangle them into a hopeless knot.

"Goodness Isabelle! Why so cross?" Sara spoke softly coming to assist with the ribbon confining Isabelle to the bonnet.

Isabelle bit her lip ceasing the angry mutterings; she lowered her gaze. She inhaled, bracing herself to confess the scene to her aunt.

"Mr. Weston said, well he is…"

"Is what, Isabelle? What did he say?" Sara asked with an interested tone.

"Well, he is horrid."

"What makes you say that?"

"He is impossible and rude. I don't know what sort of society he associates with, but I'm amazed they can tolerate him!"

"Goodness, girl, why the fluster? Did something happen?"

Isabelle furrowed her brow. "No, he was a gentleman, of a sort."

"Then why would you say these things?" Sara searched her face, taking Isabelle's hands into her own.

"He insulted my ideas. He even said I was childish."

"How did he insult you?"

"He said I was full of whimsy and fantasy."

Sara smiled chuckling softly as she lifted the bonnet from Isabelle's head allowing her locks to cascade about her shoulders. "My dear Isabelle, Mr. Weston is quite right. In that regard, you do possess a certain, childlike charm."

Isabelle lifted her chin as a wounded look glinted in her eyes. "Aunt Sara, you take his side!"

Sara fingered the pale green satin ribbon on the bonnet. "It is not a matter of whose side I take, but a matter of fact. You are young and maybe your mannerisms reflect this. But," Sara patted Isabelle's shoulder, and gave her a kind smile, "you will outgrow it." With that comment, Sara handed the bonnet to Mansfield and with an appraising glance at Isabelle, returned to the sitting room.

Isabelle stood sulking, mulling what her aunt told her. "I'm no child. There is no truth in what that snobbish man had to say!" she mumbled and in a very ladylike manner she gathered a handful of her skirts and gracefully ascended the stairs.

Lexington Estate,

"Weston!?" Walsh exclaimed as he found his cousin lounging against the fireplace mantle in the grand salon. "Why have you returned so early?"

Heaving a bored sigh Weston closed his book and looked at his cousin.

"Miss Hampton was indisposed to conversation."

"Her ailment prevails? I do hope she recovers soon."

"Oh, she is quite well," he stated carelessly.

Walsh raised an inquisitive brow folding his arms across his chest. "Yet she was indisposed? Or just disinclined?"

"Disinclined, if you will. She appeared in a disagreeable mood."

"Ah, the plot thickens. And what did you say to provoke such a mood?"

A mischievous glint flashed across Weston's features as he straightened up and replied. "I said nothing. Miss Hampton may have felt unwell." Tucking the book in his waistcoat pocket he began to move away but Walsh put out an arm to restrain him.

"I will not have you come into my home and disrupt my household, or my neighbors; do you understand me?" Walsh leaned close to his cousin's face a small frown knitting his dark brows close together. Weston seemed surprised by his cousin's seriousness.

"I have no intentions of upsetting any household cousin. But to keep peace with your charming neighbors I will apologize to the girl." He gave a small innocent smile.

Walsh shook his head, a smile creeping across his lips. "Tell me, Weston, has that silver tongue of yours never gotten you out of trouble?"

A mysterious light gleamed in Weston's eyes as he dropped his voice to a low rumble. "Believe me cousin, it serves me well."

CHAPTER 5

Brooklyn Manor,

"You cannot be serious. You are not going to wear that," Laura Millis said with disgust eyeing the dress that Isabelle had pulled from her closet.

"What's wrong with it?" she asked, defending her gown. Ever since Laura had arrived two days ago, she had been telling Isabelle how unbecoming her wardrobe was. Isabelle held out the dress at arm's length to take a good look at it.

Laura sighed rolling her dark eyes. "For one thing, yellow is hideous. And the neckline cut is far too high. It should be to about here." Laura traced her finger over the gown demonstrating her point.

Isabelle gasped. "That's ridiculous! Even in wild America," here she paused and shot Laura a look, "that low of a neckline would be considered immodest!"

Laura gave a careless shrug.

"Women in London wear them that way, more fitted too. I dare say none of them find the style inappropriate."

"Well, that's just silly. Besides, we are not in London, so we don't need to worry about that." Isabelle hung the dress in the closet with a flourish.

A smug little smile played on Laura's rosy lips. "You may dress however you wish. You can play the eccentric foreigner, but you will end up an old spinster."

Isabelle's cheeks flushed pink. "Laura Millis!" she hissed. "That's a cruel thing to say!"

Laura flipped a lock of thick hair over her shoulder batting her eyelashes. "Your fate is in your own hands. Being new and from a far away land does place you in a certain light. You may have options to marry well if you play your hand wisely. You do have a rather eligible neighbor. That makes a smart match nearly a guarantee." Laura gently buffed her nails, looking all the world like the topic bored her.

"The Dawson's neighbors have nothing to do with me," Isabelle pointed out as she passed her hand over the row of gowns in the closet.

"Your caller yesterday directed his attentions towards you in not merely a social call. He aimed to continue a previous conversation. Oh no, Isabelle, you have far more to do with the neighbors than you will admit." Laura's eyes peeped out at Isabelle from beneath the locks of hair draped around her face and they sparkled with amusement.

"It was a simple apology! Mr. Weston extended an olive branch for his behavior. You would not believe what he said to me."

"Do not be naïve, Isabelle. Do you think him to be the sort of man who goes about apologizing for anything? Far from it! He could offend people until the end of time and London socialites would still adore him. No indeed, that apology was a tactical effort."

"That's stupid."

"Definitely not. He is quite renown. Brooding yes, but he remains a Weston. They command a great deal of respect. I would almost call his apology romantic."

Isabelle laughed. "Romantic? If I'm naïve, you're ridiculous."

"Laugh if you want, but it is nothing of the sort. You would do well to make yourself more attractive. A little London fashion might help you keep his attention, since you already caught it."

"I don't want his attention. He is a pompous Englishman stuck in a bunch of old traditions."

Laura wrinkled her nose at this statement. "Old traditions that form the very basis of society. Coming from such a young country, you cannot possibly understand this and so I will let it slide on grounds of ignorance. Despite your, how shall we say, cultural lacking, I wonder if Mr. Weston would not suit you well indeed."

"Me? If he is as grand as you think, why would he choose me? I'm sure there is a woman with a title he could marry."

Laura rolled her eyes. "You are a bit daft, aren't you? A title means little. Good breeding, societal connections, family fortune, those are the qualities upper class men seek. You, my dear, have just fallen into all of those."

Isabelle paused and turned to face the girl perched on the edge of her bed. "I don't understand what you mean. I'm an orphan. I have no connections."

"Yes that, but your lineage remains. You have American roots, but do you not know the Hampton family history?"

"Well, yes, sort of. My grandfather was a seaman."

"Correct. Aunt Sara's brother. Their father was a gentleman. Aunt Sara made a smart decision in marrying my uncle since the Dawsons are by their own right a fine family, not to brag." She paused to flash Isabelle a winning smile. "The Dawsons acting as your guardians will serve you well. You are in a fine position to have your pick of eligible men. Marriage to a Weston is quite possible for you."

Isabelle frowned in thought. "Is this part of my life? Status and connections?"

Laura glanced up at her. "What was that you said?"

"Oh, nothing." Isabelle went back to searching her wardrobe. "Laura, do you really think that's true? That I have status?"

"Most definitely. While perhaps unrefined at the moment, I do believe you will be quite lovely." Laura spoke with such confidence that Isabelle felt a bit overwhelmed with the implications of what she presented. "So lovely in fact, I would consider it imprudent to discount your moody, but elegant neighbor as a potential suitor."

Isabelle sighed. Any feeling she had of fondness for Laura or intimidation at the world she painted faded. "Okay, you may be right, but I find it annoying that you're trying to find me a beau. I haven't even settled in here," she grumbled, tying the laces on her bodice.

"I cannot understand why. You would go the finest balls and parties on the arm of a most handsome gentleman." Isabelle gave her a sour look, tugging at her skirts making sure they lay straight. "Don't look at me like that!" Laura scolded with a smile. "You can't possibly tell me you have never dreamed of having a man of your own?"

Isabelle sat next to Laura. "I haven't thought about it. There were always other things to worry about."

Laura frowned. "What is going on in America that connections would receive so little attention? There is nothing worse than marrying badly! Didn't your father expect you to marry well? What could possibly be more important than that?"

Isabelle sighed. "My father expected me to do what made me happy." She looked down at her hands.

Laura gave her a pitying look. "A good marriage is the pathway to happiness."

"Maybe. My parents did seem happy."

Laura smiled as Isabelle inched closer to concession. "So do mine. Many wonderful things come from marrying well. You should be so deliciously happy, Isabelle. You are far too pretty to look so despondent."

Isabelle laughed and looked up at the girl beside her. "Marriage isn't the only happiness. Climbing trees and riding horses also bring happiness, although apparently ladies don't do these things."

Laura gave a visible shudder. "Heavens, they most certainly do not. Some ladies ride, but I consider it quite dreadful. I would never go near the saddle of one of those beasts. I shan't hold this against you, but it may not serve you in the quest for marriage."

Isabelle sighed and gave her wistful look. "Marriage wasn't a priority in my life, and I feel it still isn't. I want to pursue other things for a while." She laughed at the look of astonishment she received from Laura.

"Isabelle you cannot climb trees and ignore society. Horses are one thing, but really, you would do best to stick to walking as your outdoor pursuit." Laura gave her head a grave shake, as though discovering the task before her was more of a challenge than she thought. "Climbing trees. I am undecided if that is amusing or foolhardy."

Isabelle chuckled. "Please don't say anything. Aunt Sara wasn't impressed when she found out and I told her I wouldn't do it again."

Laura giggled. "I will not breath a word. But tell me, why don't you think about getting married? We are not so young that the possibility of marriage is far in the future."

Isabelle moved to stand by the window and looked out over the fields. Far in the east the peaks of Lexington Estate loomed above the trees.

"I'm not ready to enter someone else's world. I've already done that in a way. I enjoyed doing as I please without much thought of what others may think of me. That is already changing for me though. With marriage, the expectations are so much higher. I've already got enough expectations on me. And I enjoy spending my time pursuing things that 'proper' ladies shouldn't. There are some parts I am just not ready to let go." Isabelle paused.

"This is part of growing up. We must learn to let go and to grow. You know that your pursuits will need to change."

"Yes, but for now, I just want a rest from all the changes."

Laura stood. "Agreed. And we can still have lots of fun. Adventures will be had and some already have."

Isabelle grinned. "Yes, they have. I met you."

Laura reached out and squeezed her hand. "Yes, you have, and you have also met Mr. Weston."

Isabelle tossed her hair like a fussing horse tosses its mane. "Oh, your Mr. Weston! The first time I saw him was from the branches of a tree."

Laura's laughter filled the room. "What an unfortunate setting. One can hardly call it a romantic meeting."

Isabelle joined in the laughter. "I probably ruined my chance of ever winning his affection." The words faded on her lips as she watched a horseman riding along the Lexington border.

⁓

"Isabelle! Laura! Come here, girls, and see what has just arrived!" Sara called to her nieces from the base of the stairs.

The two young ladies hurried across the upstairs landing which opened to the entryway below. Holding their skirts aside they moved as quickly as their gowns would allow. The girls crowded around Sara.

"What is it, Aunt Sara?" Laura asked as she came to her aunt's side and peered over shoulder. "A letter? Oh, what does it say? Who sent it?"

Isabelle stood on Sara's other side, looking down at the cursive script swirling across the page. She hoped the looping hand did not convey a message of misfortune.

"Hush, Laura, and I will tell you," Sara chided before proceeding. "This has just arrived from Lexington Estate. Mr. Walsh invited us to a ball hosted at Lexington."

"Oh! A ball! I simply love balls!" Laura squealed happily, clasping her hands together. "Oh, Isabelle, your first ball! What fun we shall have!"

Isabelle smiled. "Well, that was nice of Mr. Walsh. When is the party, Aunt Sara?"

Sara scanned the page with the handwritten message. "I would be most honored if your party would plan to attend a ball at Lexington Estate on the eve of Saturday the fifteenth of June," she read aloud.

Laura's eyes grew large. "The fifteenth? Why that is this Saturday!"

Sara nodded. "Yes, that is only a few days away. Shall I accept the invitation?"

Isabelle looked at Laura who was practically jumping up and down on the spot.

"Oh yes! Please do, Aunt Sara. We simply must attend. Isabelle, say 'yes!'"

Isabelle muttered a hurried 'yes' which evoked a light laugh from Sara. "Laura, you must contain some of your zeal."

Laura raised her chin in the air. "I think only of Isabelle's welfare. It is in her best interest to attend, though she would not admit so in this moment."

"Admit it, Laura, you want to attend the party. You don't need to pretend to act in my interest," Isabelle objected, silently willing the girl to cease speaking.

Laura shot her a daring look but said nothing.

Sara folded the letter and tucked it onto her writing desk. "Alright, I will write to him this very morning and accept the offer."

Laura paled. "Heavens! What shall we wear?" she exclaimed,

laying a hand alongside her cheek. "Come on, we must go and see what we can find that is suitable for such an occasion."

Laura took Isabelle's hand and began dragging her to the foot of the staircase with Isabelle protesting every step of the way. Sara laughed; what a pair they were!

Sara seated herself at the writing desk as Isabelle complained that she did not want to pick a gown for Saturday right now.

Isabelle gave Laura a sulking frown as she allowed Laura to escort her up the stairs and to her room.

"Sit down and cease your whining. One would think you would be excited over such an opportunity."

Isabelle obliged and deposited herself on the edge of the bed while Laura went to the closet. Laura continued; her voice muffled by the clothes.

"Choosing an appropriate gown for an event is important. If you ever hope to compete with the London fashion, you will need something beautiful."

"We're not in London. Any one of my gowns will do."

Laura's tone was scornful as she glanced over her shoulder from the closet to Isabelle. "Really Isabelle, are you so simple? Need I remind you that dashing Mr. Weston is a Londoner? He will take no notice of you if you are not radiant."

Isabelle's frown lessened. It had been a week since Mr. Weston had stopped by to apologize. An entire week since she had seen him last. "I still think any of my gowns will do."

Laura turned on her with an exasperated sigh. "I am trying to help you. I am trying to make your entrance into society a success. Do you not want his attention?"

Isabelle bowed her head in discomfiture. "I appreciate that, I do, but I fear it will be for nothing."

Laura made an unladylike growl in the back of her throat. "Whatever do you mean? Cease these riddles!"

"Weston thinks of me only as a child," Isabelle blurted, feeling a little silly about the way she had reacted to his conversation.

Mr. Weston had not really done anything wrong, but Isabelle's haughty attitude practically confirmed the implication that she was immature.

"Gracious! Whatever gave you that idea?" Laura placed her hands on her hips and looked pointedly at Isabelle. Isabelle looked away to avoid her penetrating glare.

"He told me."

Laura's mouth hung open a few seconds before she realized and closed it. "I beg your pardon? This must be some sort of misunderstanding."

Isabelle ran a hand over her brow. "No, it wasn't, but maybe it was, I'm not sure. He implied I'm immature and childlike. I said he lacked imagination and a heart. It was disastrous."

Laura blinked at her. "So that was the reason behind his apology."

Isabelle gave a sad nod.

"Then it sounds to me like the matter is closed."

"But it can't be! I feel foolish about what I did. He might be right, and I am a child." Isabelle's outburst drew a disparaging look from Laura.

"Well then I suppose the best you can do now is show him that you are no child."

Isabelle's brow knit in a wary frown. "But I really have no desire to go."

"Why on earth not?" Laura's look of devastation made her look much younger than her eight and ten years.

Isabelle sighed. "I don't like your scheme to pair me with Mr. Weston. We've had differences from the start and despite his apology, we would be hard pressed to be friends let alone anything else."

"Stop pitying yourself, Isabelle. Mr. Weston is not an unreasonable man. If you can prove yourself to be sensible, I see no reason he would not put the whole incident in the past and present himself as a willing suitor." The weight of Laura's words fell heavily on Isabelle.

"You have more faith in me than I do. I should stay home. I would really like to read a book I found in the library the other morning."

Laura's eye twitched. She appeared in a battle to refrain from speaking her mind. Her voice quivered when she spoke: "A book! You would give up an evening of dancing and having fun to sit at home and read a book? You would forfeit an opportunity for connections and society for words on a page! Mr. Weston or not, you stand to lose too much. That is the most outrageous thing I have ever heard!"

Isabelle was surprised by Laura's outburst. She started to laugh. "Alright, if it means that much to you, I'll go."

A self-satisfied look crossed Laura's pretty face. "It is of little consequence to me, but you would do yourself a disservice. You will be thanking me someday. Once you have danced with all the eligible bachelors in the county, you will see I was right."

Isabelle blushed; there was no distracting Laura from the topic of marriage.

Laura clutched Isabelle's hands and stared intensely into her eyes. "I promise you this: it will be a night to remember."

CHAPTER 6

Lexington Estate,

Isabelle watched the mansion rise overhead when the carriage rolled to a halt in front of the house. An attendant opened the door and bowed low to the ladies inside as he guided each one to the ground. Several other carriages were unloading ladies dressed in fine bright colored gowns and gentlemen in elegant waist coats and tall satin hats. Isabelle stared up at the brick house rising high into the night sky above her. Light blinked from the windows that she could see, and music drifted out into the evening air.

Laura giggled and took her arm. "Isn't this going to be wonderful?" she whispered as the girls hurried after Sara.

Isabelle flashed a timid smile and nodded watching the other guests approach the door. Earlier in the evening Isabelle had felt good about her decision to attend. Now that she stood outside Lexington Estate, knowing that he was somewhere inside, she felt herself growing tense. She fluffed a curl dangling against her cheek. A quick glance at the other young ladies assured her that Laura was right and that other young ladies had similar appearance to them. She exhaled, allowing this realization to bring her some comfort.

Once inside the two girls stopped and marvelled in the beauty of Lexington. The outside had awed Isabelle, but the inside humbled her: polished wooden floors reflected her every move and glistened in the candlelight. Large paintings adorned the walls. Colorful rugs dotted the floors. The sweeping staircase twisted up towards the open landing above and the hall disappeared into the expanse of the second floor.

"Isabelle!" Laura hissed under her breath. "Stop dawdling! One might think you have never seen a house before."

Isabelle quickened her pace to match that of her friend and lowered her voice. "I have never been in a house like this. It's truly magnificent!"

Laura snickered. "You will get used to it, fine things and fancy people."

Isabelle looked at her friend. "America has fine things too. They're just different. Does everyone have a house like this?"

Laura sighed. "No, Lexington is finer than most."

Sara glanced over her shoulder at the two whispering young ladies behind her. "Come along girls," she urged, as they came to the large double doors leading to the ballroom.

A string quartet sat to the side playing beautiful music as dancers glided across the floor. The scene was cheerful. Across the hall a parlor was set with refreshments. Some ladies sat there sipping tea and catching up on the latest gossip. Isabelle and Laura joined the fray in the ballroom while Sara attended the beckoning of the women in the sitting room.

"Look, there are the Arthur girls. Come, let me introduce you. You will like them; they are quite lovely. Oh, they are standing with that dreadful Gabrielle Smart. She really is a bore," Laura babbled, guiding Isabelle by the arm through the mingled people.

"Oh Juliet, darling, so good to see you!" Laura halted and embraced a dark-haired girl. Isabelle lurched to a halt and quickly ducked to the side to avoid bumping into the girl.

"Laura, what a pleasure! How I did hope *someone* amusing would be here this evening, and here you are!"

The girls erupted into fits of giggles before Juliet continued. "I had to make an excuse to slip away. That Gabrielle has monopolized the poor Arthurs. It is *quite* dreadful." She heaved a dramatic sigh and rolled her eyes in a knowing manner.

Laura bobbed her head. "Yes, so I see. However, fortune has smiled upon us!" She turned with a flourish to Isabelle. "Miss Juliet Pierce, allow me to present my cousin, Isabelle Hampton."

The dark-haired girl squeezed Isabelle's hands and offered a dimpled smile. "Miss Hampton, delighted to make your acquaintance! Any relation to Miss Laura is sure to be a charming addition to our circles!"

"Nice to meet you." Isabelle tried to return the smile, but she felt overshadowed by the girl's enthusiastic energy.

"What is this? An accent? How exotic! Laura, you never told me you had relations in foreign lands." Juliet clutched Laura's arm, almost vibrating with excitement.

Laura's grin was mischievous. "Isn't it wonderful? She is perfectly enchanting."

Juliet's pale eyes shone. "Yes, indeed. I am so glad to meet you, Miss Hampton, and pleased to have you join us. You are a most welcome and necessary change in our modest society." Giving Isabelle's hand a final squeeze, Juliet slipped away into the parlor.

Laura regained her grip on Isabelle's arm. "See? You must be glad you came. Everyone will love you."

Isabelle pinched her lips together and made no reply.

The Arthurs turned out to be lovely, just as Laura had claimed, and Isabelle could find nothing to like about Gabrielle Smart. The group of girls exchanged greetings and then proceeded to comment on their surroundings.

"Look there. What a stunning gown Miss Murray is wearing," Rose Arthur observed, indicating towards a petite blonde woman in a dark colored dress as she swept past on the dancefloor.

Murmurs of approval rippled through the group.

"If only she danced as elegantly as she dressed," Gabrielle added with a haughty sniff.

The Arthur girls exchanged a look and Laura gave an awkward cough.

"She just got engaged to a naval captain. Evidently, she need not dance well," Juliet replied.

"What about Miss Horton? Her dress is lovely," Violet Arthur added with enthusiastic energy.

"Yes, quite lovely."

"Rather an elegant cut."

"Careful not to admire her. You know how she is when she gets rather a lot of attention."

Isabelle kept quiet and stood watching and listening. She glanced across the dance floor and tried to guess which one was Miss Horton. There was a smiling fair girl standing on the side talking to an older gentleman. Isabelle thought her dress was pretty. Then there was a tall and dark woman gliding across the dancefloor on the arm of a dashing young man. She wore a dress of dark blue and when she moved it looked like the ocean. Perhaps she was Miss Horton?

She sighed and abandoned her search for Miss Horton. Her eyes continuing searching the faces. An unexpected realization occurred to her that she hoped for a glimpse of Mr. Weston. She released the breath she had not noticed she was holding and did a quick scan of the room. She did not see him. A bit of disappointment crept over Isabelle, although she was unsure why. She felt a bit silly for letting Laura fill her head with ideas. Catching a glimpse of herself in a wall mirror, Isabelle did think she looked nice. Her dress complimented her, and her hair framed her face.

A young man approached the cluster of girls, silencing the chatter. "Good evening, ladies," he greeted them with a slight bow.

Excited titters rippled among the girls and produced a grin from him.

"I seek the pleasure of Miss Millis' company on the dancefloor."

"Me?" Laura asked, as the Arthur girls nudged her forward with bursts of giggles. "Very well, Mr. Graham, it would be a pleasure." Laura accepted the offered hand and shot a quick glance at Isabelle. "You'll be alright?" she asked quietly.

Isabelle nodded quickly. "Yes, of course. Go on."

Laura smiled and hurried onto the dancefloor with her partner. Isabelle took a few steps back from the group as another young man approached Juliet and escorted her to the dancefloor. The girls

61

resumed their commentary and Isabelle drifted further from them and closer to the wall.

"All dressed up yet standing in the shadows? That will never do, Miss Hampton. May I have the pleasure of the next dance?"

Isabelle glanced to her right where Walsh stood dressed as dashing as ever. He looked at her from the corner of his eye and smiled.

"Good evening, Miss Hampton."

She returned his smile. "Hello, Mr. Walsh, and yes, I will dance with you."

Walsh made her a slight bow. "I am pleased to have you in attendance. I saw your aunt in the parlor and if I am correct, that is Miss Millis twirling on the arm of Mr. Graham. I presumed I would find you some place."

"Well, here I am."

He chuckled lightly. "Here you are indeed. You look lovely this evening."

Isabelle felt heat rise in her cheeks. "Thank you." She suddenly felt glad Laura spent extra time fussing over her. "Your home is beautiful."

"It is quite extraordinary, isn't it? Been in the family for decades. I have the good fortune to be its latest inhabitant," Walsh replied with an airy tone as he looked around the room with some fondness. Isabelle followed his gaze and wondered how the house appeared to his eyes. He pulled her from her musing. "Is Mr. Dawson here this evening?"

Isabelle shook her head. "Unfortunately, no; he went to Southampton."

Walsh nodded. "I hope nothing serious has detained him." As he finished his sentence the quartet's song ended. Excited voices and laughter rose during the brief intermission between numbers. The dancers hurried to exchange partners and the musicians prepared for their next piece. "Shall we dance?" Walsh's eyes twinkled with pleasure as he extended his arm to Isabelle.

She smiled, looping her arm in his, allowing him to escort her to the dance floor. They took position among the other dancers and were soon twirling around the room. Partners passed back and forth between couples as they moved through the lines of people in time to the music. Isabelle found herself adrift in the sea of strangers only to have Walsh catch her repeatedly. Each time he took her arm he flashed her a dazzling smile.

"You're quite graceful," he mused as he drew her close.

"I haven't danced all that much," Isabelle muttered finding herself struggling to form a response.

She could feel his warmth as he pulled her into him protectively as another couple passed close.

"Perhaps your nimbleness comes from scrambling up trees."

She looked at him with horror to find pure amusement reflected in his features.

"I jest, Miss Hampton."

He guided her across the floor, holding her close in his warm embrace. They did not speak. For the moment, she forgot about the rest of the world. Then the song ended. Mr. Walsh made her bow and she felt disappointed as he escorted her off the dancefloor. "Thank you for permitting me the pleasure of your company."

"The pleasure was mine." Isabelle gave an awkward bow as he paused before her.

"I would like the pleasure again before the end of the evening." He smiled down at her, lowering his voice.

She suppressed a nervous giggle. "Of course."

He raised her hand to his lips. She smiled, looking away from him. He pulled himself away to assume the role of the host.

As they parted, Laura rushed over and bombarded her with questions, dripping with curiosity. "Isabelle! What was that I saw?"

Isabelle gave a coy smile, and turned away, hoping to ward off questions. "It was a dance."

Laura sniffed. "A dance! Surely a blind person could see that was more than a mere dance. What did you talk about?"

"Nothing in particular."

"You expect me to believe that? Why won't you tell me?"

"Because there's nothing to tell. Now, I'm going for refreshment. Are you coming?"

Laura bit her lip, weighing response options. "Yes, of course."

She glanced at their host who stood talking to some men in uniform. "He is an attentive host, Laura, nothing more."

Once the girls had refreshed themselves, and received the latest gossip, they returned to the ballroom. Isabelle noted she still had seen nothing of Mr. Weston, who Laura seemed to have forgotten existed. In the least she had ceased to pester Isabelle about him. One of the Arthur girls made a comment about his absence, but Gabrielle changed the subject to some awful opera she had recently seen. That was the only mention Isabelle had heard of his name all evening. Isabelle tried to follow the conversation as the girls flowed through topics, but invitations to dance interrupted the conversations and when the girls regrouped, the subject changed again. Isabelle found it confusing. She furrowed her brow in thought as she listened to a tale about Miss Horton, or was it Miss Coombes, but which Miss Coombes because there were two of them.

Isabelle was trying to sort the details when fingers brushed across her shoulder. She turned to face her visitor; a look of curiosity etched in her features. Mr. Walsh smiled at her as he clasped his hands behind his back. "I do hope I am not intruding."

The girls stopped talking and turned their attention towards him.

Isabelle replied, "Not at all."

"I trust you are all having an enjoyable time?" he inquired of the group.

Head nods and assurances that it was a lovely party appeared throughout the group.

He looked pleased. "Excellent, then I bid you carry on and if you can spare her, I should like to relieve you of Miss Hampton's company." He looked pointedly at Isabelle.

Laura wore a smug knowing smile.

"Miss Hampton?" Gabrielle raised a brow of inquiry.

"Yes, indeed. I should very much like to collect on a prior assertion of a second dance."

Isabelle swallowed, trying to find her voice. Everyone appeared anxious for her answer. Laura gave her a gentle nudge with her arm and mouthed 'go' to her.

Isabelle managed a smile at Walsh. "Yes, a dance it is."

"Then let us away. Enjoy your evening, ladies." He whisked her away from the excited chattering and onto the dancefloor.

"Goodness, you've caused a stir," Isabelle noted as they took up position.

Walsh looked back at the group with a flippant glance. "I saw no other way to disengage you. I suppose they will gossip." He gave her his easy smile and pulled her closer as the song began. "No harm will come of it."

They danced several times throughout the course of the evening. He would not let her leave the dance floor and insisted on keeping her for a few songs in a row. Finally, when she admitted to feeling a bit tired, he escorted her from the floor.

As they neared the ballroom entrance, a man laid his hand on Walsh's arm. "Walsh, our gracious host. I have been searching for you."

Walsh paused and greeted the man: "Mr. Berry, do you need something?"

The big man shook his head. "Only your time, Walsh. I wish to discuss with you the incoming changes to our fine navy."

Walsh gave a slight flinch, which Isabelle felt through her touch on his arm. "You would want to speak to my cousin regarding a matter of the sea."

The man frowned. "Yes, now, about that. I had the exact sentiment, but I have not seen Weston all evening. I fear he has not attended."

Walsh frowned. "Not attended?"

The man spied Isabelle beside Walsh. "Good heavens, beg your pardon, Miss. Here I have barged into your evening."

Walsh started and looked with big eyes at Isabelle. "My dear, Miss Hampton, I do apologize. Mr. Berry, allow me to present Miss Isabelle Hampton. She is Dawson's ward."

The man looked intrigued as he made a low bow. "Indeed? Welcome, Miss, welcome. A fine man your guardian."

Isabelle, unsure how to respond, gave a small nod. "Pleasure to meet you."

"Forgive me for being so bold, Hampton is the maiden name of Mrs. Dawson, would that make you her relation?"

"Well," Isabelle hesitated and glanced to Walsh. "She is my father's aunt."

"Ah," Mr. Berry gave an understanding nod, "that would be the son of Captain Arnold Hampton, the one who left for America."

Isabelle cocked her head to the side. "You seem to know my family well."

He shook his head. "Nay, madame. I know the name Hampton from their connection to the sea. I did meet your grandfather. He was a good man."

Isabelle felt a swell of pride as she thanked him. Walsh turned to face her, taking her hands in his. "I am afraid I have shirked my duties as host and have neglected my other guests. Will you excuse me so I can resume my role?" His expression was kind, and his touch was gentle.

Isabelle nodded. "Yes, definitely. You're the host."

"Thank you, Miss Hampton, you are the epitome of understanding!" He released her and made a quick bow. "I find you a most delightful partner."

She gave him a smile. "I've had a lovely evening. Thank you for entertaining me."

He flitted away from her as Mr. Berry began talking. He continued to glance about the room during the conversation as if he were looking for something.

Laura appeared at her side. "An attentive host indeed." She wore a sweet smile that betrayed her implications.

Isabelle turned to her with a dismissive air. "Yes, attentive. See how he tends all his guests?"

"Yes, but only after he has spent rather a great deal of time with you. If I were to guess, I would say the host has taken a fancy to you."

Isabelle smiled and moved into the hall away from ballroom. "Don't be silly. He treated me no different from any other woman."

Laura rolled her eyes as she kept pace with Isabelle. "Yes, he danced with other young ladies tonight, but you, my misinformed friend, were the one he repeatedly sought."

Isabelle blushed. "Laura, please lower your voice. No one needs to hear you."

Laura glanced around causing her tight ringlets to bob. "Let them hear. For they have all been able to see the same thing I have and, therefore, likely reached the same conclusion."

"I'm confident Mr. Walsh has other favorites. I can't think such a thing when he's likely known them longer than he's known me." Isabelle countered.

Laura raised a brow, giving her a significant smirk. "It would be pointless for them to try and woo Mr. Walsh when he so obviously has his eye on someone else."

Isabelle sighed happily. "I don't believe a word you're saying."

"Say what you like, but you cannot escape the truth."

"What about Weston? Just this morning you would have married me off to him."

Laura gave a pretty frown. "That is a puzzle. This morning I had not seen you with Mr. Walsh. Mr. Weston is certainly eligible, make no mistake, but did you notice he is not here. How could you make a man fall in love with you when he is not present? Mr. Walsh is both present and, if I am not mistaken, very much on his way to falling in love with you. It would be a sensible match and an easy one at that."

"No more of this, Laura. You're hurting my head." Isabelle ran a hand over her forehead. Laura paused in silence. "You stay here. I think I need to rest."

"I suppose now is as good a time as any, seeing how your dancing partner is engaged at the moment," Laura stated, glancing about the room. Her response annoyed Isabelle. Laura fixed her gaze on a handsome young man across the ballroom, and she smiled. "Isabelle, if you are not going, then excuse me. I see someone I simply must address." Laura gave Isabelle a wave of dismissal and then went on her way.

"Of course." Isabelle chuckled as the young man came towards Laura.

Isabelle walked down the hall and went in search of a quiet place. She did feel tired, but she continued to feel uncomfortable in the presence of all these strangers. She wanted a break from people. She also had the secret desire to read the book she stashed in her handbag. The sounds of chatter and music drifted away as Isabelle moved further away from the ball. She paused occasionally to admire a painting on the wall, or a side table adorned with ornaments. She glanced back over her shoulder as she went to ensure she did not go too far. When she felt certain she had gone as far as she dared into the house, she halted at a window alcove. A little table and a chair stood in the space away from the hall at the base of a staircase. Isabelle lowered herself into the chair and peered around the corner. The hall turned to the right of the staircase and continued along that way. How far it went, Isabelle could not tell. Glancing around the quiet hall, Isabelle closed her eyes for a moment and absorbed the peace. Then, she opened the book and started reading.

Not long had she been sitting there, when the sound of a single instrument playing a lonesome piece drifted to her. She raised her head. She could just hear the ball echoing down the hall. This melody was clearer and sounded much closer. Isabelle turned back to her book. The slight melody swirled and wandered through delicate high notes and mournful low notes, invoking her imagination, and drawing memories of things she thought she had forgotten. Soon she found herself paying more attention to the melody than the words on the page.

When the song took a sudden turn and produced lively notes of vibrant cheer, she closed the book and got up from the chair. She peered around the corner. The hall only went on about twenty feet or so before it ended. Isabelle decided she had already strayed this far into the house that she could venture a bit farther. She tucked the book away, made her way towards the music.

Light streamed into the hall from an open door. The light drew Isabelle forward and the music grew louder as she approached. The melody grew quiet again and took on a wistful edge, as if it were thinking and trying to solve a difficult puzzle. She laid her hand on the doorframe and found herself leaning in the doorway of a small, cluttered salon. The music washed over her.

She saw the man standing with his back to her. A shock of auburn hair brushed against the violin cradled under his chin. His fingers stroked the strings as he plied the bow in an elegant sweep. He played with a tenderness Isabelle had never seen before. His touch suggested a love not just for the instrument, but for the music itself. She froze, awed by the skill of the musician. The melody continued as Isabelle listened, and it betrayed an inner passion and imagination known to few. She sneezed. The violin screeched in protest as the violinist glanced over his shoulder, startled out of his musical trance. He spotted her and she recognized him.

"Weston!" she exclaimed, surprised, and embarrassed. Never would she have supposed he, of all, people possessed such skill or gentleness. Weston lowered the violin and turned to face her, maintaining a tender hold on the delicate instrument.

"Miss Hampton," he greeted stiffly bowing slightly. His expression was a tangle of feelings, and his eyes held a conflicted look. "What are you doing so far from the other guests?"

Isabelle, unable to hide her embarrassment that he discovered her wandering around and then eavesdropping, bowed her head, trying to avoid his gaze. "Please, I apologize. I didn't mean to invade your privacy. Your music was..." Her voice trailed off. "Do I need to explain myself? You're a guest in Mr. Walsh's home the same as I." Isabelle planted her feet and straightened herself to her full height.

He waved a dismissive hand in her direction turning his body away from her. "Fine, use whatever justification you will to excuse yourself. It makes no difference to me. As you said, I am a guest. Leave me."

"I'm sorry. I didn't mean any harm."

Weston gazed at the woman before him. The challenge in her eyes, the squareness of her shoulders gave her a mature air. He wondered how she changed in such a short time. Perhaps he was the one changing. Isabelle shifted under Weston's scrutinizing gaze, her stance beginning to waver.

"Weston? You're staring," she said, breaking the silence.

The sound of her voice shook Weston from his daze. He scrunched up his face like he was in pain. "Do forgive me, Miss Hampton, but the way the candlelight is reflected in your eyes causes them to look as though..." He cocked his head to one side, biting his tongue against the very whimsy he claimed was unbecoming in a woman. What was this absurd sentiment in his thoughts? He ran a hand over his face as his mind raced.

Isabelle turned away from him, allowing a lock of hair to fall across her cheek hiding him from her view. "I didn't mean to interrupt you. I need to go back. My aunt..." She turned to leave.

Weston let out a heavy breath, his shoulders drooped. Then placing the violin under his chin, he began to play. The tune was soft and beautiful. Weston closed his eyes and disappeared into his own musical world. Isabelle could feel his absence from the room though he still stood across from her. He played away her existence. Isabelle gazed at the scene before her, wondering what memories that song held for him. A shimmering movement caught her eye, and she wondered if it was a trick of the candlelight. A silent tear traced its way down his cheek. Isabelle felt like an intruder. She gathered her skirts and backed towards the ballroom as the violinist's song drifted into the night.

~

It was quite late once all the guests had gone from Lexington Estate, but Walsh did not mind. Something did bother him though as he went on the hunt for his absent cousin. He found Weston in his room staring out the window. His violin rested in his lap.

"Where were you hiding all evening?" Walsh asked, puzzled, standing in the doorway.

Weston gave a slight start as his gaze flitted towards Walsh. His expression was gray, and his eyes showed no spark. Weston sighed and blinked several times before muttering a response. "I was in the salon downstairs."

Walsh frowned. "Why?"

"I played." Weston stroked his fingers along the violin.

"All night?"

"Yes."

"Odd, but not unlike you." Walsh came and stood by the window in front of his cousin. "Why did you not come and join the fun?"

Weston shrugged. "I am not much for parties, you know that."

Walsh lowered himself onto the window ledge, concern written in his features. "Be that as it may, you never avoid them completely."

Weston made no reply; he continued to stare past Walsh. Walsh gave an exasperated sigh. "Good heavens man! What is the matter?"

Weston stood, placed the violin in its case, and began to pace. "I do not wish to burden you."

Walsh folded his arms across his chest. "Come now, I have never balked at your burdens. Why are you moping about?"

"I must return to London immediately." He snapped the lid shut on the violin case, avoiding his cousin's eyes. Walsh shot to his feet and bounded to Weston's side.

"London!? Whatever for? Has something happened?"

"Please, Walsh, don't press me."

"Do not act like madman. We have been through too much together." Walsh took hold of Weston's coat sleeve and looked him in the eye, pleading with him. "Tell me what is going on."

Weston looked down at the floor. Walsh could see the pain radiating off his cousin. All the possible scenarios began to flash through Walsh's mind and fear began to grow in his heart. "Please, my friend, do not carry this alone."

There was a long silence between the two men before Weston murmured: "I received a letter," he paused and took a shaky breath, "My mother is dead."

Shocked, Walsh swallowed hard. "Aunt Phoebe is gone?" He spoke the words slowly as if disliking the taste they left in his mouth. He released his grip on the coat sleeve. "This is terrible."

Weston nodded.

"You hid this. Why did you not say anything?"

"I could not dampen the day's events with tidings such as these."

"You buried your grief." Walsh could not keep the hurt from his voice.

"I needed time."

"I have known you to keep news of this sort to yourself far longer than this. I will not hold it against you, though you're slow to confide in me."

Weston scrubbed his hand across his face in an agitated manner. "Let us leave it for now. You know my grief and that is enough."

"I know your grief."

Weston sighed and squared his shoulders. "I will leave for London at daybreak. Her affairs cannot wait."

Walsh put his hand on Weston's shoulder. "Shall I go with you?"

Weston gripped his cousin's wrist, shaking his head. "There is no need for you to come. Besides, I am not entirely certain how long it may take."

"Will you return to Lexington?" Walsh wore a sad frown.

"I would like that. I will come as soon as I can." Weston smiled down at the leather case where his hand still rested. His voice quaked as he reflected: "She always did love the sound of the violin."

CHAPTER 7

Brooklyn Manor,

"What a wonderful evening!" Laura heaved an airy sigh at breakfast the next morning.

Sara smiled. "I'm glad you enjoyed yourself."

Laura beamed. "Oh, I did! I danced with the most interesting gentlemen."

Dawson looked at his niece over the top of his newspaper; he raised a curious brow. "Laura, your enthusiasm for gentlemen cautions me to restrict your outings."

Laura laughed, startling Isabelle so that she nearly spilled her tea. "Oh, uncle. You know it is all in fun. I assure you it is perfectly harmless. Mother has her hopes that I will marry well."

Dawson sucked in his breath. "Yes, your mother has quite the aspirations for you. I should hope you are clever enough to accomplish a good match."

"You need not worry, uncle. I shall not disappoint."

"Dawson, please." Sara laid a calming hand on her husband's arm. His mouth twitched under the weight of a withheld comment.

"What about you, Isabelle? Tell us the highlights from your first ball." Sara sipped her tea with an expectant look to Isabelle.

Laura rolled her eyes. "It seemed to me that Isabelle's first ball was rather a success. She danced only with the host! If it had been any other host, perhaps I would not regard this as a feat, but to secure the affections of Mr. Walsh, that is sport."

Dawson and Sara exchanged a look. "Really? I was unaware of this development." Sara's voice rang with suppressed intrigue.

Isabelle nibbled on her piece of toast to keep from scolding Laura. "Laura exaggerates. It was a dance, not a proposal."

"Dances may lead to proposals. If he did not like you, he would never have asked you to dance a second time," Laura defended her point while smearing jam on a piece of toast.

"While Mr. Walsh's affections remain unknown to us, Isabelle, tell me, what do you think of him?" Sara fingered her hair while awaiting the response.

Isabelle chewed her breakfast before answering: "He seems kind and pleasant. He was an attentive host." Isabelle thought back to the gushing enthusiasm with which he engaged her. A smile crossed her features.

Sara seemed pleased with her niece's praise of Walsh. "He is quite charming. There is no finer man in the county," Sara remarked.

"How true! He also happens to be very handsome! Don't you think so, Isabelle?" Laura put in, taking a sip of her milk.

Isabelle hid behind her napkin to keep from laughing aloud at Laura's bluntness. "Yes, I suppose he is handsome." Isabelle pictured

Walsh's face, with his round dark eyes and cheery disposition. His was a face she enjoyed seeing.

"Well, you could do worse than to set your cap to Mr. Walsh," Laura asserted.

Dawson folded his paper and looked at his two nieces. "What a silly pair you are," he chided. "Mrs. Dawson, why did you ever let them go spend an evening dancing when they only come home full of foolish talk? I fear they have lost their senses."

"I don't know, Dawson," Sara replied, placing her teacup in its saucer. "I had thought that dancing all night would make them tired and less troublesome."

"Really, my dear, it seems to have had the opposite effect. They are more trying than ever."

The young ladies giggled.

"Aunt Sara, did you really think we would have a miserable time?" Laura asked.

Sara chuckled, patting Laura's hand. "Not at all. I had hoped you girls would have a wonderful time. It seems you have." She shot Dawson a pacifying look.

"Although your minds are swimming with ridiculous ideas," Dawson added in his exasperated tone though his expression softened towards his wife.

Isabelle glowed as she recalled how Mr. Walsh had remained close to her most of the night. Perhaps their ideas were not entirely ridiculous.

After breakfast, Isabelle convinced her uncle to let her ride while Sara and Laura went out to call on an ailing neighbor. She hurried to her room to change into riding clothes. Rummaging through the closet, she pushed aside party dresses and everyday dresses and took out a calico she had selected for riding. She pulled her dress over her head and slipped into the calico. Once she was ready, Isabelle went to the stables in search of Sam, the groom.

The stable had a cobblestone floor and stalls lined both sides. Horses poked their heads over the stall walls, nickering softly as she passed. She stopped to pet their noses and mutter compliments to them. They nuzzled her hands, causing her to laugh.

A man was leaning on a stall door down the corridor, talking to the horse inside. Isabelle peered into the stall to see a mare with a colt by her side. She smiled, as the man continued to speak to the small horse. The colt snorted, nuzzling his arm. He chuckled. Isabelle cleared her throat.

The groom turned around and smiled. "Well, 'ello, Miss. 'ampton. What can I do for you?"

Isabelle brushed a lock of hair under her hat. "Sam, my uncle said he spoke to you about a horse?"

His smile grew larger as she addressed him. "Right you are, miss. Mr. Dawson would 'ave only the best for you," he said with a swell of pride. "Come, I 'ave just the gal for you." He led her to a stall where a black and white mare stood dozing inside. She raised her head when Isabelle peeked over the door. Sam gazed at the mare as he slipped into her stall. "This 'ere is Tafata. She'll take good care of you." He rubbed her neck with a loving hand.

Isabelle smiled. "What a lovely horse and so pretty."

"Aye, she be a perfect lady, this one."

"I think she will suit me. Could you get her ready, Sam?"

He ran a hand over Tafata's nose. "Aye miss, that's me job."

Isabelle smirked at his cheek.

Isabelle and her patchwork mount roamed close to the house for the first bit of their ride as they got to know each other. As Isabelle gained confidence, she pointed the mare towards the open field and soon they were flying across the ground. As the mare leapt a fallen log, Isabelle noticed a rider coming towards them. She reined the mare in as the horseman approached. Isabelle smiled, taking a firm hold as the horse gave a little prance.

"Good morning, Mr. Walsh."

Walsh tipped his cap. "Miss Hampton, what a pleasant surprise to find you out here. It is a fine morning for a ride."

Isabelle nodded. "Yes, that it is." She moved her hand up to smooth some of her hair down. Walsh watched as she attempted to untangle her hair, an amused smirk lighting up his face.

"No need to fuss, Miss Hampton. You look lovely as always."

Isabelle chuckled. "I should have tied my hair."

Walsh glanced around. "Are you alone, Miss Hampton? I do not see your uncle."

"Yes, I'm alone."

"I take it Miss Millis does not ride." He chuckled at his own joke.

She raised a brow in good humor. "I see you are also alone," she noted when no other rider joined them. "Your Mr. Weston doesn't ride either?"

"He does actually. Has rather a splendid seat that man. Unfortunately, Mr. Weston left early this morning for London on a matter of significant importance."

"Oh, I hope it will be okay." Isabelle gave him small smile.

Walsh heaved a sad sigh. "Yes, I hope so too. Might I accompany you on your ride?"

Sudden shyness mixed with pleasure washed over Isabelle at his question; she bowed her head. "You can, although I think we're going in circles," she replied moving the mare forward.

Allowing his horse to walk on a long rein, Walsh fell in beside her. "Where did you wish to go?" he asked, ducking under a low hanging branch.

"Not really anywhere particular."

"You are on the journey to nowhere? Sounds like quite an adventure." Again, he chuckled.

Isabelle shot him a look. "I just wanted to get out and enjoy some fresh air."

Walsh nodded. "Ah, yes, one of those days. I understand that feeling." He looked across at Isabelle. "Sometimes being indoors all the time starts to turn a person mad."

"I never really thought of it that way."

"Oh yes, boredom is the catalyst for most inventions."

Isabelle laughed. "What?"

"It is true! Invention exists to give people something to do or to give the inventors something to do."

Isabelle smiled looking down at Tafata's mane. "That's silly."

Walsh shrugged. "Perhaps."

The two rode on in silence, each enjoying the scenery. They passed a creek bordered by large boulders and a few trees, and they halted to let the horses drink. Isabelle slid from the mare's back and looped her reins over a tree branch. Once Isabelle was sure the mare was content to nibble bits of grass, she started to hike up a small ridge. Walsh fell in step with her, and the pair made their way to the top of the ridge.

The roar of the distant surf reached their ears. Isabelle held her breath as she gazed down at the rocks below her as a sea breeze tickled her nose and played with her hair. She watched as waves built up speed on the open waters and then came hurling into the cliffs shattering into sparkling water droplets on impact. Walsh stood in silent wonder by her side.

"Fascinating, isn't it?" His statement was more observation than question.

Isabelle nodded. Again, and again the waves grew to enormous sizes then roared to a close. Isabelle reached down and picked up a small rock. Walsh watched with mild interest as she tossed it over the edge. It seemed to fall forever before it disappeared. Isabelle looked at Walsh. "That's a long way down."

A small smiled tugged at Walsh's lips. "I dare say it is."

How long they stood there looking out over the sea Isabelle did not know; she felt surprisingly comfortable in the company of the man beside her. She stole a glance at him. Walsh's tall, well built, person stood elegant; his dark hair ruffled, and his coat tails swayed in the breeze.

Neither took any notice of the skies where large dark clouds were forming. Soon, it started to rain. Walsh began laughing as water dripped from his hair into his face; his eyes danced as he looked at Isabelle and shrugged. Isabelle smiled and turned her palms upwards, catching the water in her hands. Walsh took Isabelle by the arm, and they hurried back to the horses. The rain began to fall harder. They tried to shelter their heads from the downpour but to no avail. The pair dripped with water.

"I can't believe how quickly the storm came upon us," Walsh mused assisting Isabelle into the saddle.

Isabelle smiled blinking back the water from her eyes. "I had no idea it was coming."

A funny smile played in Walsh's features as he stood below Isabelle, looking up at her seated on the horse. Her hair hung wet and clung to her face. Water trickled down her nose and ran onto the calico dress. Her cheeks were rosy, and her eyes were bright despite the storm.

Curiously, she cocked her head to one side. "Mr. Walsh, is something wrong?"

Slowly he shook his head, his eyes never straying from her face. "Not at all, Miss Hampton."

He turned from her briefly to swing onto his horse's back and turned the animal to face her.

"I will see that you arrive home safely. I could not live with myself if I allowed you to ride alone in a storm."

Isabelle's cheeks flushed as she bowed her head.

They rode without much conversation. The steady creak of wet leather and the jingle of the horse's equipment were the only sounds as rain fell in sheets making it difficult to see across the land.

"I have never seen rain like this in all my life!" Isabelle exclaimed, directing the mare around a dip in the trail.

Walsh chuckled ducking around a tree. "Welcome to England. We generally do not have pleasant little showers."

Isabelle was surprised at how far they had gone when Brooklyn Manor finally came into view. There was a bit of clatter as they rode into the courtyard. Sam came running from the stables, pulling his hat over his eyes as he greeted them. He took Isabelle by the hand, helping her slide to the ground and disappeared with the mare back into the stable. Walsh stood next to his mount, holding it by the bridle as Isabelle scrambled to the door of the house.

"Won't you come in?" she called over the pouring rain, brushing hair from her face.

Walsh shifted his weight from one foot to the other. "I do think I should be getting back to Lexington."

Isabelle glanced up at the dark sky. "But the storm. You can't ride in the rain."

Walsh shrugged his shoulders. "It will not do any harm. I am already sopping wet."

"But Lexington is another mile from here!" she protested. "You can get out of this rain and warm up a bit. It might let up. Please?"

She smiled slyly. "I couldn't live with myself if I allowed you to ride home in this storm and you caught pneumonia because of it."

Walsh chuckled, a warm sound in the chilly air as a groom ran from the stable to collect his horse. Walsh hurried through the rain and soon stood dripping wet beside Isabelle.

"As you wish, my lady," he said, bowing crisply.

Isabelle laughed as the pair slipped into the house and Heather met them at the door.

"Miss Hampton!" she exclaimed, rushing to Isabelle's side. "You are absolutely drenched! You must get out of those wet things at once or you will surely catch cold."

"I'll be fine Heather..." Isabelle started to say.

"Certainly not, miss! I will send for Mr. Dawson if you do not come willingly."

Isabelle looked at Walsh. "Will you excuse me a moment? Mansfield will see you have fresh tea and someplace warm to rest."

Walsh nodded. "Certainly, I am perfectly aware how overprotective maids can be."

Isabelle smiled apologetically as Heather took her by the arm and whisked her away to her room. Isabelle was glad for the opportunity to make herself a little more presentable.

Soon she returned dry and warm. She found Walsh before a crackling fire, sipping steaming hot tea. He set the teacup on the mantle when she entered the parlor. His eyes scanned over her. Isabelle felt embarrassed by his intensity, and she glanced at the writing desk beside the wall.

"Are you well, Mr. Walsh?" she asked looking back at him.

He grinned. "Yes Miss Hampton, I am beginning to dry."

Isabelle poured herself some tea from the pot on the table and sipped it carefully as they sat across from each other before the fire. Isabelle admired the firelight reflected in Walsh's dark eyes as they chatted about everything that was on their minds.

CHAPTER 8

London, England. August 10, 1820

It had been several days since his arrival in London and Weston found himself sitting at a desk with hundreds of papers scattered before him. Some were letters of condolence; others were notices and bulletins his mother had collected over some years and still more were of legal matters. Weston leaned his elbows forward on the desk and heaving a shaky sigh rubbed his throbbing head.

"I wish I had brought my violin," he muttered staring at a letter of sympathy.

His clothes were clean pressed, but his complexion was pale, and his eyes glazed with a faraway stare as he tossed the letter aside watching it lie lifeless on the desk. The chair scrapped along the floor as he stood up to stretch and contemplate the office. As he stood in silence his mind drifted back to twenty years earlier when the study had been his father's and he himself had been a young boy.

Weston ran his hand over the bench running along one wall of the study. He recalled how as a child he used to sit and swing his short legs above the floor while watching his father work. He remembered the smile and the gentle speech of the man who used to sit behind the desk.

Mr. Weston had only one more voyage before he could retire altogether. He left his family for that final obligation to the sea. Weston was just a boy when they received the news that his father would not return. He became the centre of his mother's world. And now, she too was gone.

Why Isabelle would be on his mind at this moment was beyond him, but he longed to see her again. Weston wished to return to Lexington, but he could not leave London yet. The memory of Isabelle would have to do for now.

Brooklyn Manor. October 4, 1820,

"Do you have to go so soon?" Isabelle asked wringing her hands as she watched Laura pack her belongings. Laura straightened up and sighed clutching a gown between her hands.

"Father said in his last letter that he misses me terribly and wishes I would come home. I have been gone for several months by now. I do not think the younger children can make up for my absence. Father has always been very fond of me."

Laura gave Isabelle a mischievous smirk before placing the gown in the trunk. "Besides, you will not need me here now that you have a handsome gentleman friend. I dare say he makes a fine companion."

Isabelle smiled her cheeks turning soft crimson. "Walsh is only a friend of the family."

Laura laughed. "Indeed. A friend who calls regularly and speaks mostly to you. He escorted you to a party even. Friends certainly, if not something more."

"Nothing more as of yet," Isabelle mused with a little smirk.

Laura shot her a look while closing the lid on the trunk. "Time will tell. But I suppose I am set to go." She turned and gave Isabelle a hug. "Perhaps I will return at Christmas."

Isabelle nodded. "Yes, that would be lovely."

Arm in arm they walked downstairs to the entryway. Laura paused and faced Isabelle. "Now, promise me you will keep yourself out of trouble."

Isabelle laughed brushing a lock of hair behind her ear. "I promise."

Sara arrived and gave Laura a hug. "I am so glad you came, Laura. I always enjoy your visits," she said holding the girl close.

Laura nodded. "Thank you for inviting me. I enjoyed my stay very much and I should like to come again."

She hugged Dawson who patted her dark head fondly before she was loaded into the carriage and on her way. Laura waved as the carriage pulled out of the drive. Isabelle stood sadly, watching her friend go.

"Have Tafata saddled. I want to see Laura off," she asked of a passing footman he nodded and hurried to the stable. Isabelle stepped back into the house and selected her cloak from its peg, and draped it around her shoulders, tying the ribbons at her throat. As she moved down the steps, she met Sam leading Tafata.

"Your 'orse, Miss."

She smiled at the groom. "Thank you, Sam."

He nodded as he helped her onto the horse's back. Isabelle turned the mare towards the road and set off at a gallop with her cloak trailing out behind her. Isabelle rode along the estate fence beside the road until she caught the carriage. Laura noticed Isabelle after a moment and, smiling, she waved a handkerchief at her friend. Isabelle slowed the horse and waved until the carriage was out of sight.

Isabelle decided to return home the long way. Clucking her tongue, she encouraged the mare to trot. The horse moved with swift ease over the hills and jumped with grace over fallen brush. Isabelle sighed, feeling content in the peace of the fields with nothing but the rhythmic squeak of leather to interrupt her thoughts. Gazing out over the land Isabelle thought she heard music. Glancing about her she shook her head.

"That's odd. I must be hearing things."

Again, a gentle song burst out then faded to nothing. Tafata's ears pricked forward, and Isabelle smiled patting the mare's neck. "Well, I know now I wasn't dreaming," she said to the horse. "We definitely heard something."

Tafata stopped and looked towards the trees. Isabelle followed the mare's gaze. A horse stood tied to one of the trees. The horse raised its head and whinnied. Tafata pranced and snorted stomping her feet. A man came from inside the grove of trees to check on the horse. He reached out to soothe the animal and Isabelle recognized him at once.

"Mr. Weston?" she exclaimed, cocking her head to one side.

He looked up and saw her not more than twenty feet away. Holding onto his horse's bridle he stared at Isabelle a moment before returning her greeting. "Miss Hampton, what are you doing so far from Brooklyn?"

Isabelle mulled the question. Tafata trotted on the spot. "We're enjoying some fresh air. Riding is peaceful." The mare's movement was making Isabelle uncomfortable, so she slid from her back.

Holding the reins, she stepped closer to Weston. "And why are you out here hiding in the bush?" she asked raising a curious brow.

He gave a weak smile. "I too was in search of peace."

Isabelle nodded stroking the mare's nose as the horse buried into her cloak. "I didn't realize how many thoughts are in my head until I found myself alone with them."

"Indeed."

Isabelle looked up at him. He appeared as though he understood how heavy private thoughts could be and that he sympathized with anyone who had to carry such a burden. An opportunity for connection hung in the air, but neither reached for it. Either shame or fear restrained them. "I understand you have been in London. When did you return?"

Weston sighed, rubbing the back of his neck. "Not long over an hour."

Isabelle looked surprised. "Does Mr. Walsh know you've returned?"

"Yes. I collected my violin at the house before coming out here."

He looked tired. His clothes had wrinkles, his hair stood mussed, and dark circles underlined his eyes. She pitied him. He did not seem unwell, yet he was not himself.

"We are far from London. You must be tired."

"Most assuredly. Upon my arrival, my cousin bombarded me with questions."

"He worries about you?"

"He is inquisitive."

"So, you're hiding from him?"

Despite his weariness, a lopsided smile tugged at one corner of his mouth. "Well, he does not know where I am right this moment."

They stood a few minutes in awkward silence.

"How was your trip?" Isabelle inquired.

Weston's last bit of spark went out as darkness washed over his features. "There is no possible way to describe what torment I experienced." He turned away from her.

Isabelle was taken-aback. "If I spoke out of line..."

"Please, no apology is necessary, my lady. You have done nothing wrong."

Isabelle fell silent wondering if he would continue.

"The evening of Walsh's ball I received a letter from an old friend in London containing news of a very distressing nature," he paused, closing his eyes as though reliving the moment. "The letter informed me of my mother's death."

Isabelle gasped covering her mouth with her hand; sudden memories of the loss of her own parents came flooding back. His brief comment transported her back to the colonial home where she could hear the crackling wood and smell the consuming smoke. She trembled.

Weston took a deep breath. "I returned to London to arrange her affairs. It took rather a while longer than I had anticipated." He heaved a heavy sigh and looked to the violin case resting on a nearby stump. "My mother gifted me this violin when I was a boy. It supported me through some of the most troubling times."

Isabelle recalled the countless books she had read since the death of her parents. She spent hours buried within their pages, finding a reprieve from the reality of grief. "I think I understand."

Her voice was small, and he continued his speech as if he had forgotten her presence. "It is an instrument of comfort during days of grief. Unfortunately, in my haste to make for London I forgot the violin." He levelled his gaze at her as if slowly emerging from the spell that held him captive to his memories of London. "I had to settle for the pianoforte, but no comfort can be found in such cacophony."

Isabelle smiled. "I'm sure you play well."

Weston gave a humorless chuckle. "Certainly not, I know my playing is ill. The neighbors have told me so."

Isabelle laughed gently. "Ridiculous."

"Perhaps," he muttered.

Their eyes met and held for a moment. A sudden torrent of wind howled through the trees startling both the horses. Tafata leapt to the side jerking the reins free from Isabelle's hand. Isabelle's arms flew to cover her head as the fleeing mare swung her head over top of Isabelle. Eyes wide with horror, Isabelle watched the mare bolt for home. She stood in shock as the horse gained speed and the sound of her hooves grew distant.

Weston started to laugh.

She frowned and spun to face him. "I don't find this funny," she spat the words at him.

Weston looked amused. Still chuckling, he turned away from her. He retrieved the violin from the stump and proceeded to strap it to his saddle. Isabelle stared out across the countryside placing a hand on her hip.

"I can't believe this," she muttered, her eyes snapping, showing her disgust.

Weston looked at her over his horse's back. A slight smile played on his lips as she folded her arms and stood with her back towards him. "Come then, my lady," he called to her.

She turned to face him, a flush in her cheeks. He extended his hand towards her. "You would let me borrow your horse?" She stepped towards him, eyeing the animal.

"That's an absurd notion," Weston replied swinging onto the horse's back in one swift move. "We are several miles from Brooklyn and even further from Lexington. Nay, madame, I am a gentleman, but this is no walking distance." He looked down at Isabelle and offered her his hand. "Would you care for a hand up?"

Isabelle stared at him. "You're not serious."

Weston shrugged. "You have but one alternative."

Isabelle looked towards Brooklyn. She could see the peak of its roof in the distance. She also spied her horse marching home at a brisk trot. Muttering something inaudible, she accepted his hand. Weston leaned over to help her onto the horse. He had no trouble pulling her up behind him. She perched sideways on the horse's back with her skirts and cloak draped over the side.

"I can't ride like this! I will fall."

Weston glanced over his shoulder at her, sensing her apprehension. "You will be quite safe."

"Really, that can't be possible. You have a secure seat in the saddle. I have nothing but fur to keep me here."

"Then I suggest you hold onto something."

As the horse stepped forward, Isabelle felt as though she were going to slip. She threw her arms around Weston and laced her fingers at his waist. Weston started and jerked the hose to one side. "What are you doing?"

"Holding on."

⁓

"Where is that girl!" Sara exclaimed, wringing her hands as Sam took Isabelle's horse to the stable.

Mansfield had alerted the Dawsons moments after he noticed the riderless horse. Dawson paced the courtyard; his hands clasped tightly behind his back. "I am going to look for her," he announced and was about to call for his horse when a horseman trotted up to the courtyard and slowed his mount to a walk.

Relief washed over Sara as she spotted Isabelle seated behind the horseman. She hurried over to meet them.

Weston halted the horse and carefully dismounted so as not to upset Isabelle. Once on the ground, he looked up at the girl. His expression was unreadable, but Isabelle thought he still looked amused. "I trust you are well, Miss Hampton?"

"Yes, very well." She gathered her skirt over her arm so it would not catch on anything as she slid from the horse's back.

Weston caught her around the waist and lowered her to the ground. Their gazes held a moment as his arms lightly rested about her. A strange sparkle lit Weston's eyes as he looked down at her as he held her close to him.

"Isabelle, what happened?"

Weston withdrew from Isabelle as her aunt came rushing over to inspect her.

Sara cupped Isabelle's face in her hands and studied her features. "Are you hurt?"

Isabelle smiled chuckling softly. "No, I'm fine," she replied with an air of ease.

"That horse returned over an hour ago. I worried something dreadful had happened to you," Sara explained as she looked over Isabelle.

Isabelle shook her head, brushing away her aunt's fussing. "I'm not hurt. Tafata spooked when I stopped to talk to Mr. Weston."

"You weren't thrown?"

Dawson stepped in and laid his hand on his wife's shoulder. "Sara, she shows no indication of injury. She does not have a speck on her."

"I was on the ground when Tafata bolted then Mr. Weston offered me a ride." Isabelle felt sudden shyness as she smiled at Weston. He swallowed and gave her a slight nod.

"Well so long as you are unhurt..." Sara said concern still etched in her features.

Isabelle grasped her hands. "Really, I'm fine."

Dawson turned to Weston. "Thank you for returning my little lady."

Weston nodded as they shook hands. "It was no trouble at all."

Dawson glanced at Isabelle. "Perhaps your experience with her has been different from mine."

Weston directed a slight smile to Isabelle. "Yes, sir. That it may be."

CHAPTER 9

Lexington Estate,

"I see you have decided to return after all," Walsh stated dryly glancing up from his book.

Weston paused in the door of the study. "I take it you speak of my untimely disappearance."

"I had thought you would say a little more than 'hello' after being gone so many weeks," Walsh replied turning his attention back to his book.

Weston leaned his shoulder into the doorframe clutching the violin case in his hand "I am almost certain you found ways to entertain yourself in my absence."

Walsh slammed his book shut, tossing it onto the table and stood. "Weston, we both know this had nothing to do with me." Walsh' voice raised a notch in frustration.

Weston pushed himself away from the door to face his cousin squarely. "If this conversation has nothing to do with you, would you please be so kind as to explain to me what it is about?" Weston asked, baffled.

Walsh paused a moment his expression soft but sad. "Weston," he said, reaching out and taking hold of his cousin's sleeve. "You have just been through one of the greatest horrors of life: the loss of your mother. Have you nothing to say?"

Weston lowered his eyes to the floor. "I do not care much for speaking of one's feelings, particularly my own. I have no desire to hear about anyone else's struggles, why then would anyone be interested in knowing mine? They would gain nothing but information to be useful for starting unwanted gossip."

Walsh shook his head. "You have a low opinion of people, my friend. They are not as bad as you presume. Not all are in search of tidbits of gossip."

The two cousins stood in silence, each considering what the other had said. "Is everything alright in London?" Walsh asked, breaking the quiet.

Weston nodded, meeting his cousin's gaze. "I suppose things were as well as they could be under the circumstances. I will keep the house in London. Someday I may wish to return there."

"Yes, some day maybe, but you can't very well live in that big house all alone, can you?"

"Does this mean you wish me to stay?"

"Certainly. I am here alone. I enjoy the company."

Weston blinked. "As do I. I suppose I never really thought I would be alone in London." An image of Isabelle stroking her horse's nose entered his thoughts.

Weston gave his head a slight shake, as Walsh continued. "We will face that change, if need be, but for now, let us be here."

Brooklyn Manor,

"Ouch!" Isabelle exclaimed shaking her hand before sticking her finger in her mouth. That was the third time this morning she had pricked herself with her sewing needle.

Sara looked up from her work an annoyed frown creasing her brow. "Isabelle, you must keep your mind on your work."

Isabelle gave her aunt a sheepish smile. She could not keep the dashing Walsh from her thoughts. He was so kind, so attentive, and he seemed rather fond of her. Just thinking about him tied her stomach into knots; he was a fine gentleman whose situation in life would make any young woman quite comfortable and happy. She sighed as the handsome face and playful eyes of Weston invaded her daydreaming. Isabelle frowned at her sewing, attempting to shake the man's image. What was it about him she found so interesting? True, he was very rich, and very handsome, but his personality was quirky and proud, both characteristics that Isabelle did not like. He seemed elegant, but had no zeal for life, just a bored stoicism. He was in many respects, opposite of Mr. Walsh. Walsh was both exuberant and charming. Isabelle held a certain fondness for him. She determined that of the two men he was the better choice. Forcing the brooding cousin from her mind, she again let her imagination begin to wander...Lexington was a beautiful estate and would thrive under a lady's hand...Isabelle had an idea or two for the front gardens...Mrs. Edmond Walsh... "Oh dear!" Isabelle pulled her hand away from the biting needle sending a guilty glance at her aunt.

Sara set down her own work and frowned at the younger woman. "You are not going to be of any use to your sewing if your mind has free rein. Go on, be off with you before you do yourself harm." Sara shooed the girl from the room with a twinkle in her eyes.

Isabelle floated up the stairs to her room. Falling onto her bed, she stared at the ceiling. Heaving a sigh Isabelle frowned, that Weston! If only he would stay in London. Isabelle worried about his connection with Walsh, especially since Walsh held such respect for his opinion. Mr. Weston had called her childish. What would stop him from telling Walsh this? He would convince his cousin to find a more suitable woman! Isabelle sat up on the bed.

"I have no intention of losing Mr. Walsh to you or anyone else!" she said determinedly into the silent room, rising from her bed. She took a seat at the dressing table and stared at her reflection in the mirror. "Look at you, the future Mrs. Edmond Walsh." She picked up a brush and began to comb through her long locks.

~

"Miss Hampton?" Heather stuck her blonde head into Isabelle's room with its ruffled maid's cap covering most of her tight ringlets.

"What is it, Heather?" Isabelle's voice came from the dressing table the next morning where she sat combing her hair.

Heather came to her side and looked critically at her. "Miss Hampton, you are not even dressed!"

Isabelle looked up at the maid. "I haven't decided what to do with my hair." She played with the ruffled sleeves on her dressing gown.

Heather made a face at her mistress. "Well, I suppose you should decide soon. Mr. Walsh has just arrived, and I am certain he will want to see you."

Isabelle put down her brush hastily and proceeded to pin back her hair. "Heather! Why didn't you say so? Fetch my brown dress!"

Heather nodded and started rummaging through the wardrobe to retrieve the dress. Isabelle pulled off her dressing gown as Heather tossed the dress over her tousled curls and hurriedly tied the laces of the bodice.

"Do you know why he's here?" Isabelle asked, lying her hand at her throat while Heather tied the laces.

"No miss," she replied. "Mr. Dawson received him in the library and requested tea."

Isabelle smiled, straightening her dress. "That means he will likely stay for the afternoon."

Heather shrugged. "It seems Mr. Walsh is on a social call."

Soon her rustling skirts were the only sounds Isabelle heard as she hurried down the hall to the top of the sweeping staircase. She glided down the stairs, her hand flowing along the banister as she descended. Isabelle walked past the parlor where her aunt and uncle usually took afternoon tea. She gave a fond smile. It had not taken her long to become accustomed to the ways of the household; meals were prompt, and tea was available any time night or day.

Isabelle halted at the library door and could hear her uncle talking with Mr. Walsh. She adjusted her dress and gave her cheeks a slight pinch before entering.

Walsh stood and gave her a charming smile while making her a bow as she stepped into the room. "Good day to you, Miss Hampton."

Isabelle returned his greeting with a smile. "Good morning, Mr. Walsh."

Isabelle's gaze then fell on her aunt and uncle seated on the sofa. Dawson gave her a pleasant smile.

"Won't you join us for tea, Isabelle?" he asked.

Isabelle nodded. "Of course, uncle." While she settled herself on the sofa across from her uncle, Walsh sat once again in the chair next to the fireplace.

"You're looking well, Miss Hampton," Walsh stated as the tea arrived, and a servant set about to serve it.

She smiled. "Thank you."

There was a brief silence before Sara asked, "Do you enjoy having your cousin at Lexington?"

Isabelle winced, nearly spilled her tea; couldn't there be a moment's peace without someone bringing up that insufferable man?

Walsh grinned over the rim of his teacup.

"Certainly! Weston and I have been the best of friends since childhood. I enjoy his company. It has been a pleasure to have him with me these last few weeks. He will always be welcome in my home."

Isabelle gazed out the window a moment. If she did marry Walsh, his relatives would most likely visit, a possibility of which she did not look upon favourably. The thought of Mr. Weston staying with them for any length of time almost made her gag. The man had a house in London. Why didn't he just stay there? Picturing the wooded lane leading up to the elegant Lexington gave her the answer. Even without seeing London, Isabelle knew she would choose Lexington over a townhouse too. Walsh could encourage him to purchase his own country home. He certainly appeared rich enough to do so and he might listen to his cousin.

Dawson inquired after the horses Walsh kept in his barns these days and the two men babbled for a bit about their favourite mounts.

Isabelle listened with partial interest when Walsh suddenly looked at her, capturing her gaze with his.

"Miss Hampton," he began, scooting to the edge of his seat. "Might you be persuaded to take a walk?"

Aunt Sara shot Isabelle a significant look, urging her to accept his offer. Isabelle nodded. "What a nice idea. I would be happy to."

Walsh looked pleased as he excused himself. He rose to his feet and extended his arm to Isabelle. A spot of color rose in her cheek as she permitted him to tuck her hand into the crook of his arm. "It seems to be a beautiful day, but I won't keep your young ward out of doors too long," Walsh commented to Dawson.

Dawson waved his hand.

"I have not the slightest fear for Miss Isabelle's constitution. She did take a solo journey across the ocean."

Walsh regarded her with a curious gaze. "She did indeed. I would like to hear more about such travels."

She gave a nervous titter. "The trip consisted of wind and water. I don't think there's much you would find particularly interesting."

Their conversation began to fade as the young people slipped from the room.

Dawson glanced at his wife with a satisfied twinkle in his eyes. "Well, what do you think of that, my dear?" he asked.

Sara flashed a bright smile over her shoulder when she turned to watch them go. "I like it very much indeed, Phillip."

Heather met her mistress at the door with her cloak and bonnet. Isabelle quickly slipped them on before stepping outside. Isabelle took a deep breath of fresh air.

"I always loved fall," she said glancing about at the fading green grass and the dried flowerbeds dotted here and there by late blooms.

"I prefer spring to fall," Walsh stated as the pair ambled along. "I would much rather see new growth bringing hope of summer than the dingy, dreary and death of autumn."

Isabelle nodded, stopping to pluck a blossom from its pale plant. "Spring is more promising, but all seasons are beautiful in their own way."

Walsh looked at her, a sly smile lighting his expression. "If you were to be a season, Miss Hampton, it would be summer."

Isabelle gave him a puzzled look over the flower petals. "Oh really?"

"Because of your warmth and radiance; summer is when all nature is at its peak and overflows with beauty." Walsh bowed his head. "Summer's beauty is incomparable to your own," he added softly raising his eyes to meet hers. Isabelle flushed slightly gazing deeply into his eyes. His look was tender. "Miss Hampton, might I make a request of you?"

Isabelle's heart skipped a beat at his earnestness. "Certainly."

"Would you consider accompanying me to the Horton party?"

Isabelle touched the petals of the delicate flower. "Yes, I couldn't go alone." She playfully batted her eyelashes once.

Walsh grinned enthusiastically; quickly he leaned towards her, kissing her cheek. "I shall come for you on Thursday, my lady, until then farewell!" he called over his shoulder hurrying off to collect his horse. Isabelle stood in silent but happy shock as she raised her hand to the spot where his lips had brushed her cheek.

CHAPTER 10

Lexington Estate,

Weston plunked on his violin, the melody filling his room. He stood facing the window that overlooked the estate below with his back to the door.

Walsh walked by the door fiddling with his tie, taking a step back he paused in the doorway silently watching his cousin. Mr. Collins stood with Walsh. He was discussing something with his master.

When Collins hurried off Weston half turned and, looking at his cousin, gave a low whistle. "My don't we look dashing tonight!"

Walsh chuckled stepping into the room. "I happen to be on my way to the Horton party."

Weston's blue eyes lit up. "Surely you are not out to catch the attention of Millie Horton!" he teased with a slight grimace.

Walsh frowned. "Miss Horton is a very charming young lady and I dare say you need to speak more respectfully of her."

Weston nodded while he continued to plunk. "Perhaps, but might I remind you that I am a Weston therefore giving me the power to say whatever I wish of a person without them being able to take offence."

Walsh rolled his eyes. "And might I remind you that your grandfather would turn over in his grave if you use the name that he spent his life earning its respect for lording over other people."

"True enough, dear cousin. I shall bring no dishonor to the family name." Weston chuckled at Walsh's bright smile and dancing brown eyes. "What are you so smug about?"

Walsh could not hide his pleasure. "I will pay a call this evening on the most eloquent, charming young lady."

"Good for you," Weston replied absently.

"Yes, I do think I have fallen in love, and I am almost certain she returns my feelings," Walsh gushed, pausing before the dressing table mirror to straighten his tie.

"Oh really? And who might this young lady be? Certainly, someone of fine breeding." Weston asked, finally catching intrigue via his cousin's statement.

Walsh smiled. "The finest."

"Well speak up, who is this angel? For an angel she must be for she certainly cannot be human and yet be all the things you say she is." Weston's curiosity piqued.

Walsh stopped his fussing and faced his cousin. "Mss. Hampton."

Weston hit a sour note and removed the violin from under his chin.

"I-Isabelle Hampton?" he sputtered.

Walsh nodded unaware of his cousin's reaction. "Yes, she is the most delightful young woman I have ever met."

"I recall you saying you had no interest in pursing Miss Hampton?"

Walsh bobbed his head. "Oh, it is quite possible I said that. I say a lot of things. In the last few weeks though, we have been thrown together so much I took rather a fancy to her. It seems foolish not to pursue it. I cannot imagine a better match."

Weston fell into stunned silence as he thought over his next move. Could it be possible they had both fallen in love with the same woman? The very idea was utterly ridiculous!

"Well, I must be off, have a pleasant evening," Walsh bubbled on his way out the door.

Weston murmured a farewell, sitting on the edge of his bed. Lying the violin next to him he ran a hand over his eyes. "I cannot believe that after being gone only a few short weeks, I have lost the woman I love to Walsh before I could even have a chance to win her."

CHAPTER 11

Brooklyn Manor. December 18, 1820,

My Dearest Laura,

So many things have happened since you have left! Mr. Walsh has called so many times I have lost count and he has taken me to every one of the neighborhood parties; it has been truly delightful. He is to come to dinner tonight, unfortunately though, he is bringing that dreadful cousin of his! Luckily, Uncle Dawson may be able to entertain him, so I won't even have to speak to him ('him' being the cousin, but of course you know that). Oh Laura, I feel like I am walking on clouds. Everything is so wonderful right at this moment. Christmas is fast approaching, and Aunt Sara and I have been busy calling on all the neighbors, not one of my most favourite tasks, but one I must do, according to Aunt Sara. We have also been doing a bit of shopping to get ready for the big Christmas Eve party we are having. Will you come to visit over the Christmas holidays? I hope you will because I miss you terribly. Uncle Dawson and Aunt Sara would be pleased to see you again.

Please write soon, your loving friend,
Isabelle Hampton

Isabelle folded her letter and sealed in into an envelope. She sighed while watching the snow swirl around the window. Fingering the quill pen she wondered why she felt so sad when everything was going well. Walsh was doting on her, and it had been several weeks since her last encounter with Weston.

Weston had been polite but reserved. She felt he did not seem genuine but rather a little preoccupied or distracted. Isabelle had found his silence odd when he often spoke his mind without any invitation. She allowed the thought to pass. Sometimes people change. Isabelle herself had changed since the time she had first walked down the gangplank of the ship arriving in England. When she first arrived at Brooklyn Manor she felt so alone and frightened at suddenly being in a new country in the company of strangers. Sara and Dawson had given her time to adjust to her new surroundings, and she was grateful to them for understanding her pain. Isabelle replaced the quill pen in its jar ad stood up from the little writing desk in the library.

Removing a book from the bookcase she began to read about princesses locked in towers, guarded by fierce villains, and rescued by knights in shining armour riding white horses. Isabelle closed the book. She glanced at the clock on the library wall: ten to six. Her stomach let out a little gurgle as she got up from her chair and went out to find her aunt. The company should be arriving soon.

Sara met her in the hallway. "There you are, Isabelle."

Isabelle returned her aunt's greeting.

"What have you been doing all afternoon?" Sara inquired.

"I was reading," she replied with a small smile as Dawson came down the stairs.

"Have you enough reading material?" he asked, coming to stand next to the ladies.

Isabelle nodded as they moved into the sitting room. "Yes, I am not bored, uncle."

Dawson smiled and settled back into the settee. "Excellent, there are fine books to read."

Sara nodded, lowering herself down next to her husband. "He is right, perhaps you will find a new favourite."

Isabelle agreed.

There was a knock on the door and Mansfield bustled past the sitting room.

"Should we go out and find our Christmas tree tomorrow?" Dawson queried of his ladies.

Sara smiled "Why that sounds like a fine idea! Don't you think so, Isabelle?"

"I do! I like Christmas. I would be happy to decorate a tree!"

Dawson beamed. "Wonderful, because Sara and I very much enjoy Christmas ourselves."

Mansfield entered the room followed closely by the two men from Lexington Estate.

"Good evening gentlemen, you are very welcome in our home." Dawson rose to greet them.

Both men gave crisp bows. "Thank you for inviting us, of course the pleasure is all ours," Walsh replied glancing significantly at Isabelle. She smiled before turning away. Weston who stood tall and resolute beside his cousin, appeared distracted.

"You have been well, Mr. Weston? I hear there is a terrible cough going about?" Sara asked while gesturing that their guests sit.

Weston gave a sharp nod and lowered himself into a chair. "Yes, I have been fortunate enough to remain in good health."

"We have also had that good fortune."

The room grew quiet, but everyone smiled warmly to his neighbor. They all seemed oblivious to Walsh and Isabelle stealing glances at each other. Mansfield arrived and announced dinner.

Dawson got to his feet. "Come, let us go into dinner," he said, offering his arm to his wife.

Walsh stepped up to Isabelle's side. "Might I escort you into dinner, Miss Hampton?" he asked with a timid smile.

Isabelle smirked with joy. "Why thank you, Mr. Walsh."

Weston rolled his eyes sarcastically at her response.

She placed her hand in the crook of the arm Walsh offered her and walked by his side into the dining room. Weston followed along behind the couples. As the party seated themselves around the table, a bustle of servants served a steaming creamed soup.

Sara lifted her spoon to her lips, studying Weston who sat across from her. Dabbing her lips with her napkin she asked. "Have you been to London recently?"

Weston looked up and set his spoon aside before answering. "No, I have not. There has been no reason for me to return."

Sara nodded. "Do you plan to spend the winter at Lexington?"

"I will stay only as long as my dear cousin will have me." He glanced at Walsh who grinned.

"I could never tire of Weston's company," Walsh exulted.

Isabelle took a sip of water from her glass, giving a doubtful smile. *I could* she thought.

As the evening wore on the meal began to draw to a close, Walsh placed his napkin on the table and looked at Sara. "Mrs. Dawson, you keep a very fine table and please allow me to express my sincerest thanks to you for having us this evening."

Sara's cheeks flashed a rosy hue. "My, such kind words, really having you dine with us is always a pleasure."

Walsh smiled. "My praise is nothing compared to the things Weston says, he has a charming little way with words."

Isabelle glanced at Weston surprised. *Surely, that can't be true. I have known him to be a man of very few words and some of those were rather unpleasant.* She speculated, scrutinizing the man across from her.

Weston shook his head. "Walsh has a tendency to exaggerate, but in the case of your fine hospitality he has been perfectly accurate."

Sara looked pleased with the praise. "Would you care for tea?" she asked, as the maids cleared away the dishes. There was consensus around the table. Over steaming hot cups of tea, the party visited for a long while.

"Have you spent any time with maps?" Dawson was asking Weston.

He nodded. "Actually I have. My father studied maps and taught me a great deal."

Dawson seemed thrilled. "Really? Well then, you must allow me to show you a map of the East Indies I have recently acquired. It truly is most fascinating."

Weston smiled. "I would be happy to see it."

Dawson excused himself and his guest as they got up from the table and headed to Dawson's study to stare at maps for the next hour or so.

Sara looked at her niece with a mischievous smile. "Isabelle, why don't you and Mr. Walsh take a walk around the gardens? It really is quite a beautiful evening. I have a letter to which I must reply, and I simply cannot put it off another night."

Isabelle looked at Walsh. "I can fetch my wrap?"

He nodded eagerly. "Please do. I would be happy to have a little fresh air."

As Isabelle hurried to get her cloak, Sara chatted with Walsh a moment until she returned. Sara excused herself to the library.

"Have you been out walking much lately?" Walsh asked as they stepped out into the lightly falling snow.

"Yes, I enjoy being outside. Walking gives a person an opportunity to do some thinking."

Walsh looked at her curiously. "What is it that you think about?"

Isabelle was unable hide her slight blush. "Many things really, but mostly of how I came to England. Sometimes I wonder what my future will look like." Isabelle stopped walking, a puzzled frown on her face.

Walsh paused beside her. "Is something wrong?"

Isabelle gave a slight tug on her cloak, glancing back over her shoulder. "It's caught on something."

Walsh chuckled, bending over to untangle her cloak from a snagging rose bush. "Hold still or you will most likely pull the little plant up by its roots."

Isabelle obeyed, waiting for him to rescue her. "Is it badly tangled?" she asked, fiddling with the ribbons on her bonnet.

"Not badly, but it seems to have caught on a thorn," came Walsh's muffled replied. A twig snapped, and the cloak wrapped itself around Isabelle's ankles. Walsh straightened, a self-satisfied look on his face. "There you are, my lady, free at last."

Isabelle smiled. "Thank you."

He stood not more than a few inches from her, gazing down into her face. Isabelle could hear him breathe and could feel his warmth in the snowy night. Cocking his head to one side, he studied her. Narrowing his eyes, gently he reached out and brushed a lock of hair from her cheek. She trembled at his touch.

"Miss Isabelle Hampton, you truly are a beautiful woman," he said softly, dropping his hand to his side.

Isabelle's gaze fell to her shoes at the compliment. "Mr. Walsh, I..."

Walsh's finger silenced her lips. "There is no need for thanks nor bashfulness. I have simply pointed out the obvious." Isabelle looked up, her eyes meeting his as his finger still lingered on her lips. "Miss Hampton, might you grant me permission to say..."

Footsteps crunching in the snow interrupted his words as a figure approached. Walsh drew back from Isabelle. "Walsh, I believe we have intruded on these good people's hospitality long enough,"

Weston said, gently but in a voice of authority as he walked up to them.

Walsh nodded, staring down at the gloves clutched in his hands. "I did not realize it was so late. Miss Hampton, you must be freezing. How very inconsiderate of me."

Isabelle's smile hid her frustration with the interruption. "I'm comfortable, really."

"We shall return you to your uncle and then say our farewells," Weston said, glancing pointedly at his cousin.

The threesome walked in silence back to the house. Isabelle was burning with a desire to know what Walsh had intended to say and an intense annoyance with the man who kept getting in their way. The men stood a moment at the door thanking and complimenting their hosts before saying goodnight and heading out into the lightly falling snow. Isabelle lingered by the door a moment watching them go, a thousand questions racing through her mind.

CHAPTER 12

Lexington Estate,

Walsh sipped his morning cup of tea while opening a letter he had received that morning. Weston sat nearby with nose buried in a book; he had been unusually gruff in his mannerisms that morning which came as quite the shock to Walsh. An almost eerie silence hung over the parlor.

"Weston, would you look at this?" Walsh exclaimed suddenly breaking the stillness.

Weston only grunted in reply.

Walsh frowned "Aren't you even the least bit curious?"

Weston heaved a weary sigh and finally looked at his cousin. "I have been trying to contain myself."

Walsh ignored the tone. "It's from Irene."

"Lovely, what could she have to say that could possibly interest me?"

Walsh swatted him on the arm with the empty envelope. "She is requesting that I come and visit them for Christmas."

"Charming of your sister. Does Henry-the-Great approve?" Weston replied, returning his gaze to his book.

Walsh frowned at his cousin's remark about the man his sister married. "Henry Billingsley is good to Irene even if he thinks too highly of himself at times," Walsh explained, rereading the letter. "I am certain Irene's invitation includes you. She knows that you are here."

Weston chuckled, closing the book, and tossing it onto the side table. "Henry may be willing to allow you into his home, but I doubt he would tolerate me."

Walsh set down the letter and clutched his teacup. "You are probably right. I do not know many people who have been chased out of the house with a broom by his own mother, on several occasions."

Weston smirked at the memory. "I believe you have just enforced my earlier statement."

Walsh rubbed his chin thoughtfully. "Perhaps I have. If your own mother could not stand you, who in this world possibly could?" he teased with a twinkle in his brown eyes.

"My sentiments exactly. I would much rather stay here, if you would allow it," Weston replied.

Walsh blinked in amazement. "You have no plans to return to London for Christmas?"

Weston shook his head. "I would like to spend Christmas in the country. I am not ready to face the chaos of London quite yet."

"Certainly, you are most welcome to stay if you so choose, but I leave for Irene's on the twenty-first."

"That is quite fine by me; the quiet will do me good."

Walsh chuckled shaking his head. "I fear that if you have any quieter, you will forget how to be social."

"The possibility is inviting, but highly improbable, I assure you."

"Weston, you are the only person I know who would spend Christmas alone."

Weston sat silently, considering his cousin's words. "Christmas is a time for reflection," he said at last.

Walsh nodded. "True, but it is also the season for spending time with family and friends."

Walsh snapped his fingers suddenly remembering something. "But then again, everyone knows you have no friends."

Weston chuckled. "Yes, and I will be glad to be rid of you if only for a week."

Walsh smiled, patting Weston on the arm. "I shall miss you too."

Brooklyn Manor,

"Miss Hampton?"

Isabelle stirred when Heather gave her a gentle shake. "Miss Hampton, your aunt has requested that you get up and get dressed."

Isabelle buried her face into the pillows her tangle of curls covering her face. "Go away," she mumbled.

"Please do wake up!" Heather pleaded as footsteps sounded in the hall and Sara bustled into the room with her dark blue skirts billowing behind her.

"Isabelle, you get up this instant!" She roused her niece before drawing back the heavy curtains flooding the room with the morning light. Isabelle yawned trying to shield her eyes from the sudden brightness while she propped herself up on her elbow. Sara stood framed in the window with her hands on her hips.

"What's the matter?" Isabelle asked, dazed.

Sara smiled. "It is nine o'clock and time to get on with this day. We are going to visit the orphanage and bring the children some Christmas treats. I would like to get to Southampton before it is dark so come along get up."

Again, Isabelle yawned while she rose to a sitting position. "Alright, Aunt Sara. I'll be ready soon."

Sara smiled fondly and shook her head before exiting the room. Heather had already searched the closet and selected a deep emerald dress. Laying it on the bed she watched as her mistress tiptoed across the cold wooden floor to the washstand. Isabelle slipped her hands into the water and proceeded to splash some on her face, neck, and arms. Opening her eyes, she stared at her dripping wet reflection before reaching for the towel and dabbing at her face.

Heather helped her into the dress. "This color goes lovely on you, miss, matches your eyes" she mused tying the laces in the back.

Isabelle pinned back her hair with its loose curls bobbing at the back of her neck, she allowed one to fall along her cheek. Offering a small wave to Heather, Isabelle picked up her skirts and hurried off to find her aunt. Her shoes padded down the stairs while Sara watched the descent from the bottom.

"You look lovely, my dear," Sara commented.

Isabelle did a small twirl. "Do you like it, Aunt Sara? It's one of the few that survived the fire," Isabelle explained with a small smile, but her eyes held a look of sadness and confusion.

Sara's heart ached for her young ward, who had endured so much in so short of a time. "It is beautiful." She gave Isabelle a quick hug. "Are you ready to go?"

Isabelle nodded. "Yes, is Uncle Phillip coming with us?"

Sara glanced about. "I thought he was."

"Was and am," Dawson interrupted as he strolled down the hall towards them, a basket slung on his arm. "Good morning, ladies, you both look ravishing this fine morning."

Sara smiled coyly. "Ah such talk!"

Dawson raised his eyebrows. "My dearest, not one of the finest compliments in the world could do justice to you."

"Shall we be off?" Sara asked, chuckling.

Dawson stepped forward offering his arm to his wife. "We shall."

He led the way outside. Isabelle picked her way through the snow covering the ground as snowflakes swirled around her. She smiled as a large snowflake landed on her nose. Laughing, Isabelle flopped into her seat in the carriage across from her aunt and uncle.

"I can't believe how beautiful it is outside!" she exclaimed, ruffling her skirts trying to get rid of the flakes still clinging to it as the carriage began to roll down the drive.

The Dawsons smiled. "It is the eighteenth day of December. We usually have a bit of snow this time of year," Dawson said as the carriage passed Lexington Estate.

Isabelle leaned back into the seat giving a contented sigh she settled in for the ride.

Kingsview Orphanage,

"How do you do Miss Hampton?" Miss Bronte, the headmistress of Kingsview Orphanage, greeted upon meeting Isabelle.

"Very well, thank you," Isabelle replied, feeling a little frightened of the tall, thin gray-haired woman.

"We brought some sweets for the children. Might we hand them out?" Sara inquired giving a kind smile.

Miss Bronte raised a suspicious brow above her spectacles and gave a thin smirk. "The children will be pleased."

She led them to an open room with tables and benches at one end. At the other end of the room about twenty-five children from toddlers to age ten played with a few battered toys. Three little girls had a long strip of leather, from a broken horse's harness, and were using it as a jump rope. Miss Bronte clapped her hands and called for attention. Instantly the room was silent and eager little faces waited for her to continue.

"Children," she said with lips drawn in a tight line. "The Dawsons and Miss Hampton have brought a Christmas treat to share with you all. You may come one at a time to receive one in an orderly fashion." No sooner had Miss Bronte finished her speech when a single file line formed at Isabelle's elbow. She had to smile at the large eyes staring at her with anticipation as she opened her basket to allow each child a cookie. The little boys smiled, and the little girls curtsied as they said thank you.

Sara smiled down at a little girl who gently pulled at her skirt for her attention. Sara reached into her basket and handed the child a Christmas tree cookie. The little girl curtsied causing her tattered green dress to swish against the floor before she skipped off to share the cookie with her stuffed bear.

Isabelle watched her go. "They're so adorable," she said trying to count the children. "Where do they all come from?"

Miss Bronte gave Isabelle a sidelong glance out of the corner of her piercing eyes. "Well Miss Hampton, Southampton is a seaport. Many people arrive here thinking they can build a better life. Unfortunately, for some, they are unable to get jobs and in turn end up living in the streets. Most of the children come from such families after parents pass away. A few of the children have simply been abandoned while others have been given up. Kingsview Orphanage tries to take in as many as we can but sadly, we have not the room to take in all of them," Miss Bronte replied stone-faced not taking her eyes off the little children running about the room.

Isabelle could not help feeling a little sick. "They have no family to take them?"

"No one has come to claim any so far, Miss Hampton."

Isabelle swallowed hard and averted her gaze.

A girl sitting alone in the corner caught Isabelle's eye. Setting her basket down she slipped a cookie into her cloak pocket and stepped around the other children until she reached the girl.

"Hello there." Isabelle spoke quietly and crouched down to the child's level.

The little girl raised her head and shook her curls away from her big eyes. "Hullo," she returned timidly.

"What are you doing all the way over here all by yourself?"

The little girl shrugged drawing her knees up under her chin. "I don't have any parents."

"But don't you like playing with the other children?" Isabelle queried trying to get the child's mind on something else.

Again, the little girl shrugged. "Some of them have lived here for a long time and they all know each other. I've only been here a few months. Some of the older ones don't let me play with them."

Isabelle smiled and brushed a lock of hair out of the child's eyes. "Well, I suppose you will just have to show them how fun you really are and that you can play games too."

A slight frown crossed the little face. "But what if they still won't let me play?"

Isabelle chuckled. "You won't know unless you try, will you?" As the girl pondered this Isabelle asked. "What is your name?"

The girl lit up. "Maria."

"What a pretty name!"

Maria nodded causing her curls to bounce. "It was my mother's name," she added.

Isabelle leaned towards the child and smiled. "Well, Maria, I have a little something for you." The girl stared at her as Isabelle reached into her pocket, pulled out the cookie. Maria tentatively took the cookie murmuring her thanks.

Isabelle stood and began to go back to where she had left her basket. A small tug on her skirt caused her to halt and glance down. Maria's big tear-filled eyes looked up at her.

"Please, don't leave." The child's voice cracked as she held her arms out to Isabelle. Isabelle gathered the child into her arms, feeling her own loss with such force she gave a slight tremble as she held the child.

~

"Weston, I need to stop at the tea house to pick up a package of Irene's favourite tea." Walsh announced as the pair strolled down the Southampton sidewalk. "Do you suppose you would be able to entertain yourself for an hour without getting into trouble?"

Weston sighed, glancing around at the shops and streets. "Southampton. I shall find something to occupy myself."

Walsh grinned. "Good, I don't want you nosing around the tea house."

Weston chuckled glancing mischievously at his cousin. "I take it you still remember that one time in London?"

Walsh sighed, hooking his thumbs in the pockets of his waistcoat. "Yes cousin, sometimes I relive it." Weston bowed his head, hiding a smirk. "Very well, I shall leave you to the tea house and I will meet you at the livery by one-thirty."

The men parted and Weston glanced about at the shops trying to find one that tickled his fancy. "Books and gifts," he read aloud from a sign swinging in the breeze above a shop door. "Does that include music?"

He made his way across the cobblestone street. A bell jingled when he entered the little shop. Shelves lined with hand fans, small paintings, books, toys, and a few types of candy greeted Weston as he stepped aside so a lady exiting the shop could get by. Walking past a colorful display of hand fans, Weston picked up a light blue and cream colored one. He tried to let it fall open. He failed. Weston frowned. "Surely this can't be that difficult," he muttered. Trying again to get the fan to open, he failed.

"Excuse me sir, but you are doing wrong. It opens the other way." Surprised Weston looked down upon the little girl who had spoken to him. She appeared to be around seven and stood with her hands on her hips staring at him as if he were stupid.

"See like this," she said taking the fan from him and allowing it to fall open.

He chuckled. "Oh, of course."

The little girl fanned herself batting her eyelashes flirtatiously at him while peeking out from under the brim of her little hat. Weston gave a wry smile; a girl so young yet she already knew the tactics of a woman. The girl passed the fan back to Weston as a lady down the aisle called the child to her. She flashed Weston a smile before taking the child by the hand and exiting the shop. Weston played with the fan a little longer before returning it to the shelf.

Rounding the aisle, Weston faced rows of books. Weston discovered a book about music. Plucking it from the shelf, he began flipping through it. Taking a step back from the shelf, he nearly tripped over a young woman seated on the floor. She was pouring over the pages of a book. Her dark green skirts flared out around her. Weston had to take a step to avoid stepping on them. He smiled; knowing only one woman who would sit on the floor of a shop engrossed in a book. He watched as she turned the page and continued reading. The curls in her hair bounced when she moved her head. Absently she brushed a curl away from her cheek.

"Hmm," Weston harrumphed as a sly grin crossed his face. He crouched down behind Isabelle. Reaching out he gently pulled one her curls straight and then released it. Isabelle's lock bounced back into a curl. She half spun around to glance over her shoulder and gave a start when she saw Weston. He chuckled at her look of utter confusion.

"It's you," she exclaimed her cheeks flashing pink as she closed the book. "I never thought I'd see you in Southampton."

"Well, I had no previous arrangements for day. I thought a stroll along the pier would do me well," Weston said standing.

Taking both her hands in his, he guided her to her feet. He gazed into her eyes still standing so close to her with her hands buried in his.

"Thank you," Isabelle said avoiding his gaze, and freeing her hands took a step away from him.

He nodded curtly. "The floor is for walking not for sitting. It would not do have someone step on you. Besides, it looks as though you have found what it is you wanted?"

Isabelle shook her head. "I'm afraid I didn't. The book I'm looking for is no longer in print."

Weston tucked the volume in his hand back among the other books before glancing at her. "What book are you looking for?"

Isabelle replaced the book she had been reading on the shelf before answering. "*Where Violets Grow*. I lose my copy in the fire. I don't even know where we got it." She gave a sad sigh. "Alas, there are other books."

Weston nodded. "I am certain there are, but things still hold special memories. However, to romanticize things leads to sentiments which do nothing to foster reason. In the end, we must realize that they are just things and consider them nothing more than trifles," he mused as they walked slowly down the book aisle.

Isabelle was quiet and he stole a glance at her. He caught the movement as she swiped away a tear. He stopped walking and faced her. "I have said something to upset you." His features softened with compassion. "I have spoken out of line. Please, accept my sincerest apology. I had no consideration of your feelings. My thoughts were engaged elsewhere."

Isabelle shook her head, wiping her eyes. "It's alright. You didn't do anything wrong."

Weston reached into his pocket removing a white handkerchief and handed it to her. She took it and dabbed her eyes.

"It's like you said, memories. My father would read to me. That book became our favourite." Isabelle gave a teary smile. "Oh well, it was just a thing." She gave a sad chuckle.

A worried frown crossed Weston's brow. "Yes, but things become special because of the memories they hold. I should have spoken more carefully of the subject."

At this comment, Isabelle's tears fell freely, and she buried her eyes into the handkerchief.

Weston looked around a little panic stricken. "Is your aunt

somewhere near?" he asked, trying to get the girl's mind on something else, but not seeing any sign of Sara.

Isabelle shook her head causing some loose curls to fall in her eyes. "No, Aunt Sara is at the dressmakers picking out fabric for a Christmas cape. She asked me to meet her there when I finished looking," Isabelle murmured as they slipped from the shop out into the chilly winter air.

"Might I escort you to the dressmakers?" Weston asked, falling in step with the teary-eyed woman. "A young lady shouldn't go wandering about by herself."

Isabelle frowned at him through wet lashes. "Please, Robert! I'll be fine. You can do what you like, but I don't need a chaperon."

Weston stopped and stared at her. "Robert?"

She handed back his handkerchief. "Thank you, but I don't need your help." Her words were crisp as she tried to compose herself while brushing the locks from her eyes. Weston frowned.

"Perhaps then it would be best if I go. I agreed to meet Walsh at one-thirty," he said, turning in the other direction.

Isabelle's sad eyes lit up. "Walsh is in town?"

Her sudden interest sent a chill of jealousy down Weston's spin. He answered in a bored, off-handed manner: "Yes, he needed to purchase some gifts. He plans to visit his sister over the Christmas holidays." He added a disinterested sigh.

Isabelle's face fell. She had hoped Walsh would be at Lexington over Christmas. "I see," she replied slowly. "Well, I hope he has a merry Christmas with his sister. Will you return to London?" She felt eager that he should go and leave Walsh's affairs alone. Her enthusiasm for his leaving pricked his pride.

"No, I plan to stay on at Lexington until spring." His reply sounded a little more rigid than he had intended.

"Oh," Isabelle failed to hide the disappointed note in her voice.

Weston cringed.

"Well, I need to go. My aunt is expecting me." She adjusted her curls, her attention averted from him.

Weston made her a crisp bow before turning away and heading off to keep his own appointment.

Lexington Estate,

Walsh frowned as he snapped the latches on his suitcase closed. Something was wrong. Weston could be moody but this morning at breakfast he was plain grumpy. Usually, he was in a sort of mischievous mood covered up with a brooding exterior. Walsh sighed; something had happened. Ever since their trip to Southampton three days ago Weston had kept to himself. His behavior grew more like that of when he had first arrived at Lexington. Last night he had frightened one of the maids with his sulking in the halls.

Walsh shook his head. "That is just the way Weston is, he hasn't changed since we were boys," he muttered as soft violin music filtered into his room from somewhere in the house.

"Are you ready to go, sir?" Collins asked standing in the doorway with his hands clasped behind him at the top of the tails on his black waistcoat.

Walsh nodded. "Yes, the small trunk in the corner will go as well as this case," Walsh said pointing out the two pieces of luggage.

Collins nodded sharply. "Very good sir. Will that be all?"

Walsh ran his fingers through his dark hair surveying the room around him. "I believe it is. I will stay with Irene only a week or two. I should like to say goodbye to Weston before I go."

Collins frowned. "I am afraid Mr. Weston is in a bad way this morning."

Walsh raised a brow as a few fears quickly leaped to mind. "How so, Mr. Collins?"

"He frightened one of the maids."

"Good god, not again."

"Yes, sir. She happened upon him in your study, and he grew quite upset over the disturbance. Poor girl apologized and fled. He has not your skill with people, it would seem."

Walsh stared at the ceiling. "No, that he has not. However, he tends to be a bit more civil than this current state we have been experiencing. I will speak to him."

Collins frowned in puzzlement. "Forgive me for saying, sir, but a very strange man your cousin."

"No harm done, Collins. I do fear leaving him alone at Lexington that upon my return I will find the house with no staff. He might drive you all away from my service."

Collins looked unmoved. "Do not consider us so disloyal, sir. I speak for the staff when I say that we are content in our employment. Your cousin will be in our care, and it shall be as if you never left."

"Good man, thank you. I will rest easy knowing that Weston will be fine."

"Sir, one more thing regarding Mr. Weston: he requested to remove the large Henley rug from his room and place in your study. He called it something like a change of scenery."

Walsh groaned flopping down on the bed, startling Collins.

"Are you well, sir?" he asked worriedly.

Walsh began to chuckle. "That explains some of his nonsense."

Collins looked confused.

"He's searching for reminders of home."

Walsh sat up and looked at Collins. Collins shook his head.

"Grief does terrible things to a person."

"Indeed, it does, Mr. Collins. Now, be off with you while I say goodbye to Weston."

Collins nodded and departed with Walsh's luggage to deposit in the waiting carriage.

Walsh turned down the hall, heading to Weston's room. He knocked on the door as he opened it. Weston stood staring out the window.

Soft music emanated from the violin nestled under his chin. Walsh folded his arms across his chest and cleared his throat. Weston turned to face him.

"Good afternoon, cousin. I had assumed you had already left."

Walsh shook his head gazing calmly at Weston.

Weston tipped his head to the side. "Is something wrong?"

"No, nothing is wrong, I just had to ask you something before I left."

Weston nodded lowering the violin from his shoulder. "I'm listening."

"The rug, Weston, from Henley is now in my study. Any reason why you've put it there?"

"None that leaps to mind."

Walsh sighed. "You're well then?"

Weston frowned. "Yes, quite."

"Fine. Now, I really must go. The carriage is waiting. I suppose I will leave you to yourself. Unless you have changed your mind about joining me?"

"Nay, I shall not impose upon the festivities. I will be more comfortable here."

"Very well then."

Walsh extended his hand. "Merry Christmas, cousin."

Weston shook the offered hand but as he did, so Walsh pulled him into an embrace. Weston grinned, thumping his cousin on the back. "And to you as well. Have a safe journey. Give my regards to your sister and her husband."

Walsh nodded taking a step back from Weston. "I will. Enjoy yourself here all alone."

"I wouldn't have it any other way." Weston picked up his violin as Walsh exited the room.

Later that evening, Weston knelt on the floor in his room rummaging through the trunk he had brought with him from his last visit to London. Collins knocked on the door frame causing Weston to look up.

"Will you be coming down to supper, sir?" he asked folding his hands behind his back.

Weston glanced up at the clock on the wall; it was just past six-thirty.

"Yes, Mr. Collins. I will be there shortly."

"Very well, sir." Collins gave a stiff bow before excusing himself.

Weston frowned as he returned his attention to the trunk. "I was sure I took it when I left."

He flopped onto his backside and rubbed his chin in thought. After a minute, he reached into the trunk and set a small stack of books on top of a few shirts and continued to dig through the assortment of things in the trunk. A few minutes later, he stood and tossed a book on his bed. The flickering candlelight picked up the gold lettering on the book. *Where Violets Grow* twinkled from the cover of the book as he passed the bed. Weston gave a satisfied smile as he strode from the room and went downstairs to the dining room.

When Weston entered the dining room, a delicious smell, and a welcoming spread of biscuits and cheese greeted him. He sat down and a maid set a bowl of steaming soup before him. She wore a worried frown.

"Ah, I believe we met last night," Weston noted as he reached for the spoon.

Her cheeks flushed and she averted her gaze. "Yes, sir. Again, I apologize sir."

"No need to apologize. I had not intended to frighten you."

She swallowed and gave a quick nod. "No harm done, sir." She took up her position at the edge of the room. Weston regarded her rigid posture with a curious gaze.

"You don't need to stay for my sake," he said, dipping his spoon into the soup and blowing on it.

The young girl shook her head. "This is my place. I waited on Mr. Walsh when he dined alone, before you came to Lexington, sir," she replied, in little more than a shy whisper.

"Just the same there is no need to hover about so."

The maid looked confused. "Am I a bother, sir?"

Weston shook his head tearing a biscuit in half. "Not at all. I rather like the company, but you don't have to watch my every move."

The maid stood up a little straighter and looked over Weston's head at the far wall. "My station is to serve you, sir."

Weston stared at the girl, chewing thoughtfully. "Well, since I can't seem to get rid of you, why don't you join me?"

A look of fright crossed her face. Her wide eyes met his gaze. "Oh no, sir. I could not do that."

"It was my request."

"Then thank you, sir, but no. Would not be proper." Her skin grew redder even as she spoke the words. She continued to stare at the wall.

Weston frowned. "You might as well eat if you are just going to stand there."

"I've already eaten, sir." She clasped her hands before her.

Weston took a sip of water from the tall crystal glass. "Perhaps then you could just sit and keep me company."

"Mr. Collins would not permit it, sir."

"That is ridiculous. I will not have you standing over me. You may sit or you may go. If you were to prefer the pleasure of your own company elsewhere than mine, I would not hold it against you."

The maid looked as if she would refuse again. She weighed the risk of offending him over receiving a lecture from the butler and she finally consented to taking a seat across from Weston.

Weston finished his soup in silence. When he laid his spoon down next to the bowl, the maid began to rise.

"Would you care for more soup, sir?"

Weston frowned. "I know where the kitchen is should I want more soup. You can sit." He spoke firmly, but not harshly. Slowly the maid lowered herself back into the chair, shooting a quick glance at the door.

Weston smiled. "Now was that so hard?"

She shook her head. "No, sir."

Weston poured himself another glass of water. "Since we seem to have gotten on poorly in the last while, let us rectify this. Tell me, my young dinner companion, what is your name?"

"Penny, sir," the maid replied surveying the empty dishes on the table, longing to go back to work.

Weston pushed his chair away from the table and rested a tall, polished boot on the knee of his other leg oblivious to her desire to clean.

"Penny, what a pleasant name. Do people use it when they address you?"

Penny looked at him sceptically before nodding. "Yes sir, they would have no other way of getting my attention."

Weston leaned back in his chair tousling his hair. "An interesting observation. No one calls me by my given name, always by a surname. It makes a person wonder why we bother to have names at all."

"Perhaps people feel it is improper to use first names," Penny offered softly.

"Probably. We English seem stuck on propriety."

They sat in silence.

Weston fingered the glass, pondering his encounter with Isabelle Hampton. It was frustrating yet intriguing simultaneously. Weston shook himself from his reverie. He thanked the girl for her company and allowed her to go back to her duties. Weston watched while the girl cleared away the dishes and wiped the table clean. She appeared comfortable in her tasks and almost looked happy. He shook his head. "I shall never understand maids."

CHAPTER 13

Brooklyn Manor,

"To the right, Isabelle," Sara called up to Isabelle who stood on a stool placing a star atop a large fir tree. Isabelle reached out and adjusted the star.

"Is that better?" she asked glancing over her shoulder at her aunt.

Sara chuckled. "No not my right, child, your right."

Isabelle smiled. "You could have told me sooner," she muttered moving the star the other way.

Sara smiled. "Perfect."

Isabelle took one last look at the star before climbing down from the stool, gathering her skirts in her hand.

She stood beside her aunt and admired the tree adorned with colorful clay decorations, small candles, and strings of popped corn. Dried fruit dotted the branches with bits of color. Isabelle looked around the room; the entryway opened into the large room and the marble staircase and other rooms on the main floor branched off it as well. Tree boughs twisted with holly, ivy, and mistletoe, hung along the banister and on the doorframes. The Dawsons would have hung these on the dining room door too if it had one. The dining room had a large archway adorned with a large swag. Isabelle smiled at the beauty. She felt quite in love with Brooklyn Manor.

Sara placed her arm around the Isabelle's shoulders. "What do you think?"

"It is the most beautiful thing I have ever seen, other than the gardens in the summer," Isabelle replied in awe.

Sara smiled. "I am glad to hear that. I think so too. Now, off to bed with you. Tomorrow is going to be a long day." She kissed Isabelle on the forehead.

"I hope the party tomorrow will be fun," Isabelle said with a slight furrow in her brow.

Dawson chuckled. "It shall be a fine time. There will be games and sleigh rides and plenty of tasty treats."

Isabelle smiled hugging both her uncle and aunt before heading upstairs to her room. She hurried herself into bed and forgot all about decorations and parties as she slipped into a dreamless sleep.

When Isabelle woke, it was late morning and Heather was creeping about her room. Heather jabbered happily, as she dressed Isabelle in a heavy dress suitable for a crisp winter's day. Isabelle rustled as she moved down the hall leading to the top of the stairs.

Dawson was just coming up them with his nose buried in a book. Glancing up he smiled at her. "Good morning, my little lady." His warmth chased away any apprehensions she had about the upcoming festivities.

"Good morning, Uncle Phillip."

He closed his book and tucked it into his waistcoat pocket. "And where are you going?" he asked leaning on the polished banister looking up at his niece.

"I thought I'd take a walk before breakfast. Care to join me?" Isabelle replied.

"I would be honored." Dawson extended his arm to her. Isabelle accepted and allowed her uncle to guide her down to the step he was standing on before he escorted her the rest of the way down.

Once bundled in cloaks and mittens Mansfield pulled open the front door ushering them out into the wintery morning. The pair walked silently through the snow-covered gardens each taking in the peace of the sunny morning.

"Are you excited for the Christmas eve celebrations tonight?" Dawson asked breaking the silence.

"Yes, I think it will be fun," she replied with a nod.

Dawson chuckled. "Well, I hope you will be able to enjoy yourself."

Isabelle smiled. "I'm sure I will."

As they moved further into the gardens and away from the house Dawson patted Isabelle's gloved hand. "There is something I desire to address with you," he started gently. Isabelle looked at him expectantly.

"Of course, uncle."

He took a moment to gather his thoughts before beginning. "I want you to enjoy your time as a young lady and not spend any time worrying about Mrs. Dawson's visions for your life."

Isabelle looked surprised. "What do you mean?"

He sighed. "Sara means well, but her plans for you to marry are premature. There is no need for you to rush and marry the first man you meet. Neither Sara nor I want to be rid of you, I want to be certain you know this." He gave a quirky smile "But Sara seems enthusiastic about the potential of having you marry well despite the lifestyle shift you've already encountered."

Isabelle giggled. "You don't want me to go?"

Dawson nodded.

"Uncle Phillip, I'm happy here with you and Aunt Sara. I've only begun to love Brooklyn, but I'd like to stay forever." A soft frown crossed her brow at the reality of the situation. "I mean, my arrival has been a substantial change for all of us. I also don't want to be a burden to you."

Dawson squeezed her hand. "My dear you are not a burden; you are a blessing."

"Thank you for saying that."

"You've brought life into our home, and I would hate to lose that for Sara's sake as well as my own."

"Would you tell me what started the marriage talk?" Dawson swallowed, as Isabelle gazed at him expectantly. "Was it Aunt Sara's comments?"

Dawson shook his head. "No, I suppose it wasn't." He took his time getting around to saying what was on his mind. "I just wonder if that charming young neighbor of mine has not become rather fond of you. I mean, I do not find this surprising, you are a delight, but it happened so quickly. I do not think you shall ever be in want of a suitor if you happen to let this one pass by."

Isabelle laughed. "Really? You think if he asks me to marry him, I should say no?"

"I cannot tell your heart what to do, but in my selfishness, I would hope you would choose to remain with us for a little while longer."

"Do you think he is a good man?"

Dawson squirmed at the question. "Why must you ask these things? I have to say yes and speak his praise and that will only fill your head with more infatuations."

Isabelle leaned her head into his shoulder. "I don't mean to hurt you, uncle. I don't understand how marriage works here. My father encouraged me to pursue my own life, but people here say a good marriage is all that matters. I feel it's now my duty to you."

Dawson chuckled. "I know all that. One day you will marry, but this is only one goal in life. I also want you to be happy and if that is here with us, so be it. You have no obligation to seek marriage."

Isabelle cocked her head. "Honestly? Laura thinks I'm well on my way to spinsterhood."

"That is absurd," Dawson scoffed. "Laura knows only what her mother has put into her head. Yes, a good marriage can make for a fulfilling life, but I know some women who live a comfortable single life. There is no curse in remaining unmarried. I imagine you would have seen that in America."

"You're right." Isabelle looked up into his face.

Dawson nodded. "I am. Heed my advice, Isabelle. Any man would be lucky to have you, but you owe us nothing. Do not embrace our customs at the expense of your own. Remember what your parents taught you and live in a way that will honor their legacy."

Isabelle's eyes brimmed with tears as she nodded.

Dawson took her hands in his. "It is in a family's best interest to have a daughter marry well, but" he spoke before she could interject. "It is in a daughter's best interest to listen to her family so as not to be disinherited."

CHAPTER 14

Later that evening, Isabelle glided down the stairs to the chatter of guests. The clinking of glasses mixed with soft music. The skirts of Isabelle's gown trailed along behind her as she swept down the stairs.

"Good evening, Miss Hampton." The dark-haired girl who greeted her curtsied fashionably.

Isabelle returned her greeting. "Miss Horton, how nice to see you."

Miss Horton fluttered her fan heaving a bored sigh. "It was charming to go to a party on Christmas eve, even if it was at Brooklyn."

"Well, I'm sure you will manage to enjoy yourself," she quipped with a forced smile.

Miss Horton raised her chin stubbornly as Isabelle excused herself and went to mingle.

"Hmm pretty much the who's who of Southampton have come this evening," observed Juliet who sidled up to Isabelle.

The elder of the Arthur girls stood nearby and nodded while offering a small giggle. "Oh yes, they have. The Olivers are here, so are the Fords and let's not forget the Hortons."

Isabelle chuckled.

Juliet rolled her pale eyes. "I dare say Miss Millie Horton does think she is the finest thing in the assemblies."

The younger Arthur sister appeared then and cast a scornful glance at Miss Horton. "She does think she is special, doesn't she?"

"I can't understand how Isabelle can be so kind to her," Juliet mused glancing at Isabelle, who gave a pretty smile.

"I'm a hostess, at least in part. Aunt Sara expects me to be courteous to all the guests. Besides, she isn't all that bad."

The girls glanced over at Millie Horton as she fluttered her fan and batted her eyelashes at a gentleman.

Juliet wrinkled her nose. "I find it distasteful the way she throws herself at them."

"Yes, it is. Her behavior really is quite unseemly. Millie Horton aside, something that I would like to know," said Rose Arthur. "Is that strange gentlemen from Lexington Estate present this evening?"

Juliet cocked her head to one side. "Do you mean Mr. Walsh?"

Rose shook her ringlets. "No, I have met Mr. Walsh. I meant the cousin."

"Oh, the cousin," Juliet added with chuckle. "Yes, I have heard much talk of the infamous Mr. Weston. I have never met him myself. My family has never had the good fortune to mingle with the Westons."

The Arthur sisters shook their heads admitting that they had never met Mr. Weston either.

"He was allegedly at the Lexington ball this fall, but I don't recall ever seeing him," Violet Arthur mused.

"Laura Millis knows the family, it seems, but she's not here. Isabelle must have met him," Juliet continued, giving Isabelle a pointed look.

Rose's brown eyes lit up. "Of course! Isabelle and he are neighbors. Tell us Isabelle! Is he a strange man? I hear he is very mysterious."

"Yes, do tell us. Is he as handsome as the rumors say he is?" Juliet added.

The girls fell silent and crowded closer, waiting for the information Isabelle would divulge. Isabelle could feel her cheeks flush at her friends' interest in Mr. Weston.

"Well, first I don't believe Mr. Weston is here. I haven't seen him," she paused, a little uncomfortable with the gossip. "I don't know how mysterious he is. He isn't exactly forthcoming, but I don't think that means he has anything to hide. He's rather odd." Excited murmurings rose within the small group. Isabelle started to feel a little guilty for saying that, thinking she had added to the gossip. "Lots of people do odd things. That doesn't make him different from anyone else," Isabelle said, trying to defend Weston from her friends.

"Isabelle," Juliet soothed. "We are not going to have him cast into the river for witchcraft. We simply want to know a little more about the wealthy young man who may make one of us a fine husband if he is not an eccentric."

"Juliet is right. My father spends a great deal of time in London on business. He confirms that the Weston family is very well known and respected. I do believe one of the older Mr. Weston's is an Earl," added Violet Arthur.

Juliet nodded. "Of course, my sister in London spoke about the Weston family. She told me about the wealth and prestige of the family. She also said the Weston men are some of the most eligible bachelors in the country. They are quite prized."

The girls became quite animated at the mention of fortune and position. Isabelle made a face. She had difficulty picturing the Mr. Weston she knew as a prized young man.

"Wait, though, was there not a Weston involved in some societal crisis several years ago?" Rose Arthur's question broke through the murmurings.

"Oh, that sounds familiar. I remember my mother mentioned something about an ill-fated love affair." Juliet practically danced with excitement as all eyes turned to her.

"I heard this! Do you know who the young lady was?"

Juliet shook her head. "No, but she was poor and had no connections. I think she died!"

"Gracious! Was this the same Mr. Weston that is Isabelle's neighbor?"

The girls all shrugged. Isabelle felt baffled by the stories she was hearing.

"I don't know. It might be the same man," Isabelle confided, feeling that Laura would be much better at answering their questions than she was.

"Gah, Isabelle, how can you not know? The man lives next door!" Juliet's chiding was more teasing than angry, so Isabelle took no offense.

"What do you think of the whole situation, Isabelle?" Rose asked, pulling Isabelle back into the conversation.

"I just don't see why a name can cause so much fuss. Having a certain name does not mean he is a good or bad person. Why would his name influence anything?"

The girls all laughed.

"Oh, Isabelle! You have yet to learn about proper society," Violet said with a chortle.

"The Weston's have a reputation of being decent, and respectable people. Money and titles just add to those attributes," Juliet noted.

"I believe anyone can be mean or whatever. If they are mean they can be so with a fancy name too. My parents would never respect one person more than another because of a name," Isabelle said with a shrug.

Rose frowned. "Isabelle, is Mr. Weston mean spirited?" she asked.

Isabelle's shoulders sank. "I don't think so. I wanted to make a point..."

"I am not convinced what you have just said can possibly be truth," Juliet stated. "A person's name has a great deal to do with who they are. I do not think it possible for a child to be loathsome if its parents are amiable."

Isabelle's gaze drifted from her party to the roomful of people. "Perhaps," she muttered.

Once again, the conversation shifted, and Isabelle stood listening for a moment before excusing herself. She picked her way through the guests to the refreshment table filled with pastries, sweets, and sandwiches. Isabelle selected a piece of toffee and popped it in her mouth. The sticky candy began to melt in her mouth as she turned from the table. She had moved maybe a foot when she bumped into someone travelling the other direction.

"I am terribly sorry." His hands went round her shoulders as he steadied her on her feet. Isabelle tried to reply but found that the toffee had caused her teeth to stick together making any response impossible. Putting on what she hoped was a pretty smile, she looked up.

"Mr. Weston!" she exclaimed, the surprise of seeing him jarring the candy lose. "I didn't know you were here."

Weston gave a slight nod. "I have only just arrived." He looked very elegant and a little uncomfortable. He worse breeches with tall boots, a waistcoat with long tails, and a vest with matching silk ascot tied at his throat.

Isabelle felt a bit in awe of the man. They stood in an awkward silence for a moment.

"How are your uncle and aunt?" Weston inquired.

"They're fine; they're here someplace."

"Of course." He cleared his throat and took a step back.

"Not big on conversations for a Weston," Isabelle muttered turning her head away from him.

"Beg pardon?"

"I just asked if you have you plans for tomorrow?" She tried to sound like her interest was genuine.

"Nothing particular. It will be quiet. How will you spend Christmas?" Weston asked stepping aside so a young couple could pass by.

"Well, my cousin will come sometime tomorrow. She will likely stay until the new year."

"Yes, I did notice the absence of your Miss Millis this evening."

Isabelle stopped and studied his face. His expression gave nothing away. She continued her answer to his original question.

"Yes, because she will be here tomorrow."

"That must be delightful for you."

Again silence.

Isabelle shifted uncomfortably as music began to play and the young people paired off to dance. As she stood there beside Weston wondering if he would say anything else, a young man come to ask her to dance.

Weston took a step back. "Please go ahead." He indicated she accept the young man's offer.

Isabelle excused herself and joined her partner on the dancefloor. Isabelle caught glimpses of Weston lingering alone at the edge of the dancefloor. He looked neither bored nor amused. She caught herself trying to guess why he had come when he did not participate. She felt eyes on her while she danced and looking his direction she wondered if he were watching her. When the song ended, Isabelle curtsied and thanked her partner. She noted Weston had moved before Juliet and the Arthurs hurried her way.

"Who is that dashingly handsome gentleman we saw speaking to you before you accepted an offer to dance?" Juliet inquired in muted tones while her eyes sparkled with excitement.

"Mr. Weston," Isabelle replied running a hand over her pinned up hair to make sure it was still in place. Looks of astonishment crossed their faces.

"That extraordinary gentleman, who is no older than our eldest brother, he is Mr. Weston?" Rose asked, glancing at him with little discretion.

Isabelle could not help but follow her gaze to where he had gone to the other end of the room.

"I dare say he does look very rich indeed. Look at the way he holds himself. He has almost a proud manner about him," Juliet whispered.

The Arthurs nodded.

"Indeed, he seems to be. He should have asked you to dance, Isabelle. Surely, you are one of the prettiest young ladies present this evening," Violet announced, rather too loudly for Isabelle's liking.

Weston briefly glanced their way. He raised a curious eyebrow. The girls froze and grew quiet as his eyes flickered over them.

"Perhaps he will ask me to dance," Juliet said hopefully, as she stood a little straighter and raised her chin a little higher.

Isabelle gave Juliet an odd look before shaking her head. "I doubt it. He doesn't strike me as very social," she paused as Weston engaged himself in conversation with Dawson.

"That is absurd Isabell. From what I have heard of the Westons they are very fashionable, and they attend the most elegant parties in London. It seems in most of the country that it is an honor to have a Weston on the guest list," Rose said matter-of-factly.

"If that is indeed true, Mr. Weston will be acquainted with the mannerisms expected of a gentleman of such rank; therefore, he must be an accomplished dancer which gives no reason as to why he should stand silently by the wall all night as if it would fall down without his presence," Juliet pointed out.

"I have yet to see him dance," Isabelle interjected.

Violet frowned. "Well, if that be the case then he sounds rather queer."

"Come now Violet, you know a well as I do that rich men are always queer. I believe that is partly why they are so rich," Rose said fluttering her fan in a fashionable manner.

Isabelle frowned. She was growing tired of talking of Mr. Weston. He did nothing to warrant such attention.

"I would like to dance again. I will be back in a bit." Isabelle escaped from her friends before they could object. No sooner had she gotten away from them when, a young man approached her for a dance, and she eagerly obliged.

As a fresh song commenced, Dawson ladled punch from the bowl into his matching glass. You aren't going to dance, Mr. Weston?" he asked taking a sip.

Weston shook his head. "No, I much prefer to watch."

Dawson nodded absently. "I suppose that makes for an amusing pastime, but there does seem to be a shortage of young men."

"That seems to be the case, but I don't believe it is the truth."

Dawson raised an amused brow. "How so, Mr. Weston?"

"There are certain ladies who remain unchosen," Weston replied indicating towards a young lady who looked at her shoes and not the person talking to her. "See there, that poor creature will never have a chance unless she displays a bit more confidence."

Dawson chuckled. "I dare say you may be right."

Weston smiled. "It is a gentleman's duty to see to it that each young lady has had the pleasure of at least one dance throughout the course of an evening."

"Then you had better see to it," Dawson said with a grin jabbing Weston with his elbow good naturedly.

Weston shook his head. "I am afraid I won't be dancing this evening."

Dawson laughed heartily at this. "Come come, Mr. Weston, a man of society is never out of practice at such things as dancing."

Weston shrugged heaving a sigh. "I haven't danced for several years."

Dawson set down his glass of punch and clapped Weston on the shoulder. "Then it is my duty as a gentleman to see this lady shall dance since you are unable to fulfill the role."

Weston gave a weak smile.

"A noble gesture, Mr. Dawson. I leave you to it."

As the evening developed and the dancing and laughter continued Weston watched the festivities from a corner of the room. He often caught glimpses of Isabelle as she moved among the other dancers. Her gold dress swayed gently with her movements as her partner guided her about the floor. She had a partner for each dance, which was no surprise to Weston for she appeared a graceful dancer. Weston determined to go when a woman bumped into his arm on her way past.

"Oh, excuse me!" she exclaimed as her hand fan fell to the floor. Weston forced a smile as he leaned down and scooped up the fan. "I am so sorry. I meant no harm." She batted her long lashes over dark eyes.

"No harm done, miss," Weston assured stooping to retrieve the fan.

As she accepted the fan, her hand brushed his. "I'm very glad. I would hate for our first encounter to be ill," she remarked with a giggle fluttering her fan.

Weston sighed, weary of the game she set before him. "No."

"But for it to be a proper introduction, you will need to ask my name. You neglected to do so." She bowed her head coyly.

"Please excuse my mistake." He ended the conversation by stepping around her and walking away.

Appalled the young woman gapped in amazement. "I have never been so disregarded!" she huffed to another young lady nearby. "Of all the inconsiderate people I have never in all my life met one such as him!" She glanced back at him over her shoulder as if to ensure he had heard her.

Weston narrowed his eyes. He had been abrupt, but he grew tired of overbearing women who wanted his name and money. To him, they all seemed so silly. Weston hurried through the crowd after he had said his farewells to the Dawsons. Once at the door, he paused a moment while waiting for his cloak and scanned the crowd. Isabelle stood off to the side of the room with a few other young ladies. She looked disengaged from the chatter around her. He stood for a moment admiring her from a distance; she seemed different to him than other young ladies. Isabelle must have felt Weston's gaze upon her for she raised her head and looked at him. Their eyes met. For a moment she looked welcoming. Walsh's declaration echoed through Weston's mind as he swept his cloak over his shoulders and in a fluster of black was gone.

Weston walked into his room at Lexington and closed the door behind him. Stepping over to the window he stood staring into the winter's night. Absently he loosened his tie and removed it from about his neck. Tossing the tie onto the bed, he unbuttoned the top buttons on his shirt and shrugged out of his waistcoat tossing this onto the wingback chair. Feeling more comfortable now, Weston collected the little black case from beside his bed. He removed the violin with tenderness. In a moment, he had tucked the instrument under his chin. He twirled the bow around in his fingers.

"What shall I play?" he muttered watching his reflection in the window.

Gently Weston swiped the bow across the instrument. It whimpered as he grimaced giving the tuning knob a slight twist. Repositioning his fingers on the strings, he pulled the bow over the strings. This time the violin offered a mournful sound. An image came to Weston's mind. A second mournsome chord followed the first and then a third before a melody of complexion and loneliness began to unfold. Every note carried an emotion that otherwise would go unnoticed.

CHAPTER 15

Brooklyn Manor,

Isabelle uncurled herself from the large chair, tossing her book onto the end table. Gathering her skirts, she hurried from the library. The doorbells had rung.

"I've got it, Mansfield," Isabelle called as she flew past the bewildered butler.

"Yes of course, miss," he muttered as he watched her swing back the door.

A rush of cold air swept into the room and whipped at Isabelle's skirt as a young woman hurried into the house. The visitor pushed back her bonnet which had fallen over her eyes. "Merry Christmas, Isabelle!" she exclaimed opening her arms.

Isabelle grinned and hugged her friend. "Merry Christmas, Laura!"

Laura pulled back and admired Isabelle as Mansfield stepped around them to assist the footman. "You are still just as beautiful as ever; have you been behaving?" Laura asked, her eyes dancing as she removed her bonnet and cloak.

Isabelle laughed. "Yes, I've been an angel since I last saw you."

Laura laughed. "I hardly believe that. I heard talk that there was quite the Christmas Eve party here last night. Juliet wastes no time in spreading tales."

"No, she does not. We missed you last night."

Laura waved her gloves in her hand.

"I felt it all the way from Bristol. My parents would have no part of my coming last night. This morning was the earliest my mother would even consider letting me travel again after our adventures to Bristol."

"You'll have to tell me all about your trip."

"Oh, it was nothing exciting. I shan't bore you will it. I want to hear about this party I missed. I dare say that a certain young gentleman was present?"

Isabelle rolled her eyes. "Please, I'll tell you anything else but let's not talk of him."

"Why on earth would you silence the subject? Have you had a row?"

Isabelle sighed. "No, not exactly. It's just…" She thought back to her encounter with Weston the night before. He lingered but didn't address her. It just felt awkward. "There's nothing to talk about and I don't want to hear any more about the Weston fortune," Isabelle begged.

Laura looked at her searchingly. "I was going to enquire after Mr. Walsh. Did he not attend last night?"

Isabelle looked surprised. "Oh yes, Walsh. He has gone away for the holidays."

Laura's lips turned upside down in a perfectly practiced pout. "What a pity, for your sake."

"I enjoyed myself without him, so it really doesn't matter."

"Wait did you say Mr. Weston attended? And without his cousin?"

Isabelle narrowed her eyes. "I thought we agreed not to discuss him."

Laura sighed. "Yes, certainly, but you know he is quite good for your status. The fact that he attended without Mr. Walsh speaks to the fact that something other than his family drew him here...."

"Laura, I know what you're going to say, that catching a man of fortune never hurt anyone, but I'm still sorting everything, and life is complicated."

"I know, I know, and you have someone else in mind. Still, what harm would it do to keep an open mind? You have nothing yet established."

"Maybe, but that could backfire and be a disaster."

"You worry too much, Isabelle. It will all play out as intended. I just suggest you should not limit yourself to a single potential outcome, especially if you have options."

Isabelle smiled. "You certainly seem to be yourself. Not tired at all after your travels. Why don't you tell me about your trip?"

Laura linked arms with Isabelle and waved her hand as the pair made their way to the parlor. "Traveling becomes all the same after a while. It really is a bore."

"Your hands are freezing. Come on then, let's get you settled. You must need a rest." Isabelle patted Laura's arm. Laura grinned.

"Actually, I slept the whole way here. I am feeling very refreshed."

The girls giggled as they entered the parlor.

Sara looked up from her needlepoint and smiled. She reached over and rested her hand on Dawson's arm. He paused in his reading aloud and glanced first at his wife. She gestured towards the young ladies standing before them. With a grin, he closed the book. "Ah, so you have returned, Miss Laura. How was your trip?" he said rising to greet his niece.

Laura who was shorter than almost everyone at five foot two looked up with a smile. "Very good, thank you, uncle."

Sara chuckled and came to hug her. "Such a pleasure to have you again."

Laura sighed happily. "It is very a pleasure to be back. I enjoyed myself ever so much on my last visit I have been dying to return."

Dawson tossed the book onto the sofa. "Well, we are glad to see you again. Perhaps you can keep Isabelle out of trouble," he added with a wink, Isabelle cocked her head to one side.

"Have I been trouble?" Isabelle's brow creased with a hurt frown.

Dawson's features softened. He reached out and squeezed Isabelle's hand in a tender manner. "Not at all. I was merely teasing you."

"Pay him no mind, girls. He missed his midmorning tea."

Dawson frowned. "Madame, I resent that statement." He folded his arms across his chest.

Sara placed her hand on his arm. "Come now, Phillip, do not be sore. We are all here now and it is Christmas after all."

Dawson looked down at his wife out of the corner of his eye. "I suppose it is at that," he remarked heaving a sigh before placing a light kiss on Sara's hand. She touched her fingers to his cheek.

"Alright my girls, why don't we have lunch and then we can open presents," Sara suggested, turning back to the girls.

The girls exchanged glances.

"Alright," Isabelle agreed.

"Yes, I am simply starving," Laura added.

Sara chuckled, wrapping a hand over Dawson's arm, and placing the other on Laura's back. "Oh poor, dear! Come along then we shall see what is for lunch."

CHAPTER 16

After a hearty meal of cold meat, a variety of cheese, biscuits, and steamed vegetables the group retired to the parlor where stood the decorated fir tree with the pile of presents tucked under its branches. The girls sat on the floor, crowded close to the tree, and the Dawsons settled onto the sofa.

Laura scooted closer to Isabelle and handed her a small box. "It's not much of a gift, I'm afraid, but I just couldn't decide what to get for you," she explained as Isabelle accepted the package.

"Oh, very pretty! You really didn't need to bring me anything."

Laura frowned. "Nonsense. It's Christmas."

Isabelle untied the ribbon from around the box before removing the lid. Pulling back a layer of tissue paper revealed a set of white handkerchiefs. She read her initials embroidered on them in blue thread. "Laura, these are so nice!" Isabelle exclaimed removing a handkerchief and running her fingers over the lettering. Laura looked pleased with her choice.

Sara leaned over the box. "Are they ever pretty." She took a handkerchief to admire and showed it to her husband. "Don't you think so, Phillip?"

Dawson took the little cloth from Sara and inspected it a moment before handing it back.

"I suppose I'm not the best of authorities on the subject."

Sara scoffed and gave him a gentle rap on the arm. "You can't just offer a simple compliment?"

Dawson just smiled tenderly at his wife. Isabelle and Laura exchanged happy smiles, watching the playful affection between their aunt and uncle.

"I did you get you a little something too," Isabelle said, pulling a package out from under the tree. Her cheeks grew pink as she passed the thin box tied with a yellow ribbon to Laura. "I must admit compared to those handkerchiefs this is a small gift. I did not know if you would like it."

Laura grinned. "It seems we both had the same problem. Perhaps next year we could drop each other little hints." She laughed while untying the ribbon and tossing it aside before taking off the lid and peering into the box. "Isabelle, I think this is a very thoughtful gift," she exclaimed, plucking a piece of fudge from the box, and popping it into her mouth.

Isabelle caressed one of the handkerchiefs. "I thought fudge was sad choice."

Laura laughed. "Not at all, I enjoy fudge. Thank you for my present, cousin."

Isabelle grinned. "You're welcome. Thank you for the handkerchiefs. I really like them."

Laura smiled and stuck another piece of fudge in her mouth.

"Laura, don't spoil your appetite," Sara chided frowning slightly.

"Oh, Aunt Sara, dinner is ages from now. You have no need to worry for I will be hungry again by then," Laura replied nonchalantly replacing the lid on the box in her lap.

Isabelle chuckled. "True, I don't think you could ever spoil your appetite."

"And still, she remains as petite as ever. You must share with me your secret," Sara added with a laugh.

Dawson glanced over the top of his book. "My love, you are perfect. Now let the girls have some fun." His dark eyes returned to the page.

Sara lowered herself to the floor by his feet. "I suppose you are right. Though I would hate to have your sister thinking I allow Laura to do as she pleases while she is with us."

"After all these years, my sister would think no such thing." Again, the dark eyes appeared over the top of the book as Dawson gazed at his wife seated on the rug; he could not help but smile with pleasure. "We do our best when she is in our care, but ultimately she is not our charge."

"Indeed, but I should not tolerate any ill behavior while in my home."

"Is that irony, my dear?" The humor in Dawson's voice caused Sara to look up. "You would never rule with an iron hand."

"Is that what it takes to raise a young lady?" Sara's gaze fell on Isabelle. "Sometimes I worry I don't know what to do for Isabelle."

"Tut tut, my love," Dawson replied as Isabelle got to her feet. "Just look at her, she already is as fair a maiden as the princess herself."

Isabelle flushed. "Please! That is not true."

"Of course, it is true. Your parents were good people. I can see their influence."

"May we be excused?"

Laura looked up at Isabelle who was running a hand over her wrinkled skirts. Isabelle met her gaze. Dawson gave a quick nod to the request.

"I think I need some fresh air," Isabelle observed.

Laura removed a pile of wrappings from her lap. "I would like that. It is a lovely day, and I could do with a little exercise after that carriage ride," she said with a grin, untangling her skirts from wrapping paper.

Sara looked to Dawson with a confused frown after the girls had gone. "I fear your banter has offended them."

"Ah, if so, they won't be for long."

"Are you certain? Did you see Isabelle's face? She looked quite overwhelmed."

"All in good time, my love." Dawson slid down from his seat to position himself next to his wife on the rug. "Now, I must say I find your gown quite becoming."

Sara raised a brow. "What?"

He ran his hands over her arms. "You look very fetching, and I think I am in love."

CHAPTER 17

"Where did you have in mind?" Laura asked as the girls walked down the hall and the chatter of the two adults drifted away.

"Oh, I don't know. Anywhere really."

"How about the orchard?"

Isabelle rolled her eyes. "I did say anywhere." Taking her cousin by the arm, the girls hurried to the cloak room to get their wraps and hats.

"It really is a charming day for a walk," Laura commented pulling on her mittens as she stepped out the door. Isabelle nodded while tying the ribbons on her bonnet.

"Yes, I haven't had anyone to walk with since your last visit."

Laura shot her a playful look. "Not even with that young man from next door?"

Isabelle swatted her on the arm with her mittens as the girls walked out into the sun and snow of the beautiful Christmas day. Birds chirped and fluttered about in the trees knocking sparkling frost from the branches as the girls wandered in the orchard. Laura cast a sidelong glance at Isabelle who seemed lost in her thoughts.

Licking her lips Laura asked: "How are things with Mr. Walsh?"

Isabelle started and looked at Laura. "Excuse me?"

Laura giggled. "Oh, you know, Mr. Walsh your neighbor, the charming bachelor."

Isabelle nodded. "I know who he is, Laura. I told you; he went to spend Christmas with his sister."

Laura looked surprised. "His sister? You said he had gone but not where. Why would he go there?"

"Laura!" Isabelle chided. "She is his sister. That is a good enough reason."

Laura shrugged brushing back a lock of her hair behind her ear. "Maybe, but last I heard Mr. Walsh and Mr. Billingsley were not on the best of terms."

Isabelle flew to his defense surprising them both. "How could someone not agree with Walsh? He is the kindest man! Is there something about him I don't know?" Isabelle stopped walking and stood in thought.

"I don't recall the incident, but I believe it was of a delicate nature." Laura's tone was gentler now.

"Does everyone in this country know everyone's business? Nothing seems private."

Laura halted by her side; her expression pained. "No, but you have seen how gossip circulates. It becomes a pastime."

"That isn't a good reason."

"Be that as it may, information often has a way of becoming public."

"So do you know what happened?"

Laura shook her head. "No, but I do think Mr. Weston had something to do with it."

Isabelle rolled her eyes. "I am not surprised to hear that. He has a hand in everything Walsh does."

"It has always been that way, although more so in recent years. Mr. Weston spent most of his time in London up until now. I do find him rather odd. What is your impression of him?"

Isabelle gave a snort of disgust. "I have nothing to say about Weston. I think he's arrogant and overrated."

"Really Isabelle, that's your opinion of the handsome mysterious young man?" Laura looked skeptical.

Isabelle kept her eyes trained in the direction they were walking. "I don't like mysteries. I believe if a person has something to hide, he should just keep it a secret instead of allowing subtle hints. There seems to be a lot of lore around him, but no one knows if any of it is true, and he doesn't bother correcting it."

Laura chuckled. "But where would be the fun in that? A hint of mystery makes a person more intriguing."

"You don't care if the gossip is true?"

"No, of course I do, especially if it is bad gossip. There are rumors of some scandal involving Mr. Weston, but I do not believe those parts are true. The family would disinherit him if he had conducted himself as the rumors suggest he has."

"You think the rumors are lies?"

Laura shrugged. "For the most part. I mean, they may have stemmed from partial truth, but surely, people exaggerate."

"I wonder what is true. I think there's something unnatural about him. He always looks like he's plotting something," Isabelle paused and looked squarely at Laura. "He's busy interfering with everyone else's problems and doesn't appear to have time for his own."

Laura chuckled. "Perhaps you distrust him because he reminds you of yourself."

"Excuse me?" Isabelle halted.

Laura smiled. "I mean no offense. You and Mr. Weston are not dissimilar."

Isabelle looked appalled. "I'm nothing like him! He is proud and stubborn."

Laura laughed. "I won't comment on that, but he does have other quirks that you have as well."

Isabelle stuck her nose in the air. "Such as?"

Laura sighed. "You're both head strong, blunt and have a tendency of being reclusive." Isabelle shot her friend a withering look, but Laura continued before she could comment: "There is no use in denying it. He knows his mind, and no one can persuade him into something he is disinclined to do."

Isabelle lowered her eyes to the snow hiding the toes of her shoes. "I suppose you could be right," she admitted, before looking up. "But that doesn't make me like the man."

Laura heaved a sigh. "It would be imprudent to continue these hostilities towards him. He is one of the most amiable bachelors in England." Isabelle wrinkled her nose at the word 'amiable.'

"I think you people have a distorted standard."

Laura looked amused. "As you experience more of our society you will see that I am right and that the standard is accurate. One cannot stay upset for long with someone like Mr. Weston."

Isabelle scowled but said nothing as she shuffled her feet in the snow. "You know a little bit about everyone. What else do you know about the Weston family?"

Laura scrunched up her nose in thought. "Like I said, I am not really sure if what I have heard is fact or fiction."

"What have you heard?"

"Well," Laura paused before plunging ahead: "Mr. Weston lived with his mother in London before he came to Lexington."

Isabelle made a face. "Everyone knows that."

"You let me finish. Now hush, and I will tell you something you want to know." Laura sat on a bench in the garden and pulled Isabelle down next to her. "The story goes that while in London, Mr. Weston lived somewhat of a reckless life like any man would who had too much time on his hands and too much money to spend."

Isabelle cocked her head. "What do you consider reckless living?"

"Drinking, gambling, carriage races and things like that. He seems to have remained a perfect gentleman despite the speculation regarding his character. Rumors yes, but no scandals have sullied the Weston name on his account." Laura tossed her hair over her shoulder and continued:

"One of the most popular rumors involved a woman. This story is the most interesting of all. There was talk of marriage at one point. Rumor indicates that her father was a fool with money, and he lost everything. The family forbade Mr. Weston to marry a woman without rank or fortune. Doing so would risk losing his own fortune though disinheritance. Not even two months later, she died. People said she died of illness although others claimed she really died of a broken heart. I even heard one version of the story where she died in Mr. Weston's arms. I was quite young, so I liked that version the best, especially if she died of a broken heart. It seemed very romantic, even if it seems silly now. Most rumors suggested she was Mr. Weston's lover."

"A lover? Laura, do you think that's true?"

"I find that doubtful. Mr. Weston has no reputation for being a rapscallion."

"Perhaps he changed his ways?"

"You really want that to be true? No, he is a man of honor. The Weston family would have dismissed him long ago if the rumors were true. However, I do not know what really happened. It was long ago and there were varied stories." Laura stretched out her legs and wriggled her toes. "After the young lady's death Mr. Weston withdrew from society. He locked himself away with his emotions and his thoughts. The man we see now is only a shadow of the brilliant young man he had been."

"Like a shadow? Laura, that sounds dramatic."

"Hmm, one would think, but that really was the case. I remember the first time I saw him. He was so elegant, witty, and striking. Every girl batted her fan his way. Every mother made her introductions to him with hope for her daughter. Young as I was, I can see the changes. More recently he has appeared in society again. I suppose he must keep up appearances. I do not think he brings glory to the

Weston name these days," Laura paused and shrugged. "He has been a distant man ever since I have known him. My own mother will not bother about him since she cannot seem to sift truth from rumor and there are easier matches to be made on my behalf. I do not think I have ever had a conversation with him and never have I seen a smile cross his lips."

Isabelle cocked her head. "He has a conflicted past. Why people speak of him like he was made of gold?"

Laura gave a smile. "In some regard, he is. He has a fortune. He is a Weston. There is nothing he could do to lose favour with society, especially since there was never proof of any misdeed. I doubt society would disapprove of him if the family had disinherited him."

Isabelle frowned. "Even with rumors of scandal hanging over him?"

"Rumors are simply talk. They cannot overshadow years of good breeding and status."

"Despite his disregard for the assemblies?"

"He participates enough to appear mysterious. That is sufficient to quiet speculation and keep himself in all the proper circles. In a way, his lack of participation makes him more appealing."

"English society is strange."

"Whatever your opinion of our practices, bear in mind it is an aged and cultured society."

Isabelle smiled and leaned near to her friend. "Be that as it may. I got the impression that Weston has a mischievous side and enjoys a practical joke. I can see it in the way he treats Walsh."

Laura shrugged. "He is an enigma. The man has so many personalities. I feel like no one really knows him."

Isabelle nodded. "Every layer is so different; I wonder what he is like on the final one."

CHAPTER 18

Sunlight shone through the window casting its rays and sweeping away the shadows of the night. Isabelle pulled the covers up over her head to shield her eyes, trying in vain to sleep just a little longer. Mumbling an incoherent sentence, Isabelle rolled onto her front and planted her face into the pillow in a final attempt to hide from the sun. She stared into the darkness of the pillow now fully awake. She sighed. "So much for getting more sleep," she grumbled propping herself on her elbows and staring at the headboard through a disarray of hair.

Her thoughts trailed off as the sound of horses' hooves echoed up from below her window. Rolling over, she blinked up at the ceiling waiting for her eyes to adjust to the brightness of the room. Tossing the covers aside, she padded across the cold wood floor to the window and peered down into the courtyard below. Sam was leading a white horse around the courtyard in a small circle.

Stepping back from the window Isabelle scurried across the cold floor to open the wardrobe and pulled out the first dress her fingers touched. After she pulled the gray housedress over her head, Isabelle sat on the floor to put on her stockings and shoes. Pausing in front of the mirror, she ran her fingers through the loose curls to organize them a bit. Gathering a handful of skirt, Isabelle pulled open the door and came face to face with Sara who was reaching for the door handle.

"Gracious, you're up, I see," Sara stepped back and laid a hand on her chest.

"Yes, I haven't been awake long."

"I imagine. Heather returned to me stating that she was unable to wake you. Given the importance of this morning, I came to collect you myself." Sara's face paled as she spoke.

"What's wrong?" Alarm crept into Isabelle's voice.

"I don't think anything is wrong, but we will get it sorted," Sara replied with a weak smile as she reached for Isabelle's hand. Sara led the way downstairs and towards the library. Dawson emerged from the other end of the hall chatting briskly with a short well-dressed fellow with a salt and pepper moustache. Dawson looked up and noticed Isabelle standing with Sara.

"Well, here is my ward now," Dawson exclaimed guiding his companion in her direction. The fellow nodded to her before his eyes shifted to Sara. Dawson beckoned to Isabelle. "Isabelle, come along. I would like you to meet Mr. Martin."

Isabelle stepped forward with a shy smile and gave a gentle curtsy. "How do you do?"

The man bowed slightly at the waist. "Very fine thank you Miss Hampton. Your uncle has told me a lot about you."

Isabelle grimaced. "Oh?"

Martin chuckled. "I can assure you there was not a thing that he mentioned which would cause you to be ashamed. From what I have heard it is obvious that Dawson is fond of you."

Isabelle blushed slightly. "I'm very grateful to both him and Aunt Sara. I owe them everything."

Dawson stood quietly watching, a twinkle of pride shinning in his eyes. "We have been thrilled to have her," Dawson said, joining in the conversation.

Martin smiled. "You don't say?"

Dawson nodded, taking his wife by the hand. "Try not to look so troubled, my dear. Martin has never steered us wrong. Shall we talk in the library?"

Mr. Martin nodded. "Most definitely. Mrs. Dawson, I assure you I have not brought unwelcome news."

"Yes, historically your presence means something is about to change," Sara said, leaning into her husband as the group moved into the library.

"Ah, yes, you're getting ahead of us, Mrs. Dawson," Martin returned, seating himself at Sara's writing desk.

Dawson sat on the couch still holding Sara's hand so that she sat next to him. Sara reached for Isabelle and pulled her down beside her in a protective embrace. Isabelle shot her aunt a worried look as Sara laid a hand on her arm.

Dawson cocked a brow at the women. "No need to look so concerned. Martin, get the point before my women fret to death." Dawson kept a comforting grip on Sara's hand.

"Of course, yes." Martin cleared his throat and pulled a pair of spectacles from his jacket pocket. "Well, I will try to be concise, but there are many details regarding the estate of Colonel Fredrick Hampton."

"The estate?" Isabelle leaned forward, the color draining from her face.

"Yes, miss," Martin affirmed with a nod. "It took some time for all the information to cross borders, but I think we have it sorted. The passing of Arnold Hampton caused a great deal of confusion for the estate which forced my office to seek information from America. The law firm managing the Hampton estate in Virginia received word of the...erm...misfortune befalling the heir in Virginia, but they lacked information regarding the fate of the family. They thought the entire family had perished and so they searched records to locate a next of kin. The Hampton estate was to return to the Hampton family of London. Because of this, we did not contact the Carter family of Virginia, who would be your mother's relations, Miss Hampton. Of course, the next of kin, your brother, Mrs. Dawson, has passed. It became quite a mess as Arnold Hampton was the last eligible male to inherit. My office received notice about the American affairs as it all linked to the Hampton estate."

"Wait, what do you mean by 'eligible' man?" Isabelle interrupted.

Dawson and Sara exchanged looks. Sara addressed the question: "That means there may be other men in the family still alive, but unable to inherit the fortune due to being outcast from the family."

"But is there a man?"

Sara squirmed and heaved a sigh. "My brother, Arnold Hampton, had two sons. Donald Hampton, your father's brother, still lives. He no longer associates with the family."

"Wait, I have family?"

"Well, in a way, yes. But Donald Hampton no longer legally has claim to the Hampton family. The family renounced his position quite some time ago."

Isabelle looked distressed. "How does this happen?"

Sara looked at Dawson. "It was long ago, and many factors influenced the decision. I am sorry to have to tell you this. You must remember that if Donald Hampton had been eligible to inherit you would have gone into his care."

Isabelle leaned deeper against Sara's hand pressed to her arm. "Oh, I would not have come to you."

Sara shook her head. Dawson reached over to touch Isabelle's hand. "But you are here and that's all that matters."

"That is all that matters, and this all brings me here today," Martin resumed his speech. "With no one to inherit the Hampton estate, it remained tied up in our office, waiting for an heir to appear. And now she has." He smiled at Isabelle.

"Me?"

"Yes, of course," he replied with a chuckle. "With no eligible male heir my office remained uncertain what to do. We knew there was a child of the late colonel but had no word of your whereabouts, until Mr. Berry brought news to London of your arrival here. Given the nature of your unique situation, the firm has agreed to accommodate your circumstances."

"Martin, get on with it," Dawson interjected with a sigh.

"Ah, certainly," Martin stumbled over a few words before picking up a page and reading it while talking. "Miss Hampton legally remains an American citizen and with Fredrick Hampton's immigration to America, the entire estate transfers to American law. The death of

Arnold Hampton saw the entire English estate—thus, combining the English and American estates—transfer to Fredrick Hampton who is no longer living either. There is no living male heir, as would be required by English law, but there is a living female heiress, which satisfies American law. Miss Hampton, although she is a woman, will inherit the Hampton estate in whole when she comes of age, of course." Martin turned to Sara. "Like you said, Mrs. Dawson, I did bring a change, but I hope you will find it a positive one." He smiled and peeped over the rim of his spectacles.

"Yes, that is the best news," Sara said with a light laugh.

Dawson smiled. "Will that be all for today, Martin?"

"Yes, Mr. Dawson, I need Miss Hampton to sign a few documents and then I can return to London." Martin stood and brought a pile of papers and a pen to Isabelle. She accepted the pen and looked to Dawson for guidance. He nodded and indicated she go ahead.

"I must say, I am pleased with the outcome. I am glad we were able to locate you and could reunite you with what is rightfully yours."

Martin collected the pen and papers before bowing to Isabelle. "I never would have envisioned a woman to inherit, but I feel like we are part of something very progressive. It was truly a pleasure to meet you, Miss Hampton."

"Yes, likewise. Thank you for finding me."

Martin waved away her words. "I've done my duty, miss, nothing more."

The group rose and Dawson stepped ahead to escort Martin to the door.

Martin tipped his hat and headed out to where his own horse was waiting. Swinging up onto its back, he gave a final wave. "Dawson," he called, "Take care of that girl. She is part of something special."

"You mean she is something special," Dawson corrected, laying a hand on Isabelle's shoulder.

CHAPTER 19

Isabelle stood in the parlor watching from the window as the carriage carrying Sara and Laura rolled down the snow-dusted driveway. Sighing, she wrapped her arms around herself. She felt a little guilty for refusing to join them in visiting the neighbors. She could have gone, and it would not have been as awkward as she imagined it. Scowling, she stared out at the bleak winter's day, at the gray and lifeless countryside. Between the morning's unexpected turn and this, she needed something to cheer her. The only thing she could think that could do the trick would be a visit from Walsh, and that was impossible with him being away.

Dawson came and stood beside her, a faint smile in his features. "Come now my dear, there will be plenty of time to worry about paying social calls."

Isabelle's frown vanished, as she looked up gratefully at her uncle.

"People will just have to accept that you need time to adjust without expecting you to do things our way."

A smile spread over her lips as she threw her arms around a startled Dawson's neck. "Thank you, uncle!" she exclaimed, squeezing him tight. "I want to be settled above anything else, but everything keeps changing."

Dawson kissed her forehead. "If I can understand your needs, Sara shall be able to as well."

Isabelle looked up at him with round eyes. "Do you think people will gossip about me? I've noticed rumors spread here."

Dawson chuckled. "Rubbish! There are more interesting topics of conversation than anything pertaining to you."

Isabelle sighed, relieved.

"Now," Dawson continued, rubbing his chin thoughtfully. "Worry no more about it. I will speak to Sara and ask her to excuse you from what she feels your regimen should be."

"Thank you."

Dawson waved his hand as if to wave away her thanks. "Now then, I will not have you looking so despondent. Might I recommend a ride? You have neglected your spotted mare."

"Poor Tafata. You're right. If I go now, I should be back before Laura sees me and I'll miss her lecture about how disgusting horses are," Isabelle teased as she bounded from the room, throwing a wave to her uncle.

Dawson chuckled and shook his head affectionately.

Isabelle stepped through the snow making tracks as she crossed the courtyard towards the stables. Sam whistled happily as he approached with Tafata in hand. "I say there's a dampness in the air today miss, best be ready for sudden changes in the weather," he greeted.

"Why do you say that?"

He chuckled, slapping his right knee. "Ere since I got kicked, the leg lets me know when the weather's a'changing," he replied, leading the horse to the mounting block. Isabelle noted he walked with a slight limp.

"I will keep an eye on the sky," she commented as he helped her into the saddle.

Passing her the reins, he tipped his hat. "Aye, miss, enjoy your ride."

"Thank you, Sam. We'll be back soon."

Isabelle steered the horse out of the yard, enjoying the rhythmic squeak of the saddle.

~

Tafata's head bobbed with each stride while Isabelle's thoughts began to drift. She wondered if being an accomplished horsewoman would help her fit in or would others think like Laura and consider her odd for choosing a dirty hobby? The thought gave her a queer feeling.

Touching her heels to the mare's side, Isabelle smiled as she felt the horse's surge of power beneath her. The wind whipped at her hair trailing out from under her bonnet as the ribbons fluttered around her cheeks. As they covered the ground in long easy strides, Isabelle began to feel free from her worries. Cantering through a bit of brush, a fallen tree blocked their path. Unconcerned, Isabelle pointed the mare towards it. Gracefully, Tafata leapt the tree and cantered on into the trees. Not wanting to get the horse too hot Isabelle brought her down to an easy trot. She noted they had already traveled quite far from the house. The slower pace offered Isabelle an opportunity to admire her surroundings.

The sky had darkened with brooding clouds that forbid the sun to offer any of its warm rays. Snow floated down from the sky. All around them birds hopped from branch to branch, knocking bits of snow off as they went. They chirped noisily as horse and rider passed.

Tafata dropped her nose to the ground jerking the reins from Isabelle. Leaning forward in the saddle Isabelle pulled the horse's nose away from the boulder she sniffed. The horse gave a heavy but submissive sigh. Isabelle noticed a gray mist began to creep along the ground, hiding stumps and rocks as it skulked along. In some places it was closing in against the sky and starting to cloud visibility.

"We better go so we don't get caught in the fog," Isabelle spoke to the horse, watching the smoky-white substance warily.

The snow began to fall heavier as she turned towards home. Suddenly, she heard twigs snap and a rustling in the woods beside her. Something was moving towards her hidden by the cover of the trees. Isabelle froze, unsure of what she would do if an animal came upon them. Tafata's ears flicked back and forth aware of the movement, but she did not seem afraid.

Isabelle started as a figure stumbled its way out of the brush muttering as it did so. The person stopped ranting and stared at Isabelle. His expression betrayed his surprise at seeing her. "Miss Hampton." His greeting was awkward and stiff as a slight frown crossed his face.

"Weston," Isabelle exclaimed. "What on earth are you doing way out here on foot?" Isabelle pursed her lips to avoid smiling in amusement at seeing him trudging through the snow. He cleared his throat while brushing away snow and branches clinging to his overcoat.

"I stopped to take a closer look at a small bird I saw hopping along the ground. I stepped down from my horse and while I was investigating my horse broke free and ran for the stables." He gave a weak smile. "I am now simply making the most of my predicament."

Isabelle gave a brief nod of understanding. "I think I know this story. But we've reversed our roles from the first time we lived it." She forced a polite smile. "Since you offered to help me then, I can give you a ride now."

"I do not think I ought to accept your offer."

Isabelle chuckled awkwardly, a little irked at his impertinence. "I don't think you are in a position to say no."

He looked towards Lexington standing solemnly in the distance. "I would make it there eventually."

She shrugged. "I won't stop you if you'd rather walk."

He hesitated a moment, before taking a step forward. "You are quite right. With this fog, I would be a fool to refuse aide. Thank you, Miss Hampton, I was fortunate you happened upon me."

He stepped up beside the horse and sprang up easily behind Isabelle. Isabelle felt small seated on the horse with the powerful man so nearby. She grew aware of his presence as her skirt fluttered against his long legs with the motion of the horse. She could feel his warmth. He sat close to her, astride on the animal. His arm brushed against her back, sending a tingle racing through her body. The sensation frightened Isabelle. She had never felt something so powerful. Sitting rigid in the saddle, she hoped to avoid touching him again before they reached Lexington.

They rode across the fields in silence, neither inclined to speak to the other. The fog grew thicker and began to close in around them. Soon it became difficult to see the path. A shiver of fear ran through Isabelle. Weston noticed her tremble. Concerned for her health in the growing cold, he unwound a scarf from around neck and gently placed it about hers. Startled, Isabelle glanced back at him.

"What are you doing?" she asked, afraid of his touch.

"You must be freezing out here," he replied.

Isabelle's fingers reached up to touch the scarf. "How thoughtful."

He made no reply, instead, he stared into the fog.

An eerie silence hung over the land. Isabelle began to wonder if they were going the wrong way, but soon the large stone mansion appeared in the fog up ahead. Relief washed over Isabelle, as she would soon be rid of Mr. Weston's company, and she could make her way home. Isabelle had the mare follow the path through the snow leading to the house.

Once they arrived in the courtyard, Isabelle halted the mare and Weston slid to the ground. Isabelle removed the scarf from around her neck as Weston glanced about at the fog. "This is terrible weather for riding. Will you be all right, Miss Hampton?" He appeared concerned as he stood next to her horse, gazing intently up at her.

Isabelle's anxiety became apparent as she glanced around. The weather had turned miserable, but she had no desire to spend more time with him than she already had. Isabelle forced a confident smile. "I will manage," she said, with more certainty than she felt as she passed the scarf back to him.

Weston took it but did not seem convinced. "Perhaps I could saddle my horse..."

Before he could say anything more, a gust of wind tore through the courtyard. It picked up Isabelle's cloak and whipped it around the horse's face. Unable to see, the mare began to panic. Weston tried to grab the frightened horse's bridle as she leapt sideways, but he was unable to catch her. Isabelle let out a startled scream and grabbed for the horse's neck. The mare shot backwards before rearing up high, thrashing out with her front legs. The horse's sudden movements proved too much for Isabelle and she could do nothing to save herself. She felt herself slip from the horse's back. She heard Weston shout before there was nothing but darkness.

CHAPTER 20

Distant voices spoke in soft tones as a damp cloth wiped across Isabelle's brow. Isabelle did not understand what they were saying. Stirring in the luxury of the bed, her eyes fluttered open. The room was unfamiliar. The fading light of day mingled with that of the candle, casting strange shadows along the ivory walls. A warm hand rested atop the cold compress held on her forehead for a moment. Isabelle's eyes roved over to her nurse.

Weston sat in a chair pulled up alongside the bed, his brow creased in worry. He moved the compress from her forehead and dipped the cloth into a porcelain basin. He had removed his waistcoat and his tie hung undone around the collar of his shirt. He stared into the basin as his hands wrung out the excess, unaware that curious eyes watched his every move. Turning his attention back to his patient, a small smile softened his features when he realized she was awake.

"How are you feeling?" He placed the fresh cloth on her skin. Isabelle let out a breath.

"I feel tired."

He nodded. "I am not surprised. You had quite the fall."

Isabelle reached up to steady her pounding head when she started to see shadows. "Thank you for looking after me." Her words were a mere whisper.

Weston placed a finger to her lips. "Save your strength. There will be time for words once you are better."

His keen eyes studied her for a moment as she gave a slight nod. Reaching out, his fingers brushed aside the locks of hair which had fallen across her cheek. Isabelle's heart gave a small flutter at his touch. With a sigh, she closed her eyes, slipping back into the darkness with the image of Robert Weston fresh in her mind.

When Isabelle woke again, the candles had burned low, caressing the room in a soft glow. It must have been late for the house was quiet and it was dark outside. Feeling better, Isabelle glanced around the room. The chair next to the bed sat empty and the basin of water on the side table was gone.

Isabelle sat up amid thick pillows, careful not to jostle her head, and pulled back the covers. Swinging her legs over the edge of the bed, her toes brushed the soft rugs on the floor. She paused, waiting to see if her head would grow cloudy. When it did not, she rose from the bed and stepped across the room to the window. The dim lighting from the candle cast reflections of the room on the window. Isabelle cupped the glass to peek out into the darkness. She realized the ghostly fog made it impossible to see anything. Sighing, she ran her fingers along the top of the dressing table, slowly making her way back to the bed.

Passing by the mirror, Isabelle caught a glimpse of herself from the corner of her eye. Horrified, she stopped and took a closer look. In the dim light she saw her reflection wearing a short night shirt, with a lace up front, which fell just to her knees. Her bare legs looked soft and smooth in the candlelight as she studied the garment. The longer she looked at it, the more she began to question whether it really was a lady's night shirt. It appeared rather un-feminine. Her hair was down, falling about her shoulders giving her the appearance of an older woman. Turning sideways, she inspected her reflection from a different angle. It occurred to her that she had been wearing a dress when she arrived. She cast a hurried glance around the room, but it was not there. Isabelle frowned; her arms dangled by her sides. There were maids in the house. Weston would have had them help her. A shiver ran through her. Moving away from the mirror, she crawled back into the safety and comfort of the bed. Drawing the covers up to her chin, Isabelle buried her face in the long sleeves of her gown. Feeling a little uneasy, she drifted into a fitful sleep.

Weston moved noiselessly down the hall, his candle flickering in the darkened passageway. Reaching his room, he pushed open the door and slipped inside. Setting the candle down on a small table, he tossed his waistcoat onto the bed. Throwing himself into the wingback chair, he slung one booted leg over the arm. His fingers fumbled with the knot in his ascot; he pulled it from around his neck. His shirt gapped open. It was two am and he was wide-awake. Leaping up from the chair, he began to pace about the room. His thoughts tumbled about in a mass of confusion. Folding his arms across his chest, he paused and leaned a shoulder against the wall.

"Isabelle should not be here," he spoke aloud, staring into the candle flame, rubbing his chin. "She has no need for anyone to speculate about her virtue."

He gave a weary sigh. Resuming his position on the chair, he ran a hand over his forehead as his thoughts continued to roam back to events of the past. Leaning his head back against the chair, he closed his eyes. Images flashed through his mind. The Weston name and what it stood for hung over him like a shroud. Sighing, he dropped his head into his hands as a new image crept into his thoughts: Isabelle standing before him in a shirt that barely covered her, his shirt. A quiver danced across his shoulders. Soft candlelight lit the room, gently revealing her bare legs as she paused before the mirror. She was graceful and beautiful. Weston tapped his fingers on his lips; he should have let her know he sat in the corner of the room, watching her every move. He should not have been there in the first place. He had no intention to be in her room all night, but he fell asleep while tending her.

"I only wanted to make sure she would be safe," he muttered, trying to console his conscience. Weston shrugged it off and began to dress for bed.

The next morning, Isabelle lay awake in her bed staring around the room. Sunlight dulled by the fog lit the room with a grayish hue. Isabelle felt stiff this morning, but her head felt a bit clearer. However, her curiosity to explore her environment was greater than her pain. Tossing aside the covers, she spied a robe lying on the chair. Hurrying across the rug covered floor, she picked up the robe and slipped into it. It was much too large for her, but she did not mind, she just wrapped herself in it tying the sash about her. It was quite comfortable.

Cozy and covered, Isabelle stepped over to the window. The fog made seeing anything near impossible, but Isabelle determined she was on the second floor of the mansion. Leaning closer to the window, she peered into the fog, trying to catch a glimpse of anything. If she squinted, she thought she could see the carriage house or stables.

There was a gentle knock on the door. Isabelle spun around as a maid slipped into the room, carrying a breakfast tray. Isabelle's dress hung over her arm. The maid froze and gazed uncertainly at the empty bed. Her roaming eyes spotted Isabelle standing next to the window. She looked relieved but a small frown creased her brow.

"You should be in bed, miss," she said, setting the tray down on the bedside table.

Isabelle gave a weak smile. "I felt well enough to be up for a bit."

The maid laid the dress on the back of the chair next to the bed. "Yes miss, but you took a bad fall yesterday. The master insists you stay in bed. We must make certain you are unharmed." She stepped over and taking Isabelle by the shoulders, steered her towards the bed. "Master Weston would not like it if he knew you were out of bed while you are unwell."

Isabelle sighed. She had not the strength to protest. "I suppose not."

Footsteps echoed in the hall as someone approached and presently Weston appeared in the doorway. Isabelle looked up, turning to greet him as best as possible. He folded his hands behind his back.

"Miss Hampton, I had not expected to find you out of bed."

The maid looked pointedly at Isabelle. "How are you feeling this morning?" he enquired.

Isabelle smiled, leaning on the back of the chair. "Much better thank you. Your hospitality is kind."

Weston shrugged. "Yes, well, the thanks should really go to Walsh, for the house and servants are both his. I, like you, am merely a guest."

The maid fidgeted next to Isabelle. "Miss, you really ought to be in bed. Your breakfast will be cold soon."

Weston took a step backwards. "There is a great deal of sense in her words. I will leave you now." He turned to go.

"Wait a moment, please," Isabelle pleaded, ignoring the maid who tried to hustle her into the bed.

Weston halted, giving her his full attention. "Is something wrong, Miss Hampton?"

Isabelle felt small under his intense gaze. She swallowed. "Has someone gone to my uncle? Do my family know what happened?" Her eyes shone with compassion.

Weston looked a little surprised. "No, I cannot risk sending anyone out in this weather."

Isabelle gasped and her hand went to her mouth. "But they will be worried!"

"Miss Hampton, I assure you I would have sent word already had the fog not made such an act impossible."

Isabelle bit her lower lip. "Surely a man could find his way to Brooklyn?"

Weston shook his head. "I would not send a man out only to have him get lost. It is too dangerous."

A look of distress crossed Isabelle's face. "So, we wait? That's it?"

Weston shrugged, his expression not exactly sympathetic. "I will go to Brooklyn myself, as soon as it is possible to do so."

Isabelle gasped in horror. "Heaven only knows when that will be. I'll have been missing for days. Aunt Sara will be sick with worry." The image of her aunt fretting for her safety was too much for Isabelle to bear. Her headache began to return. Raising her hand to her head, she hoped to steady the pounding. "Please, is there nothing you can do?"

Heaving a sigh, Weston shuffled his feet along the floor. "I am terribly sorry, Miss Hampton, but I fear it is too dangerous to venture out in this weather. The visibility is poor, and any horse would be inclined to spook," he paused, squaring his shoulders. "I will get word to your relations as soon as I am able, but until then, you must rest. Injuries to the head are a serious matter."

Isabelle's complexion had been growing increasingly paler. She started to protest but had no strength to continue. Instead, she gave a small, understanding nod.

Weston stood watching her for a moment. "Please see to it that Miss Hampton gets the rest she needs," he instructed before disappearing back into the hall.

Isabelle allowed the maid to bustle her out of the robe as the room began to spin. The maid worked quickly and drew aside the covers so Isabelle could climb into the bed. Isabelle struggled to focus; everything turned gray as she fainted dead away.

CHAPTER 21

Brooklyn Manor,

A door opened and a gust of frigid wind whipped into the house. The door banged shut as murmuring voices and tromping feet sounded in the hall.

Sara, pale and worried, rose from her seat to greet her husband as he appeared in the doorway. Wringing her hands, she stood next to the large bay window. "Did you find her?" The words sounded calmer than she looked.

A frown crossed Dawson's wind burned features. He shook his head, removing his cloak and cap. "I did not. This blasted fog makes any search impossible! The weather unsettles the men, and the horses are skittish," he muttered, discouraged. He tossed his gear onto a nearby table. Timidly, a maid stepped forward to gather them, hustling them away to the cloak room. Sara bit her bottom lip and squared her shoulders as tears brimmed in her eyes. Dawson's heart melted. He strode easily to her side and pulled her into his arms. "No tears, my dear. I will find her."

Sara looked up at him. A tear ran down her cheek "That silly girl. Wherever did she go?"

Dawson sighed. "She could not have gone too far. I am certain she is all right," he replied burying his fingers in Sara's hair.

Sara laid her cheek on his chest, seeking comfort from her husband's strength. Laura looked up at her uncle and aunt from her position on the floor next to the window. She shuddered at the thoughts running through her imagination. Laura turned back to the window and gazed out at the fog.

Lexington Estate,

The music from his violin surrounded Weston, taking him back to days long ago. Closing his eyes, Weston listened to the sweet sound as it filled the sitting room. He stood playing before a crackling fire, yet he appeared unaware of anything around him.

"Pray excuse me, sir." A voice beside him interrupted his solitude.

The violin squeaked as Weston's eyes fluttered open. His brows knit in annoyance. Lowering the bow, he cradled the violin in his arm. "What is it, Mr. Collins?"

Collins cleared his throat. "The fog has lifted, sir. Shall I send a man to Brooklyn Manor with news of Miss Hampton's welfare?"

Weston traced his finger along the scrolling on the mantle. "No, I will go myself. The situation requires an explanation," he replied, turning to face the butler. "I prefer the Dawsons hear it from me."

Collins folded his hands behind his back. "Very good, sir. I shall send for your horse."

Making a quick bow, Collins turned to go. "Thank you, Mr. Collins," Weston muttered, settling the violin in its case.

~

A soft hand brushed Isabelle's hair back from her face. "Hello, my darling." A woman's voice spoke to her. Isabelle knew that voice. She opened her eyes, looking up into Sara's loving face. Sara smiled as she sat on the edge of the bed.

"Oh, I'm so glad to see you!" Isabelle exclaimed, struggling to sit up.

Sara placed a firm hand on her shoulder to restrain her. "Be still, Isabelle. There is no need for such excitement. You have had too much already." Isabelle nodded and settled back into the pillows. Sara folded her hands in her lap and her smile fixed on her lips. "Now then, how are you feeling?"

Isabelle returned the smile. "Much better, but oh, Aunt Sara, I felt so much worse when I thought about how worried you must be," she explained with a tearful voice.

Sara reached out and took Isabelle's hand, giving it a gentle squeeze. "There, there, child, everything is alright now."

Isabelle blinked, fighting back tears. "You're here. But the fog..."

"The weather is much improved. Mr. Weston came early this morning to explain what had happened."

Isabelle's eyes grew wide with surprise. "Weston?"

Sara chuckled. "Yes, dear, he explained that he felt the situation required his personal attention. He himself wanted to tell us where you were and that you were all right."

A puzzled frown creased Isabelle's brow. "Weston?" she repeated, amazed that he himself, the great Robert Weston, had gone to Brooklyn as a messenger boy.

Sara chuckled, leaning forward to place her hand on Isabelle's forehead. "Yes, Mr. Weston. Are you feverish, child?"

Isabelle shook her head. "Oh no, Aunt Sara." A warm feeling swelled up inside her. This powerful man had gone to Brooklyn on her behalf. The news pleased her although she was not sure why. Glancing up, she saw Weston standing outside the bedroom door. He leaned against the doorframe; his eyes fixed on her. He cocked his head to one side as he studied her. She smiled at him. Sara continued talking, but Isabelle did not hear what she was saying.

A faint trace of a smile showed itself on Weston's lips before he took a step back from the door, allowing Laura to enter. She cast on odd look at Weston before she beamed at Isabelle.

"Laura! I'm so happy to see you!" Isabelle greeted her friend as Weston disappeared down the hall.

Laura came and sat on the other side of the bed. She wore a smug little smirk. "Hmm, I dare say, Isabelle, how lucky you are to have had an 'accident' which forced you into the private company of the most eligible Mr. Weston."

Isabelle glanced worriedly at the door, hoping that Weston had not heard Laura's remark. "I wouldn't call this situation lucky at all. I spent most of the time unconscious."

Laura patted her hair. "I merely wished to point out that it was convenient to be forced into lodgings with him," she sighed, wistfully.

Sara chuckled. "Silly girl, you have read too many romantic novels."

Isabelle nodded. "Yes, she has. This incident could hardly be romantic. Neither Weston nor I have a romantic interest in each other."

The conversation came to an abrupt halt as Dawson swept into the room. He smiled lovingly at Isabelle as he stepped up to the bed. "There is my little lady." He leaned over her, placing a kiss on her forehead. "How are you, Isabelle?"

She returned his smile. "I feel better, uncle."

Dawson gave a nod of approval. "Do you feel well enough to go home?"

Isabelle's heart skipped a beat at the thought of going home. "Yes, I don't want to burden Weston any longer."

Dawson smiled and patted her hand. "Good, good, I will excuse myself then."

Sara and Laura helped Isabelle out of bed and into her dress once Dawson had gone. Laura held the nightshirt in her hands.

"What on earth were you wearing, Isabelle?" she exclaimed, examining the shirt while Sara tied Isabelle's dress.

Isabelle glanced over her shoulder at Laura, who was scrutinizing the garment. "I think it's a nightshirt," she replied, leaning against the dressing table to steady herself.

Laura dropped the shirt on the bed. "It isn't a lady's nightshirt."

Isabelle smiled while Laura draped her cloak about her shoulders.

"No, I suppose it's a man's shirt," she replied as she sunk onto the edge of the bed.

Laura looked horrified. "Dressing a woman in a man's clothing is almost barbaric," she sniffed with a righteous air.

A knock at the door cut off Isabelle's chance to retort. Sara hurried to open the door and moved aside as Dawson stepped into the room. He smiled cheerfully at is wife. "Is everything in order?"

Sara nodded. "Yes, Isabelle has all her belongings."

"Good. Then let us be off."

Isabelle looked up at her uncle. "What about Tafata?"

Dawson chuckled, bending over so he could look Isabelle in the eye. "I have the mare saddle and waiting for me. I shall ride her home myself." Relief washed over Isabelle. Dawson placed Isabelle's arms around his neck before he scooped her into his arms. Startled, Isabelle tightened her grip around him. He chuckled. "Your carriage awaits you, miss. Shall we go home?"

She nodded. "Yes, I definitely am ready."

Sara looked a bit uncertain as she walked beside Dawson as he exited the room and headed down the wide hallway to the sweeping staircase. "Phillip, please be careful. Isabelle has already had one fall; another would do her no good," Sara muttered.

Dawson chuckled. "I am not an old man, Sara. She is safe in my arms."

Sara frowned but looked a bit embarrassed. "I am simply concerned for Isabelle's wellbeing. I made no comment about your age."

Weston suddenly stepped out from a room further down the hall reading a book as he went. When he glanced up from his reading, he gave a start as an uneasy expression crossed his face. Gold lettering glitter on the book as he slammed it shut and lengthened his stride. "Mr. Dawson is everything alright?" he asked as he met up with the little party.

Dawson smiled. "Quite all right, sir. She weighs nothing."

Weston looked uncertain. "Should you be doing this?" he said, hesitantly.

Dawson frowned. "If you too think I am too old to carry this young lady, let me assure you I am perfectly capable."

Weston looked embarrassed. "Of course, I was only..."

Sara placed her hand on his arm. He looked quizzically at her. She gave a sweet smile. "Mr. Weston, Dawson is a bit stubborn about some things." She glanced down at the floor. "In his heart, he is a young man." Her voice softened.

Weston nodded, "Yes of course, I understand."

Sara looked to her husband as he reached the top of the stairs.

He chuckled and exclaimed: "I never thought I'd see the day when a man was considered aged at five and forty." Isabelle assured him that he was nowhere near an old man.

Sara gave Weston a knowing smile. "Thank you, Mr. Weston. You have been more than kind." He opened his mouth to reply, but only gave a tight smile. She stepped ahead to join her family. Isabelle eyed the stairs warily as they made their descent. Weston followed along behind Sara and Laura.

Once Dawson settled Isabelle in the carriage, he turned to Weston. "Thank you, Mr. Weston, for taking such excellent care of my little lady." Weston straightened and gave a small nod while shaking Dawson's hand.

"It was no trouble. I felt the need to dedicate myself to her care as the incident resulted directly of my actions."

Dawson gave a sympathetic smile. "No one is responsible for an accident, but we are much obliged to you."

Isabelle watched the two men talk for a moment from her position in the carriage. Dawson swung onto Tafata's back and waved a farewell to Weston. Weston tucked his hands, book, and all, behind his back as he stood watching them go. His gaze met Isabelle's in a cold stare. She smiled and raised her hand to the window. Surprised, he offered a tentative wave, and his scowl broke. Laura, who had been quiet, now interrupted the silence with a barrage of questions and speculations. Isabelle sighed, listening to her cousin's chatter above the clip-clop of the horses' feet.

CHAPTER 22

Weston sat beside the fireplace, drinking tea, and staring at a book. He traced his fingers over the golden title. He pondered what compelled him to stick it in his pocket yesterday. The fire popped, rousing Weston from his thoughts as a knock sounded at the door. Looking up, he saw the maid, Penny, peering into the room.

"Yes, Penny, what is it?" He returned the book to his pocket and rubbed his eyes.

Penny came to his side. "I found this, sir, whilst I was setting Miss Hampton's room to rights." She handed him a white handkerchief. Weston turned the handkerchief over in his hand. The initials IH appeared embroidered with blue thread in the corner.

He traced his thumb over the letters before looking up at the maid. "Thank you, Penny. I will take care of this."

The maid bobbed her red head and curtsied. "Yes, sir." She excused herself.

Weston studied the handkerchief. "Isabelle..." he murmured, drifting into a collection of thoughts. Shaking the dream like state, he stuffed the handkerchief into his pocket.

Someone clomped and clamored up the hall. A thud at the

door caused his eyes to flutter that direction. "Well, the master has returned, eh?" he quipped.

Walsh laughed, leaning on the doorframe as if his remaining upright depended on it. "Weston, you old codger! Did you miss me?" Walsh's eyes twinkled, reflecting the fresh air and excitement he encountered over the holidays.

Weston sighed, looking annoyed. "Not really, I had plenty to entertain myself." He rose to greet his cousin. Walsh pulled him by the handshake into an embrace.

"Have you? What did you do? Pray tell?"

Weston frowned, prying himself from Walsh's grasp. "Walsh, have you been drinking?" he asked, a bit irritated.

Walsh threw himself into a chair, and grinned. "Not at all my good man! A man drinks to drown his sorrows. I, my friend, have none. Tell me why the long face? Or is it exhaustion I read in those lines? My, you have had a time while I was away, haven't you?"

Weston rubbed his eyes. "No, cousin, you need not wag your eyebrows so."

"Did you not attend the Dawson's Christmas party? They host a beautiful celebration every year."

"Yes, I attended, briefly."

"Briefly briefly, how do you expect to have any fun?"

"Need I remind you, they are your people, not mine."

Walsh slung his legs over one arm of the chair and looked up at Weston with a cheeky grin. "Good people, the Dawsons, and even finer around the holidays. Ah Weston, isn't Christmas a wonderful time of year?" He laughed.

Weston shook his head. "What has gotten into you?" he asked, sitting on the arm of the sofa.

Walsh rubbed his chin. "Just the holiday spirit!"

"I would be surprised if that were the only spirit you've had recently."

"Nonsense. I am just in a good mood. I had a wonderful time at Irene's. Really, Weston, you should have come. Collins!"

Weston jumped, nearly falling from his perch. "Good heavens Walsh, bellowing like that is enough to wake the dead."

Walsh chuckled. His eyes danced. "Isn't it though? Ah Collins."

The butler appeared in the sitting room looking frazzled. "Master Walsh, I hear you have returned."

Walsh nodded. "Yes, Mr. Collins, 'tis good to be home. Be a good fellow, no more of your cheek, and see that we have tea brought up with whatever delicacies we have in the kitchen."

Collins bowed. "Very well, sir."

Sighing, Walsh settled back into the chair. "Now Weston." Weston glanced at his cousin with a look of expectancy. "I have news for you."

Weston raised a brow. "News?"

Walsh nodded. "Yes, yes, news. Now do not interrupt." He sat up and slid to the edge of his seat. The heels of his tall black boots gave a dull thump when they hit the rugged floor.

"On the evening of my arrival at Irene's, a small gathering of friends was present. One particular guest, I know quite well although we have not seen each other for—oh I could not even hazard a guess as to how many—years. Do you recall a Miss Stella Duke? Yes, of course you know her. You attended her coming out party. She and Irene, of course, have remained friends all these years," before Weston could reply, Walsh prattled on, "Of course, you know everyone, I daresay. She was a very pretty young lady, with dark hair, quite charming. She has not changed much, really. I would recognize her in an instant if I were to spot her at the assemblies or some such place. She does possess such a rare elegance and simple beauty. Delightful, positively delightful. She belongs to a small but wealthy family in Brighton. Only one other sibling, a young man who I hear is an accomplished musician. I would think your path would have crossed his, both being the musicians you are, but he sounds so young and full of life, while you—now Weston, please do not make such a face for you know well what I meant. Good heavens, where was I going with this?"

Walsh paused a moment and scratched his head. Weston sat, waiting, and growing more agitated with each tick of the grandfather clock in the corner. "Ah yes, now I remember. We were well acquainted several years ago, Miss Duke and I. I must admit, I held a certain fondness for her, but we were so young then that my attentions to her were never serious." He chuckled fondly. "However, upon seeing her again, I believe her to be more charming than ever. She truly is a fair lady, a calibre of which I have not seen for a long time. We are older now so any feelings I may have towards her I can explore, and she can consider me a suitor. Yes, I am quite enamoured with the prospect. I cannot believe my extraordinary luck."

Weston coughed, nearly choking on his morning tea. Walsh looked concerned.

"Weston, are you quite alright?"

Weston nodded, still coughing. "Surely you do not mean to tell me you are in love with this woman?" Weston asked, once he had caught his breath.

Walsh nodded. "Love may be a strong word for this point in time, but I do not suppose it premature to presume that Miss Duke will accept my offer as suitor. We make a good match."

Weston stared at him. "You're not serious."

"I am. Why wouldn't I be?"

"Walsh, are you that heartless to forget your prior obligations?"

"My what? I can recall having no such thing."

"But what about Isabelle?" He asked, leaning forward onto his knees.

Walsh shrugged. "What about Miss Hampton?"

A twinge of annoyance cursed through Weston. "Have you not left her hoping for a proposal of marriage? Surely, she expects something from you."

Walsh waved his hand. "Oh, no, I sincerely doubt that."

"You do. But does she have no feelings for you? Walsh, this is absurd. I thought you loved her."

Walsh frowned, looking down at his hands. "I must have been mistaken."

"Mistakes are what happen in games of cards not in matters of love. How could you be unsure of your feelings towards her?"

"How could I be uncertain of my feelings towards her when I have none? Once I saw Miss Duke again, feelings I had long forgotten burst to life. Miss Hampton never did elicit feelings of that sort."

"You could never love her?" Weston asked, folding his arms across his chest.

Walsh looked a bit baffled. "Miss Hampton is a charming young lady, but as you pointed out: she is little more than a child."

Weston cringed at the word "child." "Walsh you're being a fool."

"Oh, Weston, don't be such a prude. And that frown is very unbecoming. No harm will come of this."

"Don't you realize how this foolishness will impact your relations with the Dawsons?"

"They're reasonable people. It will not be a concern. You are worried for nothing."

Weston's eyes narrowed. "Whatever your flippant attitude towards all this, Miss Hampton does not deserve to be treated as a mere trifle."

"She cannot expect anything more than a neighborly friendship from me. She is several years my junior and hardly anything is known of her. Her connection to the Dawsons is her only commendation."

"You seek an excuse to justify your behavior, cousin, and I am afraid you will not find one. She is well bred and of fortune. I believe she has deeper feelings for you than I think you realize. No argument you make will excuse your callousness." Weston's voice rumbled deep and gloomily.

Walsh patted his knee. "I have not acted out of ill will. I think you have mistaken her feelings towards me."

"You have a valuable opportunity before you, yet you could care less. You treat it with frivolity as if there were no other sacrifices involved! Do not forget you did not receive her affections by chance." Weston spat the words out with a bitter snarl. "You might not have fared so well if you had some competition for her affections."

"What absurd nonsense. Of course, there are other suitors."

"Maybe others relented in their pursuit of her because you seemed intent to win her? You would have met some barriers to your path had there been any doubt of your interest in her."

Walsh shrugged. "If they did, they missed the opportunity through their own foolishness. They should have made their intentions known and let her decide who she would have."

Weston flew from his perch onto his feet. "Disgraceful! She cares about you. Your carelessness will only bring her pain." Weston's tone held a sharp edge.

Walsh frowned. "Weston, what's the matter with you?"

Weston stooped down to look Walsh in the eye. "Your wanton acts have led a young lady to believe you would have romantic intentions towards her. Not only have you permitted her to believe you loved her, but you have encouraged such beliefs. You have played a fiendish game with Miss Hampton. I will not sit by and support your Don Juan exploits."

Walsh scowled. "I never intended to hurt anyone. I love another; what am I to do?"

"You should behave as the gentleman you were born to be and conduct yourself with more integrity than you have."

"Weston, I need no lectures from you; but I suppose you would be the perfect model of how one stifles any sort of emotion."

"You cannot turn the course of this conversation. You have dabbled with a young lady's affections and caused unnecessary harm."

"No harm has come to Miss Hampton. This lecture you are intent on giving me is unwarranted."

"Hardly. It is my duty as the elder of this family to correct your errant ways. Consider the damage your actions will have upon your relations with the Dawsons. These people are your neighbors, with whom you have always been amicable. How will they respond to your treatment of their ward?"

"I have not erred! Nothing I have done is wrong. While I am fond of Miss Hampton, I do not love her. My affections are for Miss Duke alone."

Weston shook his head. "You can argue your way out of any affection you ever felt for Miss Hampton, but it will never justify your dismissal of her nor will it protect her from hurt."

"I mean her no harm, Weston, but I cannot change how I feel. Such hurts are part of life and surely, she will recover."

"Love does not come and go on a passing whim."

Walsh bowed his head. Weston continued. "You have given her reason to expect a proposal. I will not see her disappointed." Scooping his book off the table, Weston marched from the room.

Bewildered, Walsh watched him go. "Weston!" Sitting alone, Walsh heaved a sigh. "What has gotten into you?"

CHAPTER 23

Brooklyn Manor,

A light knock sounded on the door before Laura poked her head into Isabelle's room. "Isabelle, are you awake?" She spoke in hushed tones and hesitated by the door. Her eyes lit up when she spied Isabelle seated at the dressing table.

"Yes, I'm here."

Laura chuckled, stepping over to the dressing table. "How are you this morning?"

"I feel ready for an adventure after being confined to bed for so long."

"Perfect! I may have just the thing for you."

Isabelle tipped her head to the side. "Oh?"

Laura spoke in a rush and shoved a package at Isabelle. "This has just arrived for you from Lexington. Open it!"

"But who sent it?" Isabelle asked with a frown, turning over the package in her hands.

"Who sent it? Why Mr. Walsh, most certainly!"

Isabelle pulled at the wrapping. "There's no note. That doesn't seem his style."

"Maybe he forgot." Isabelle shot her a look. "Don't look at me like that. Why would Mr. Weston send you a parcel?"

"Why wouldn't he?" Isabelle pulled a book from the wrapping and read the front cover. She froze.

"It's a book." Laura sounded disappointed as she wrinkled her nose.

"How did he know?" Isabelle murmured, running her fingers over the golden etched title.

"It's a significant book?"

"Huh? Oh, yes. I wonder where he found it." Isabelle flipped through the pages, a little yellowed with age and softened with use.

Laura heaved a sigh. "Well, this was not the adventure I hoped it would be. There must be something else to do today outside of old books."

Isabelle tucked the book on her dressing table and gave it a loving pat. "Yes, we can have an actual adventure too," she exclaimed as Heather appeared in the room with a gown draped over her arm. "I would like to see the orphans again. Oh Laura, it's awful to see all the children who live there. Could you imagine someone abandoning their child?" Isabelle shook her head as her voice grew thick. "What sort of person could do that?"

Laura nodded and lay a hand on her shoulder. "Sometimes the parents have no choice. Poverty exists and grows ever more prominent. Desperation forces people into action they would typically avoid.

What choice do they have when they have no choice? Lord knows, it isn't an easy world."

Heather approached the two young ladies, fingering the hem of the gown in her arms. "Aye, right you are, Miss Laura," she kept her head bowed as she spoke.

Laura leaned down to examine her reflection in the mirror. "Are we off to Southampton then, Isabelle?" She twisted a curl around her finger, watching Isabelle in the mirror.

Isabelle nodded. "Yes, to Southampton we go. Heather, please, tell Aunt Sara we are ready to go when she is."

Heather bobbed her head and slipped into the hall. Isabelle linked arms with Laura as they left the room.

Sara met the girls at the door and together they piled into the carriage. Their conversation was lighthearted with a great deal of joking and laughter, making the drive to Southampton seem short. They arrived well before any of them were ready to end the pleasantries.

"Aunt Sara," Isabelle broke-in as Laura was finishing a sentence, "might we stop at the book and gift shop? I would like to pick up something."

Laura grinned. "Shopping? I like shopping."

Sara nodded. "I do not see why not. We have the time."

"Now this talk reminds me that I do need a few things myself." Laura mused, running a finger along her chin.

Isabelle gave a knowing smile. "Of course, you do."

Once outside the little shop, the ladies stepped from the carriage.

Isabelle hurried through what a little bit of snow there was to the door. Inside the shop was cozy and smelled of cinnamon. As each of the ladies went her separate way to the department of her preference, Isabelle headed to the shelves laden with toys.

Scanning the shelves, she spied a little doll tucked behind a wooden boat. The doll was no bigger than her hand and wore a yellow dress. Raven ringlets stuck out from underneath the matching bonnet and tumbled down her back. Moving aside the other toys Isabelle lifted the doll and admired her.

Smiling, she headed to the cashier's counter, clutching the doll in her hands. She paused in line behind a man. He stepped aside gesturing with his hand. "Please, my lady, go ahead of me."

The gesture startled Isabelle and she shook her head. "That's kind, but I don't mind waiting." Her eyes rose to his face and a smile of recognition crossed her lips. The warmth in her smile drew him closer. Her cheeks began to burn with the warmth of secret fancy. He stepped around her, forcing her into his spot in line.

"You have only one item, Miss Hampton. Do not make a great thing out of a small one."

Isabelle gave a small frown as she adjusted her feet to face the man who now stood behind her. "Weston, can I point out you also have only one item?"

He shrugged looking down at the book in his hand. "Be that as it may. I have no other errand in town this day. I see both your aunt, and Miss Millis touring the shop and I can only assume you ladies have a schedule to keep."

"Waiting in line won't ruin our schedule, if we had one."

"Then consider it a matter of principle. No lady shall wait on my account."

"You don't need to look so smug about it."

"I had no knowledge of my appearing smug. I only thought it amusing to see a doll in your hand."

"She is not for me."

"Then she is for Miss Millis, although Christmas has both come and gone."

Isabelle made a face. He gave a low chuckle. "I jest. Neither you nor Miss Millis strike me as someone who would play with dolls."

Isabelle smoothed down the dress on the little doll. "Yes. She is for a little girl I know." Isabelle smiled at the doll before handing it to the clerk for wrapping. "This doll is a trinket for a child who has suffered a lot," Isabelle continued as she accepted her change and received the small paper package.

Weston nodded. He paid for his book and stuffed it into his pocket. "Indeed, though I suspect your small friend is but one of many. What comfort will you offer the others who have suffered the same fate?"

"Isabelle!"

The conversation came to a halt as Laura appeared at Isabelle's side. Her eyes widened as she looked upon Weston. She gave him a clipped greeting. "Good day, Mr. Weston."

He inclined his head towards her. "Miss Millis, a pleasure to see you."

"Isabelle, Aunt Sara received some consuming news. She has asked us to accompany her on her errand. I am afraid we must postpone the visit to the children."

"Oh, how disappointing. Yes, if Aunt Sara needs us, I suppose the children can wait." Isabelle offered a strained smile.

"What children are these?" Weston looked at Isabelle and noted how she tucked the little package under her arm. Laura arranged her curls as she addressed his question.

"The children of Kingsview Orphanage. Isabelle has taken a liking to them."

"You were planning to visit orphans?"

"I don't need to explain myself to either of you. They are children." Isabelle's ears flushed red.

"No need for defense, Miss Hampton. I merely wondered."

Isabelle raised a shoulder. "Wonder no more."

"Children yes, but orphans they remain. Any kindness afforded to them must come from charity not duty. Unfortunately, with the pressing nature of Aunt Sara's business, any visit today would be out of duty since we have not the privilege of time," Laura added, looking impatient.

"With respect to your observation, Miss Millis, I agree in part. However, if Miss Hampton is intent on making a charitable visit today, I would be happy to escort her for I have the privilege of time."

Laura quirked a brow at his proposal and Isabelle cocked her head. "That is quite an offer, but I can't accept. That would be too much of an imposition."

"Nonsense. If it were an imposition, I would never have made the offer. If your aunt can spare you for the afternoon, I will escort you to Kingsview." Weston directed the comment towards Sara as she approached the group.

She looked perplexed. "What is this scheme you young people have brewing?"

"Weston has offered to escort me to Kingsview."

"That is very kind of Mr. Weston."

He nodded to Sara. The corner of her mouth rose into a smirk when she met his expectant gaze. "I see no reason to interrupt Isabelle's plan, if Mr. Weston will accompany her to the orphanage. Laura and I can manage without her. I will leave the decision to her."

All eyes turned upon Isabelle. She fingered the package in her arms. "I'd like to go. If you're willing to take me, I'd appreciate that, Weston."

"You don't consider it an imposition on my time?" He raised a teasing brow. She felt herself smile at his cheek.

"No, you said it yourself that you had the privilege of time this afternoon."

"Very well. We shall depart when you are ready."

Sara heaved a sigh. "My gratitude to you, Mr. Weston."

"Certainly, Mrs. Dawson. Your ward is safe with me."

Sara looked amused. "I have no concern for her wellbeing, but I worry for yours. Do not let her run you ragged."

Weston chuckled. "An unnecessary warning, I assure you."

"Very well. We will meet you at the teahouse on the corner after five. Come Laura, let us be on our way."

"Yes, Aunt Sara, we will be off then." As Isabelle waved goodbye to her party, Weston directed her towards the door.

CHAPTER 24

Southampton was busy that day. People strolled past, separating Weston and Isabelle for a moment. Weston drifted back to Isabelle's side. "Kingsview stands along the seafront, does it not?"

"Yes."

They fell instep and continued in thoughtful silence. Weston sighed, drawing a curios glance from Isabelle. She directed her gaze away to the sea when he turned to her. He slipped his hands into the pockets of his overcoat. He was not sure why he had offered to go with her to the orphanage. He felt it was the right thing to do to provide her an alternative to occupy her time. If she had a distraction, she could remove herself from Walsh. Then when that scoundrel Walsh pursued Miss Duke, Isabelle would avoid devastation. This first step of engagement was the best he could to do protect her. Regardless how he felt about the girl, he did not want to see her harmed through Walsh's inconsideration.

She looked at him as if she could read his thought. He flinched and turned towards the waterfront. Such an odd man, she thought. Odd yet alluring. She found his secrecy a bit intriguing. She gave her head a shake. Regardless of that, he was also the one who tried to sabotage Mr. Walsh's attempts to court her. He meddled quite a bit in

Mr. Walsh's affairs. A slight frown creased her brow. However much of a menace he was in past, he tended her and cared for her after her accident when the Dawsons could not be reached. Mr. Weston was a complicated man who did complicated things. She could not begin to guess his reasons for his past actions let alone his sudden amicability.

As they approached the orphanage Weston stepped ahead to open the courtyard gate. Isabelle timidly passed by, entering the dreary yard. Latching the gate behind him, Weston strode to Isabelle's side and together they went up the steps to the door of the massive building.

"Cheery place, isn't it?" Weston asked, ringing the bell.

Isabelle shook her head. "I think it's creepy old building. It might almost be better to live in the streets than stay in the haunted mansion."

Weston chuckled, leaning back against the railing encircling the porch. "You read too many books, Miss Hampton. Your imagination is getting the better of you."

She raised her chin into the air. "At least I have an imagination."

Weston folded his arms across his chest. "So long as you can maintain the distinction between fantasy and reality."

Before she could reply the door creaked open revealing the gray head of Miss Bronte. She tilted her nose up and looked over the rims of her glasses at the pair waiting on the porch. "Can I help you?"

Isabelle gave a pleasant smile. "Good morning, Miss Bronte. Would it be possible to see the children?"

Miss Bronte scrunched up her nose before giving a curt nod. "Yes, they have a break before their next lessons." Miss Bronte stepped aside allowing them to enter. She stared at Weston. He nodded in her direction, acknowledging her in a pleasant manner. Miss Bronte's mouth drew in a tight line as she closed the door behind them before leading the way to the great room. Her stiff dress rustled as she moved.

Pausing in the archway of the great room she ushered them inside. "Here you are. You may visit until you hear the lesson bell. I have other duties to attend so I will take my leave." She made no farewell remarks before continuing down the hall.

Western glanced to Isabelle. "Charming thing, isn't she?"

Horrified, Isabelle tried not to laugh as she peered down the hall praying Miss Bronte was out of earshot. Satisfied Weston's comment remained between them, Isabelle shook her head while a sly smile crossed her lips. "I can't believe you said that!" she said laughing softly. "That was quite horrid of you."

He chuckled. "I was merely pointing out that woman's disposition is as icy as Southampton harbor in February."

Isabelle found no argument in her defence. "I suppose you're not wrong, but she does mean well."

"I don't doubt that, or she would not be here," Weston replied as they walked toward a group of children playing with a few old chairs and a tattered bed sheet.

A boy around the age of nine stood between the chairs, holding a stick in his hand. He raised his other hand as the newcomers approached. "Halt!" he commanded. Weston and Isabelle stopped moving. The boy's chest swelled at their compliance. He lifted his chin in a proud manner. "Who dares approach the vessel of the dread pirate Gavin?" He raised his stick sword towards Weston. Weston stepped forward when he beckoned with the sword.

"Seaman Weston, at your service, sir. Might I join your crew?"

The young captain stroked his chin in thought. "Hmm, a seaman, you say?" He began to pace the deck of his ship, his gaze travelling up and down Weston. "Have we need of a seaman, Mr. Smith?" He directed the question towards another boy around the same age. Mr. Smith gave a sharp nod and when he did the navy cap on his head slipped down over his eyes. The captain set his ragged shoe upon one of the chairs and sized up the newcomer. "Aye, lad," he said at last. "But I run a tight ship and any man who don't pull his weight will get tossed overboard!" He glared at a boy who sat on the floor next to him. The boy's ears turned pink as he leapt to his feet and hurried to help with the sail.

"Aye, captain, thank you, captain." Weston gave the boy a sharp salute and then turned to Isabelle as the boy went to bark at the boys tangled in the rigging. "Will you join us on board?" He extended a hand to her.

She shuddered. "Goodness no. A woman aboard a pirate's ship? What an idea!"

Weston grinned. "An idea indeed."

She feigned disgust with him. "That is no place for a lady. Those pirates look rough."

Weston gave a nod. "Yes, and I suppose they are mean too. Well, I better board before the captain sails without me" He stepped into the group of chairs and gave Isabelle a jaunty salute. "Farewell, Miss Hampton. I do not know when I shall sea land again."

She could not contain her smile. "It could be a long time."

He looked into her eyes a moment. His mouth parted as he moved to speak, but the young captain marched to his side.

"Put me on your shoulders so I can see where we are headed." The boy had to crane his neck to see Weston's face.

"Aye, aye, captain." With ease, Weston hoisted the boy onto his shoulders.

Isabelle watched in silent wonder while the boy ordered Weston from one end of the ship to the other. Here was this brooding man, playing on a pretend ship, and seeming to enjoy it. She shook her head in disbelief and went in search of her own thing to do. She joined a group of girls who were coloring on a large reem of paper they had spread across the floor. The faces of the girls lit up with smiles as she knelt beside them and arranged her skirts around herself. One girl with dirty cheeks passed her some pencils. Isabelle scribbled on the page with lines and circles going this way and that. She decided the shapes looked like a horse and the girls crowded close as she began to draw. The lines on the page took the form of a sorry looking animal.

Isabelle gave a weak smile. "Oh, well, I am not much of an artist."

One girl looked up, wide-eyed. "I think it is a lovely horse."

The child beside Isabelle gave a wistful sigh. "I would like to ride a horse." She looked sad as she studied the sketch.

"Maybe when you grow up you can," Isabelle said, feeling optimistic.

A shout echoed through the room, ending their conversation. A band of ruthless pirates raced across the room and invaded the drawing space. The girls squealed as they ran from the pirates who now all wore hats of folded paper. Some waved their hats as they whooped and chased the girls around the room. Isabelle laughed and ducked to avoid a boy swinging his arms and running past. The children ran after each other, hollering and laughing. Some got caught and others got away and there were cries of dismay and shouts of victory. Suddenly a fight broke out amid the pirates. She covered her mouth to muffle the laughter as a group of shouting boys surrounded Weston. They dove at him and dragged him down. Weston hit the floor with a dull thump. The boys were on him in an instant, pinning him.

"Surrender! Surrender!" The pirate captain shouted, as he knelt across Weston's shoulder.

Weston peeked at Isabelle from beneath the brim of his wrinkled paper hat. His cheeks flushed, but he grinned. He held her gaze a moment.

The boy across him jabbed him with a bony elbow. "Do you surrender?"

Weston flinched. "Ouch, I yield, my captain. I yield." He raised his hands in a defenceless gesture.

The boys jumped off him and cheered. "We removed the traitor from our ranks! Carry on, men!" Gavin shouted and led his boys back across the room.

Weston appeared in no hurry to remove himself from the floor.

Isabelle got to her feet and stepped over to hover above his prone form. "Are you alright?"

Opening one eye, he peeped at her. "Yes, fine. I need a moment to catch my breath." He propped himself on his arm, watching the pirates disband and each go their own way.

"Have you given up your pirate ways then?" Isabelle said with a smile in her voice.

He plucked the paper hat from his head. "Not given up by choice, necessarily. My captain marooned me!"

"Marooned?! You mean they cast you overboard?"

"Yes, it seems the dread pirate Gavin did not want me as a member of his crew after all." Weston tousled his hair and got to his feet. Isabelle laughed as he drew near. He looked down at her hands. "I see you still have your package. You have not found your little friend then."

Isabelle shook her head. "I haven't seen her anywhere. I don't know where she could be."

"There's Miss Bronte across the room. We could ask her?" Isabelle's nose wrinkled instinctively at his suggestion, and he chuckled. Taking her by the arm, he steered her in Miss Bronte's direction. She looked up at them as they approached.

"Miss Hampton, I trust you have finished with your visit? The children have had quite enough excitement and must return to class."

On impulse, Isabelle shrank back into Weston's shoulder. His hand moved to the small of her back. "Nearly," Isabelle replied stepping forward to put some space between her and the man at her side. "I had hoped to see Maria. The little girl with blonde curls?"

Miss Bronte gave a curt nod. "Yes, yes, I know the one."

"Would you be so kind as to tell us if she is here?" Weston's tone had taken a more serious note.

225

Miss Bronte peered at him over the rims of her spectacles. "The child you seek, Mr. Weston, died of a fever two nights passed."

"Oh," Isabelle's breath left in a rush. "How awful!"

Weston's hand returned to her back as she once again pressed into him.

Miss Bronte's gaze was level at them. "Not an uncommon occurrence in places like these, unfortunately. We do our best, but we have limited supplies, and the children often arrive with ailments we cannot treat."

Isabelle pressed the small package into her hand. "Please use this however you can." She turned away in a whirl of skirts and headed for the door. Weston nodded to Miss Bronte before hurrying after Isabelle.

CHAPTER 25

Weston caught up with Isabelle outside as she swept onto the porch. He placed a hand on her arm as her foot touched the top stair. "Miss Hampton?"

She spun to face him, tears pooling in her eyes. "I must look ridiculous." She bit her trembling lip.

"No, not at all. You look grieved."

She sighed and blinked up at the sky. "I don't know why, but I am. I didn't know her well."

He raised his hands in a helpless gesture. "A life snatched away just as it had begun is a great tragedy. It is an event worth grieving." He joined her on the top step and together they wound their way down the path towards the gate.

"I suppose some heavy thoughts struck me as Miss Bronte told us the news."

Weston reached out to open the gate and stood rubbing his thumbs along the cold iron. "What sort of thoughts?"

Isabelle laid her hand on top of the gate between them, her gaze downcast. "I am an orphan too. I could have easily ended up in a place like this." She looked back over her shoulder towards the mansion, so stony and cold. "I might have had a similar fate as that child if not for the Dawsons." She shuddered at the thought. "I could have died in a place like this without anyone to mourn me."

Weston appeared thoughtful. "Do you visit these orphans because you feel you are one of them?"

Isabelle's shoulders rose in a shrug. "Perhaps. Why was I saved when these children aren't?"

"Your situations are not the same. You must understand that."

"Well, yes, but you don't need to look amused about it. What life would there have been for me without my guardians?"

Weston sighed and ushered her through the gate. "Let us not speculate what may have been. Instead let us focus on that which is."

They fell into silence, walking toward the pier. Their footfalls sounded hollow on the wooden walkway as ships bells rang in the harbor and gulls cried overhead. Isabelle leaned her elbows on the railing and resting on the point overlooking the bay. She watched the buoys bob in the surf offshore. The sea breeze brushed against her cheeks and played with her hair as she admired the scene before her. A large sea vessel sailed into the bay. It had three tall masts, along proud peak, and several sails fluttering in the wind. The massive ship moved with the utmost grace into the bay gliding noiselessly across the water. Its flags fluttered high in the sky from the tip of the masts. The crew scurried about the rigging getting ready to dock. Isabelle lit up at the sight.

Pointing to the ship, she smiled. "Look at that one! Isn't it magnificent?"

Western came to her side. "Yes indeed, what a beauty. She is a war galleon armed with seventy-four guns, known for speed and maneuverability. A galleon is likely the best vessel on the sea, definitely the most distinguished," Weston added looking over the bay his eyes scanning over the ship. "She is in her homeport," he commented. "See that flag on the middle mast? That is the Tudor Rose, the identification mark of England." Weston leaned towards Isabelle and pointed out the flag. Isabelle followed his gesture and spied the flag waving proud. Isabel regarded him curiously as he stepped back and returned to his position leaning against the rail.

"How do you know all of that? These things about ships?"

Weston raised his gaze to be hers. "My father was in the navy."

"He must know many things about the sea."

"He did indeed. He taught me about maps, ships, and ways of the sea."

"It must be fascinating. I'm sure he has many stories."

Weston's expression clouded over. "I don't care for the sea." He turned away from her, his easy stride taking him away from the pier. Isabelle trailed behind him.

"Why not? The sea is beautiful and filled with such excitement. You must have heard legends of the adventures had upon the sea."

"Miss Hampton, you speak more whimsical nonsense. I will agree the sea is beautiful, but as far as adventures go, I say we would do well enough without ocean voyages," he growled at her. His sudden darkness surprised her.

"No exploration would happen if everyone had your attitude. I would never have gotten to England if not for an ocean voyage. Just think how much would have been missed if men had never ventured onto the sea! Exotic discoveries and places are hardly whimsy."

Weston stewed in sullen silence. He spun so quickly to face her that she wheeled backwards to avoid him bumping her. He paused as if facing an internal struggle. Finally, he blurted out the words: "My father's ship was lost at sea when I was a boy."

Isabelle struggled to contain her surprise. Her mouth hung open for a moment before so noticed. "I had no idea."

He shrugged. "It happened so long ago many have forgotten it."

"What happened?" The question seemed to ask itself.

His brows rose in a way that suggested he was about to make a curt response. He seemed to think better of this and instead said: "Speculation was that the Ainsley ran among the reefs. The ship sank off the coast of France. They discovered it in pieces. There were no survivors." His words were little more than a muttering, nearly drowned out by the screaming gulls and ringing bells. The breeze had grown colder. It tousled Isabelle's hair. She shivered against the chill in the air, pulling her cloak tighter around her shoulders. She suddenly felt very tired. He stirred as if awakened from a dream. "Are you well, Miss Hampton? You look a bit pale." He reached out and gathered her hands in his. "Cold as ice. You must be freezing. How inconsiderate of me." He tucked her hands into the crook of his arm and rubbed his hand over hers. "I had best return you to your aunt."

Isabelle shivered and leaned into him. Her head felt unsteady. She sighed against the ache building behind her eyes. "Yes, I think so. I worry I've had too much exertion for the day."

He regarded her with slight frown. Was that concern she saw in his face? "Yes, maybe you should still be resting so soon after the accident." He disappeared into his own thoughts as they began walking back towards the shops where they were to meet Sara and Laura.

CHAPTER 26

Brooklyn Manor,

Late the next morning Isabelle stood by her window watching Dawson climb onto his horse. Isabelle smiled as he turned the horse towards the open field. A knock drew her gaze to the door and a moment later, Laura peeped into the room.

"Here you are," she exclaimed stepping in and closing the door behind her. "I have been looking everywhere for you. I was about to check the fruit trees if I failed to find you indoors." She threw herself into an overstuffed chair beside the bookcase. Isabelle gave a dry smile. Laura sat up and studied her with narrowed vision. "You have been out of sorts since your tour of Southampton with Mr. Weston yesterday. Did something happen?"

"No," Isabelle shook her head. "I think I'm just tired."

"Tired I will believe, but you do seem unwell. Has the pain returned in your head?"

"Maybe a little," Isabelle admitted, running a hand along her forehead.

"Mr. Weston did seem to think you were quite ill yesterday. He looked so worried when we left him."

Isabelle busied herself with untangling the curtains.

"How were the children?"

A fond smile lit Isabelle's features as she recalled certain events from the day before. "They were so amusing. We got the worst news at the end of our visit though." Isabelle recounted her news. Laura's hand went to her mouth as Isabelle told her a bit of her conversation with Mr. Weston about the fate of orphans.

"I must say I am impressed that he engaged so openly with you," Laura mused.

"Yes, but that isn't the most surprising part. He played with the children, Laura."

Laura jerked so suddenly in her chair that she almost toppled onto the floor. "What? Did you say Mr. Weston played with orphans?"

"I did and he did. He got right in on the game of pirates, allowing the children to order him around and even maroon him!"

"Marooned? What on earth are you talking about?"

Isabelle laughed. "It was a game. They had a pretend ship."

Laura raised her nose in the air. "It sounds absurd."

"It was play. They liked him." Isabelle pictured his flushed and smiling face looking up at her from his position on the floor. "I think he enjoyed it too."

Laura stood and swept across the room to lay her hand along Isabelle's forehead. "Maybe that outing was too much for you in your current state. I wonder if you are running a fever."

"Not at all. I'm fine." Isabell brushed her hand away.

"Of that, I am not convinced. You spent the day about town with a Weston and all you told me is of make-believe ships."

"We did go down to the pier on our way to meet you and looked at the actual ships."

Laura heaved an exasperated sigh. "You have extraordinary taste to have your eye on him, but I can't imagine why he would have his on you."

Isabelle pulled a face. "I don't want anything more to do with the man than that. I've told you before, I'm not interested in Weston."

Lexington Estate,

Walsh stood in the bedroom window watching the antics of his cousin in the courtyard below. Buttoning his shirt, he smirked at the pile of logs Weston had gathered and was proceeding to chop. Swinging the ax, Weston brought it down with a crushing blow, missing the log by a few inches. Laughing at the look of consternation on his cousin's face, Walsh shrugged into his coat and bounded from the room.

Reaching the staircase, he threw one booted leg over the banister and proceeded to slide from the top to the bottom, polishing the brilliant wood with the seat of his breeches. He gathered speed as he neared the bottom and practically flew off the end, narrowly missing Collins. Startled Collins reached out taking hold of Walsh's shoulders steadying him on his feet. "Master Walsh, what are you doing?"

Walsh chuckled, slapping the butler on the back. "Mr. Collins, you're looking at a changed man," he paused walking towards the door, guiding Collins along with one hand while gesturing with the other. "I, Edmund Walsh, have discovered the secret of life. The key to life is love. Without love one does not live but simply exists."

Collins gave him a worried look. "Yes, Sir, if you say so."

"Yes, most definitely, there is no greater gift in this world than love. I have seen the treasures of men within this fine nation, but no, my dear friend, none can compare with the treasure of love. It is a rare and extraordinary thing. So valuable it is that men will spend their days seeking it. Literature and art boast of it. I now understand why."

"Of course, master Walsh. Are you well?" Collins could not keep the skepticism from slipping into his tone.

Walsh's smile reached all the way to his eyes. "Mr. Collins, I give you my word, I am in perfect health. I am only sorry I have not known this sentiment earlier in life." He patted the butler on the shoulder before striding out the door.

~

The log split in two on impact and the pieces clattered to the cobblestone. Weston hefted the ax over his shoulder as he set the next log in place on the chopping block.

"Good morning, cousin," Walsh called across the courtyard as the ax fell with a ferocious heave and sliced clean through the chunk of wood. Weston looked up as Walsh approached. Beads of sweat glistened on his forearms as he positioned the next log on the chopping block. "I see you have discovered a new hobby."

Walsh looked bemused as Weston stepped back to take aim. Weston swung the ax overhead and sent it smashing into the log, splitting the wood with such force that the pieces jumped off the block and scattered on the ground. He dropped the ax and bent to move the split pieces aside.

"Is this how you amused yourself in my absence?" Walsh stuffed his hands into his pockets and poked at a log with the toe of his boot.

Weston grunted and heaved a log onto the pile. "It seemed a constructive use of my time."

"Yes, time indeed. I have seen little of you since my return."

"Pardon my privacy," Weston threw a log past Walsh, starting a new pile.

"Privacy is one thing; lack of inquiry may be cause for alarm." Walsh stepped a few paces away from the pile as Weston took aim for another shot.

"How fares you sister?" Weston did not break his momentum as he asked the question.

"Irene is well." Walsh's brow knit with a frown of suspicion.

"How is her family?"

"They too are well."

"There, now I have the news I require. Consider inquiry complete."

"Ah, not so quick, your part of the inquiry may be complete, but I still have questions. What has happened in my absence?"

"Little of any consequence." Weston set another log on the chopping block.

"You cannot expect me to believe that. My household is in a tizzy. The servants are buzzing with talk of all sorts. Christmas, balls, houseguests: what sort of mischief have you gotten into?"

The logs hit the ground with a thump. "Nothing of any consequence." He proceeded to toss the pieces past Walsh and onto the pile.

"Come come, I heard the servants mention a woman. I need to know of any indecent shenanigans that may have transpired in my home."

Weston straightened and met Walsh's gaze. "I am afraid you are the only member of this household to engage in any of those."

Walsh cocked a brow. "I feel certain this is not about the conversation you and I had upon my return. Something happened during the holidays, and I ask you for the truth."

"I went riding."

Walsh looked surprised. "What?"

"And when I stepped down from my horse to admire the view, the creature returned to the estate without me."

"This is all very amusing, but—"

"Miss Hampton happened upon me."

Walsh paused and studied his cousin. "Miss Hampton?"

Weston nodded.

"She was alone on horseback?"

Again, Weston nodded.

"Well, proceed with your story."

"I will if you would cease your interruptions. She offered her assistance, and we returned to Lexington. Once I had dismounted, however, the horse spooked, and threw Miss Hampton."

"Good heavens!" A look of shock crossed Walsh's features. "Weston, was she harmed?"

Weston gave a slight nod. "Yes, she suffered a concussion and lacked any sort of strength. I permitted her to stay at Lexington, for fear a ride to Brooklyn would subject her to further harm."

Walsh let out a heavy breath. "Yes, it very well might have. You likely made the best decision. How long was her stay?"

"Several days."

"Did the Dawsons come?"

"No, the fog fell so heavily that any sort of venture would have been too dangerous. I was unable to bring word to them for a day or two."

"Two days? Heavens, Weston, they must have suffered with worry over their niece." Walsh sunk down onto a log, his skin taking on a gray pallor. "Why didn't you tell me this sooner?"

Weston stooped and began clearing away the logs. He threw several armloads aside before responding. "You returned with news of the love of your life. The timing did not seem appropriate to mention Miss Hampton."

"Weston, Miss Duke has nothing to do with this situation. The Dawsons are dear friends and neighbors. I should have called upon Miss Hampton before now, particularly since the accident happened here."

"If you say so." Another log flew past Walsh.

"How is Miss Hampton? Has she recovered well?"

"I relinquished her care to her guardians. I have not visited them since they removed her from Lexington."

Walsh leaned his elbows on his knees. "I must go to Brooklyn immediately."

Weston shrugged. "Do as you wish."

Walsh stared at Weston with a fixed gaze. Weston's eyes were intense but empty revealing nothing of what thoughts roamed through his head.

"It is my duty as a friend to ensure Miss Hampton will recover. Her wellbeing is important to me."

"I refuse to acknowledge the irony of such a statement. You need not my blessing nor approval to act as you see fit. You know the Dawsons better than I. If you feel your presence would be welcome then go to them in the name of charity," Weston paused and seemed to search for the right words though pained to do so. "Know this, cousin, I do not condone your actions towards Miss Hampton. You have played her a cruel game and I will not stand by and watch you cater to her family while you hold a love alive for another woman. I will return to London by the end of the week." Weston turned away from Walsh and moved towards the house, dropping the ax beside the chopping block.

Walsh leapt to his feet and caught Weston's arm. Weston turned on him with a fury Walsh had not expected. He took a step back when he saw the hurt written in the lines on Weston's face. "Cousin," Walsh's voice was low as he began. "I cannot begin to excuse myself from your chiding. In truth I have acted without much sense, and it appears I may have jeopardized my connection with the Dawsons and their ward through my own impetuousness. I deserve your words though they bring much pain to me." Walsh lowered his gaze. Weston stood rooted to the spot; his lips pulled in a firm line. "Years of friendship may warrant disappointment and reproach for my actions, but this anger is more than the situation deserves." He peeked up at Weston. "Do you have feelings for Miss Hampton?"

Weston flinched. His resolve wavered for a moment before the stony expression returned. He reached out and patted Walsh on the shoulder. "Naïve, but foolish friend, not everyone can be as fortunate in love as you."

Walsh brightened and looked at his cousin. "Your sarcasm betrays you. You avoid the question. Does that mean there is some truth to it?"

"No, it means that it is a ridiculous accusation." Weston turned to walk away. Walsh blocked his path. Weston regarded him with a scowl. "You irritate me. Step aside."

Walsh shook his head. "On the same basis that permits you to lecture me, I ask you to answer the question."

"It is a ridiculous question."

"Your future is not ridiculous. The person who captivates your heart is far from ridiculous."

"That sentence in and of itself is ridiculous. Walsh, get out of my way."

"No, I refuse to move until you do. You cannot continue to wallow in your own self-misery. You have a chance for happiness, and you will not take it. Unless that is not what you want? Please, tell me. If it is not what you want, I will leave the subject and never speak of it again." Weston glared at him. Walsh stood his ground. The silence grew taught between them.

A chilly wind began to drift through the courtyard. Walsh heaved a weary sigh. "If you wish to remain in your sullen existence, I cannot stop you. I want more for you than that, my friend, but if you do not want that for yourself, nothing I say will change you mind. Carry on, then." Walsh nearly choked on the last words as he stepped out of Weston's path. He gestured to freedom with a sweeping motion of his hand.

Weston brushed past him in a purposeful stride, his coat tails fluttering behind him. Walsh felt a sorrow settle in his heart as he watched Weston retreat to the mansion. Weston faltered and the determination went out of his steps. A stride later, he stopped moving altogether. He stood still with his back to Walsh. Walsh tipped his head to the side, curious as to what was happening.

"She loathes me." The bitterness in the words bit Walsh with the same harshness as the wind.

"What do you mean? You think Miss Hampton despises you?"

"Yes, she does,"

Walsh shook his head. "She is too kind-hearted to loathe anyone. Why would you say such a thing?"

"She told me this."

"What? Why?"

"Because she loves someone else. That love drives her disdain for me."

Walsh felt the wind rush out of him. "Who does she love? Has she spoken to you of this?"

Weston spun and faced Walsh. "You."

Walsh stepped towards him. "You are certain?"

Weston nodded.

Walsh drew near to him and saw the seriousness of his expression. The hurt he saw in those blue eyes amazed Walsh.

"She brightens at the mere mention of your name. She has a special smile just for you. She watches you across the room before ducking away in shyness. Yes, those are the signs of a woman in love."

"Does she really love me? And you knew this? How did I miss this?"

"Because you are a fool, Walsh. You were in a romance that you did not even realize until the girl is in love with you and you are in love with someone else. Badly done, Walsh. You should feel ashamed."

An impish smile crossed Walsh's features. "I ought to be and I am. What a fool I am."

Weston nodded. "My sentiments exactly."

"But now what am I to do? There is no conceivable way for me to pursue Miss Duke without bringing harm to Miss Hampton."

Weston shrugged. "I cautioned you against pursuing such a connection with Miss Hampton."

"You tried, and I did not listen. I thought what I felt for her was love, but now I realize my error."

"You have a challenge before you. Any action now on your part will cause a rift between you and the Dawsons. Your actions towards

Miss Hampton give her just cause to expect an offer of engagement. Extricating yourself from such a situation will not be easy."

Walsh turned to his cousin with mournful eyes. "To cause harm for myself and Miss Hampton is unfortunate. But to be the cause of your inability to pursue the woman you admire is grievous. It is a wrong I do not bear lightly. I sincerely regret being the reason you hurt."

"All will be forgotten when I return to London."

CHAPTER 27

Brooklyn Manor,

"Oh, Isabelle, stop moping about!"

Laura stood over her friend with her hands on her hips. Isabelle sat on the rug before the fire, staring into the flames.

"I'm not moping." Her weak protest caused a wrinkle to form on Laura's brow.

"But you are! You have sunk into a depression. You don't read anymore, you don't contribute to the conversations, you just don't seem happy." Laura lowered herself to Isabelle's side and pulled her hands into her lap. You barely noticed Mr. Walsh when he last visited. He was so worried about your accident, yet you appeared unmoved." Laura sighed.

Isabelle shrugged. She had asked Walsh about the book, hoping to thank him for such a thoughtful gift. He appeared surprised and denied knowing anything about *Where Violets Grow*. That meant only one thing. But why would Weston send her a book? She certainly was not going to ask *him* about it.

"What is on your heart? Won't you tell me? You haven't been yourself since your visit to the orphanage."

"Don't worry, Laura. It's fine."

"Fine? Do you expect me to believe that? You do not look fine. Your skin is pale, your eyes do not sparkle. The doctor has cleared your health since the accident, and you say your head doesn't hurt much anymore. The only thing left is melancholy. And why you would be experiencing that is beyond me. Mr. Walsh has returned and appears eager to resume his pursuit of you. What is there that could make you unhappy?"

Isabelle's gaze remained downcast as she spoke. "I'm not unhappy."

"But something has unsettled you."

"Maybe a little."

Laura leaned closer. "Won't you tell me what it is?"

"Just thinking about something that doesn't make any sense."

"Like what?"

"Since the accident, some days my thoughts are unclear. Some things puzzle me."

"Oh," Laura looked surprised. "Do my questions tax you?"

Isabelle gave Laura's hand a gentle squeeze. "A little bit, but it's okay."

"Oh, my intent is not to make you feel worse. I worry about you."

Isabelle smiled down at their interlaced fingers. "I know you are, and you don't make me feel worse. I just don't know how to say what I am thinking." She did not want to say what she was thinking. If she admitted to Laura she had been thinking about Weston, she would never hear the end of it. Right now, he was on her mind, especially in relation to the book. He intrigued her.

"I have an idea!" Laura's exclamation jarred Isabelle from her musing. Isabelle looked to her friend and saw an excited flush in her cheeks. "You need a change of scenery."

Isabelle wrinkled her nose. "A change of scenery?"

Laura bobbed her head. "Yes! You said it yourself; you feel well enough. A little travel would do wonders towards improving your mood."

"I hadn't thought of travelling. Where would I go?"

"London!" Laura beamed at her. Isabelle's brows went up in surprise.

"London? How would I get there?"

"With me! Mother and I were planning to visit London. Wouldn't it be simply splendid if you joined us?" Laura clasped her hands together under her chin, looking all the world she would burst with pleasure.

Isabelle toyed with a lock of hair. "Me go to London? I hadn't thought of that. That would be something."

"Oh, Isabelle, please say you will come! Aunt Sara would be able to spare you for a few weeks. Mother would be thrilled for me to have a companion my own age. Please, dear, you will come, won't you? Oh, say yes!" Laura's expression was so pitiful and pleading that Isabelle had to laugh.

"If Aunt Sara agrees, I would love to go."

Laura let out a squeal of glee that startled Isabelle. "Oh Isabelle, this is wonderful! Just think of the fun we will have!"

CHAPTER 28

London, England. February 10, 1821,

The carriage wheels clattered over the cobblestone while rolling down the London street. The sights and sounds were so different from those of Southampton. Isabelle watched from the carriage window as the view rolled past. The shops along the streets had large windows overlooking the walkways, exhibiting their wares to all those passing by. Isabelle spotted all sorts of vibrant trinkets and treasures in the displays. Elegant ladies dressed in colorful gowns strolled down the walks on the arms of dashing gentlemen. Their chatter and laughter filled the air as they paused before the shops and pointed to oddments that caught their eyes. The chatter felt strange to Isabelle. The air of Southampton carried the cries of gulls and ringing ship bells. London echoed with horse's hoofs clipping down the cobblestone and the voices of people. Sweet smells drifting from the bakeries replaced the salted sea air. Isabelle felt dizzy as she tried to look at everything all at once.

A giggle across from her drew her eye to Laura. "You will get to see London, Isabelle. We will be here for a while and will make sure to take in some sights while we are here."

Isabelle released a breath and settled back into the seat. Mrs. Millis smiled at her from across the carriage. Her dark hair framed her face in an elegant manner and accentuated the dark eyes that could have been her brother's. "Your curiosity is such a pleasant change. I myself have grown accustomed to the city and neglect to admire it. It is a delight to have you along with us, Isabelle." Her voice held a light accent, like Dawson's, but she spoke with a delicate tone that betrayed a tender heart rather unlike her brusque daughter. "I do hope you will enjoy your time with us."

"I already am," came Isabelle's prompt reply as she talked her hands into the folds of her traveling cloak.

The carriage eventually pulled up in front of a large white building with many windows. A raised balcony with flower boxes adorning it and a four-step staircase stood overlooking the street. Isabelle felt the building looked quite splendid.

The footman leapt from his perch atop the carriage as they rolled to halt. He opened the door and announced: "63 Barlington Way, madame. Allow me to escort you." Mrs. Millis accepted the proffered hand, and he guided her to the sidewalk.

"Thank you, Thomas. It is good to be back. How I did miss this dear old house! Isabelle," She turned round as Isabelle stepped down from the carriage. "Welcome to our London home. I am confident you will be most comfortable here. Once your bags go to your room, Laura will show you your room." She swept up the staircase ahead of the girls and flung open the house door.

Isabelle followed behind beside Laura. She leaned over to her friend and murmured: "You must spend a lot of time in London if your family owns a house here."

Laura shrugged and responded in a normal volume. "I visit a few weeks in the year. My parents spend more time here than I do. Even so, the house stands empty most of the time."

"It's very pretty." Isabelle eyed the glass panelled door and the scrollwork creeping along the ceiling.

Laura paused in the entryway and glanced about. "I suppose it is. It belonged to mother's family."

"Did your mother grow up here?"

Laura nodded. "She was always fond of the house. My father acquired the house when my grandparents relocated to Bath. It became our vacation home."

Isabelle traced her toe over woodgrain in the polished floor, avoiding the vibrant rug before the door. "Whatever you say, Laura, it seems like an elegant vacation home."

Laura gave a light laugh. "It is very aged; my mother was born here."

Isabelle trailed her fingers along the carved railing as the girls took to the stairs. "To me, that just sounds like history. This house has stories."

Laura halted at the top of the stairs as Isabelle moved to inspect a door decorated with intricate scrollwork and inserted frosted glass. "Those doors are archaic, despite your romanticism."

"They're beautiful."

Laura tipped her head as if to see the house through Isabelle's eyes. She eventually shrugged and moved further down the hall. "It isn't as fashionable as some of the newer homes, but it's quaint." She pushed open a door directly on her left. "If you ever wish to remain upstairs in the morning, Thomas will serve tea to the yellow salon at your request. We do it quite regularly during the winter assemblies." Laura abandoned the room with the door ajar and swept across the hall to swing open the next door. "This is my room. More dreadful yellow! Gah, I hate it." She wrinkled her nose and leaned against the doorframe."

Isabelle peered past her into the room. The bed stood heaped with lace trimmed cushions in varying shades of yellow. "It looks very comfortable."

"Perhaps if you are fond of sunshine and daffodils. Let us go to your room." Laura brushed past Isabelle and opened the door across the hall. She entered the room with a flourish. "There you are! A lady's room, proper as it should be. No horrid yellow in here!" Isabelle followed behind and found herself standing amid the colors of lavender and sage with a lace trim. Laura rushed to the windows that peeped out beneath sheer curtains. "We have a lovely garden!" She cast aside the curtains and frowned down upon the land. "Although you cannot see it on this side of the house. But no matter, you can see the carriage house from this window."

Isabelle remained in the middle of the room, watching the curtains sway with Laura's enthusiastic assault.

"What? No comment? Isabelle, you surprise me." Laura sat on the bed with a small laugh.

Isabelle turned to her with a weary smile. "This is a lovely guest room. I will enjoy my stay here."

"Excellent. Once you rest from the journey, we will see about getting your things settled into the closet." Laura crossed to the double doors on the wall and flung them open.

Isabelle came to her side. "There are clothes in there. Whose are those?"

"Oh, somethings my sister or I left behind, I do not really recognize any pieces. This one may have belonged to my mother." Laura pulled at a cream-colored gown. "Regardless, you may wish to borrow them during your stay."

"What? I brought my own clothes with me. I don't need to borrow any."

Laura turned to her with a skeptical frown. "I intend to attend some events whilst I am in London, and I refuse to be embarrassed by you."

Isabelle laughed. "Aunt Sara picked my gowns. She said they were lovely and stylish."

"Aunt Sara, love her I do, has country taste. We are no longer in the country. This is London. This is the fashion capital of the country. No, my friend, country fashion will not do here."

Isabelle's smile became a stifled yawn.

Laura's expression softened. "You are exhausted. We have time before dinner to rest."

"What a wonderful idea."

"Indeed. I think I will lay down myself. I will let you settle. We will make plans for our visit after dinner."

Another small yawn escaped Isabelle.

"I'll be right across the hall if you need me." Laura waved and closed the door behind her.

Once she was alone, Isabelle tumbled into the luxurious bed. Blinking once she started to feel far away. Blinking twice she began to dream. Blinking once more she fell asleep, giving her imagination unto the desires of her heart.

CHAPTER 29

When Isabelle awoke, she found the sunlight had started to fade. A golden hue dance along the walls. She raised herself up on one elbow, breaking forth from her dream state, and swept a lock of hair away from her cheek. With an also delicate jolt, she roused herself from the bed and approach the dressing table. Picking up the pitcher off the table she poured a dribble of water into the basin. The water felt cool and refreshing splashed against her skin. She took a quick appraising glance of her appearance before leaving the room. She glided across the hall knocking softly on the door to Laura's room. She cracked the door enough to peek in and discover her friend was not there. The salon across the hall was also empty. Isabelle found herself at the top of the stairs. She glided down the steps towards the soft voices echoing from a room below.

She followed the voices to the door of a parlor. She discovered Laura seated upon an overstuffed sofa deep in conversation with a young man sitting across from her. He leaned near to Laura and murmured something that caused her to giggle. She glanced away from him in a playful manner and her gaze fell upon Isabelle standing by the door. "Isabelle! You sly creature. You have appeared out of nowhere." Laura's tone danced with humor, and she beckoned to Isabelle. "You must join us."

"I feel like I'm interrupting…"

The young man rose as Isabelle approached the sofa and seated herself in a chair by the fire.

"Nonsense!" Laura adjusted herself on the sofa so she could face them both. "Jimmy, I am pleased to introduce my dearest friend, Miss Isabelle Hampton. Isabelle, James Avery. His family and mine have been associated for ages. I cannot recall a time when the Averys were not part of my life." Laura looked at him with an expression that one could only describe as fondness.

Jimmy turned to Isabelle with a smile. "Pleasure to make your acquaintance." He made her a quick bow before returning to his seat.

"Yes, likewise." Isabelle got a look at the man as he turned his attention back to Laura. She felt the way his lips curled beneath his thin black mustache gave his smile a smug air. His was not a rich smile like the one that tugged against the lips of Weston. His bright eyes bore a sharp contrast to his black hair, but they lacked the knowledgeable depth that Isabelle saw when she looked at Weston. In her opinion, James Avery carried himself with a sort of flippant confidence, but it was nothing like the elegant strength of Weston. Isabelle gave her head a shake as she realized she used Mr. Weston as the standard for her evaluation of the man before her.

"Laura tells me you are American." The male voice jarred Isabelle from her musings and brought her full attention to him.

She nodded. "Yes, I was. I'm not sure what I am now."

"Still settling in here, are you?"

"It would seem so. I didn't exactly choose to move to England."

"You will love the country. London is spectacular. You will feel England is home in no time."

Isabelle's thoughts drifted to home. The proud house standing on a hill in the countryside dotted with trees. She could see the breeze ruffling the grasses on the meadow. As she submerged deeper into the images, she could smell the smoke from the fire. She could taste the ash on her lips. She could hear the stress on the supports as they began to give way and her home collapsed into a rubble heap. She swallowed hard. "I have no home anymore."

Laura leaned forward and placed a hand on her knee. "You needn't speak anymore of the subject." She shot Jimmy a warning frown. "It is uncomfortable for you."

Jimmy looked down at his hands. "I apologize, Miss Hampton, for prying into your affairs."

"You've done nothing wrong." The words sounded hallow, but final. The conversation dissolved into intimate murmurs. Isabelle gazed into the fire, unable to leave her memories completely for the moment.

Isabelle and Laura bustled around the garden tending the plants. Isabelle knelt in the grass plucking wilted blooms from the plants. She peered at Laura from under the brim of her bonnet.

"There's something I'm wondering," she began, drawing Laura's gaze from rich soil.

"What is that?"

"Why haven't you mentioned Mr. Avery before?"

"Jimmy? Oh, he and I have known each other for years. He is a friend of the family."

"And you like him."

Laura giggled and tossed a dried-up blossom at Isabelle. "Nonsense, he is just a friend."

"What better way to get to know a person."

"I do quite admire him, and I enjoy his company, but really, he would never have serious intentions towards me."

"I wouldn't be sure of that. He came to see you hours after you arrived in London. I think that suggests he likes you too."

Laura's cheeks flushed. "Do you really believe that?" Isabelle nodded. Laura sighed and regarded her with round whimsical eyes. "I dare not hope. His father has plans for him to overtake some family affairs. I fear that he will become so deeply submerged in business that he will go off and forget about me. We see each other infrequently as is." Laura bit her lip.

Isabelle reached over and took her hand in a reassuring squeeze. "He won't forget you. That's impossible."

"I suppose. But I long to have some reassurance of his affection."

Isabelle was about to reply that she felt the same way when Mrs. Millis came into the yard to join them. She shook her head upon seeing the two of them seated on the grass. "Look at you," she said with a smile. "You will be dirty from head to foot."

The girls glanced at each other and smiled. Isabelle plucked a small stem from her hair. "My mother used to say a little dirt never hurt anyone."

Mrs. Millis cocked an amused brow. "Perhaps not, but it is rather unbecoming."

Laura laughed, brushing dirt from her hands. "But mother, it is the latest fashion."

"I think not, Laura. Besides, that would never suit a dinner party at the Coombes."

Laura stopped her fussing and stared at her mother. "An invitation? To dinner at the Coombes?" Her mother nodded. "Already? Why, we only just arrived in London yesterday."

"Indeed. Word travels fast on the lips of James Avery."

CHAPTER 30

Time also travels fast when dinner parties are on the schedule and the eve of the event arrived sooner than the girls could have imagined. The house on 63 Barlington Way bustled with activity as the women prepared themselves for the evening.

Isabelle pulled on a dusty rose gown and admired the sweeping skirt before the full-length mirror. She ran her hands down over the bodice, feeling elegant. She had just adjusted the cap sleeves when the door slammed behind her. She whirled around.

"Laura! What are you doing?"

Laura stood with her back pressed against the door and a wine colored dressed clutched in her arms. "I didn't want anyone to see me," Laura quipped as she deposited her gown on the bed and stood there in her white underthings. "I require assistance with the corset."

"You're going to wear a corset?"

Laura nodded and turned her back to Isabelle. Pulling aside her hair revealed a bodice of intricate laces. "Will you help me?"

Isabelle stepped over and gave a light tug at the laces. She started to tie them when Laura's shoulders began to shake with laughter. "You have to pull them tighter than that!" She placed her hands on her hips and braced against the material as Isabelle pulled again, harder this time. Laura gasped as Isabelle tied off the laces. "Thank you, I can barely breathe so you've done it perfectly," she observed with a laugh as she slipped her gown over her head. Isabelle's smirk betrayed her skepticism. "You mock, but this is the height of fashion. Your laughter will cease once I marry a baron and you still live as spinster of Brooklyn Manor." Isabelle had to laugh at that.

The girls twisted up their hair, braiding in a few tiny flowers, and then Laura gave them each a spritz of perfume for good luck. Mrs. Millis knocked on the door and announced it was time to leave. Isabelle leaned towards the mirror for a final inspection. With a nervous smile at her reflection, she gave her cheeks a pinch and gathered up her skirts to follow Laura out onto the evening's adventure.

The gold lettering on the gatepost sign caught Isabelle's eye as she disembarked the carriage at their destination. *Henley Manor* glinted in the fading light. She turned to look at the stately townhouse rising high above her. She felt a twinge of the familiar as she admired the wrap around porch that stretched along side the huge house and disappeared round the back. The lack of light burning in the windows gave the house a lonesome appearance. A sudden solemness came over Isabelle as she moved past the house at the urging of Laura to hurry.

The Coombe home turned out to be the house across the street from Henley Manor. As the party approached the door, Isabelle caught strains of music carried on the evening breeze. Passing through the door Isabelle met with a barrage of laughter and conversation; the house was bristling with life. People milled about and the ladies had to weave their way through the crowd to reach the party room. Isabelle's senses felt overwhelmed with all the sights and sounds. Laura was right about London fashion varying from that of the country. Isabelle struggled not to gawk at the colors and cuts of the various gowns around the room. She also noticed uniforms were abundant here more than she had ever seen before. Officers dressed their smartest and decorated with badges and patches depicting ranks, awards, and connections strode among the guests. They seemed pleasant enough, but she still watched them with a sense of awe. She drew closer to the wall, feeling like a misfit.

Laura called to her from the edge of the dancefloor: "Isn't this wonderful?" Her cheeks bore an excited flush as she beamed at Isabelle. Isabelle gave a tight nod.

James Avery strode to Laura's side and paused, looking down at her. Her beaming smile turned to him. His features lit with a special smile as he greeted her. He pulled her hand into his and raised it to his lips. Laura's flush grew deeper, and she giggled. "Would you grant me the pleasure of a dance?" He tucked her hand into the crook of his arm. Laura nodded and moved towards the dancefloor. James Avery stayed her movement and turned to Isabelle. "Can you spare your companion for a moment?"

Laura glanced at Isabelle with a look of surprise, as if she had forgotten Isabelle standing to the side. "You don't mind, do you, Isabelle?"

Isabelle forced a smile. "Not at all."

Laura offered her the most grateful smile that Isabelle could not help but feel pleased for her friend. She watched as Jimmy leaned closer to murmur something to Laura, which caused her to laugh. Isabelle drifted towards the sideboard where an ornate painting hung on the wall. From that vantage point, she could watch most of the events, while remaining out of the way.

Everyone around her seemed enjoying themselves and she watched their revelry with a muted interest. The event seemed populated with long lost friends who greeted each other with excited babble and energetic conversation. Trapped in her own apathy Isabel began to question her decision to come to London. It was not as if she knew anyone. Feeling a twinge sorry for herself, she surveyed the room. She found herself following the movement of a tall gentleman as he slipped between the conversations pausing briefly before moving on again. His stride was determined, and he glanced about occasionally as if in search of someone. When he drew near to her recognition hit them both at the same moment. The surprise of seeing her flashed in his features for an instant before a blank stare took its place.

"Miss Hampton. Whatever are you doing in London?" He drew himself to a halt before her.

"Good evening, Mr. Weston. I'm glad to see you're in good health." Isabelle shot him a pointed look as she turned her attention to her ruffled sleeve.

"I take it you joined Miss Millis here this evening. I believe I saw her hanging off the arm of the youngest Avery boy."

"Yes."

"I will take your response as confirmation of both my observations."

"Do as you will."

"I believe that was my plan, but again, I thank you for the confirmation."

Isabelle looked up with a slight glare, but he was not even looking at her to experience the effect. His eyes scanned the faces throughout the room. "Don't let me keep you if you have to be elsewhere." Isabelle could not stop the bitterness from seeping into her tone. She felt so frustrated. Finally, a familiar face in the sea of strangers and it had to be Robert Weston. The arrogant and infuriating man himself. And he was practically ignoring her.

"Actually no, I am here at the request of Mrs. Coombes. She spied a young lady hiding amongst the decor and implored me to intervene."

Isabelle wondered if he would have bothered had he know it was she who stood next to the sideboard. "What a perfect gentleman you are," she muttered with less vehemence than her previous statement.

He pulled out a gold pocket watch and checked the time. That was when Isabelle noticed they people were watching them. The occasional glance would drift their way, followed by murmurs among the small crowds of people. She was unsure if she should feel angry or laugh. The whole thing was ridiculous. She was the new girl, standing there with one of the most well-known men in the room, if not the entire city. Of course, that would rouse some level of interest. The irony was, he seemed to have forgotten she was there.

He tucked the watch back into his pocket and straightened his waistcoat. A sudden admiration of the man crept upon Isabelle. She tried to squelch it, but she had to admit he was confident and unconcerned about the whispers going on around them. He turned his penetrating gaze up on her and she nearly recoiled at the intensity.

For the briefest of moments, Isabelle wondered if he had read her thoughts. "Are you unwell, Miss Hampton? You appear a bit flushed." His eyebrow raised in curiosity. Was he laughing at her?

She cleared her throat and fussed with her hair, hoping to hide her embarrassment. "Not at all. I'm fine."

"Perhaps you would do with a drink. Shall I retrieve a glass of punch for you?" He looked at her with expectation, his posture fit to serve at her command. For a fleeting second, she felt touched.

"Yes, please."

He gave her a quick nod before hurrying off on her behalf. The song ended at his departure and Isabelle found herself in the company of her party once again.

"Was that Mr. Weston?" Laura queried dumping Jimmy's arm for Isabelle's hand.

"It was."

"What did he have to say?"

Isabelle shrugged. She could not begin to guess his motives.

Weston glanced around with a sweeping gaze. As he drew near the refreshment table, he still had spotted no sign of his cousin. Weston selected two glasses of punch.

"Well, here is a happy evening indeed when the assemblies once again have the privilege of the company of Mr. Weston."

Weston faced the speaker. She cocked a brow above her hazel eyes as her red lips parted in a smile.

"Miss Duke."

She shook her black hair away from her face then took a step closer. "You look well. You have kept yourself away so long it took me a moment to recognize you."

Unsure if it was a compliment or a comment, Weston made no response, but inclined his head in her direction. "You all seemed to have carried on in my absence."

She shrugged a delicate shoulder. "What choice do we have? Time waits for no man. Yet, you seem very well to have born the excitement of younger years. You do appear well. I would love to know your secret to that." She gave a flirtatious chuckle. He remained silent. "Still a man of few words. How young I was then. You brought much excitement into our midst." She spied the two glasses he carried and gave a knowing smile. "Ah, so that is your secret. Am I to assume by this evidence of new love there will be carriage races later?"

He maintained a level expression though his fingers tightened around the glasses. "Examine me if you wish. You will find nought but the evidence of living well."

"Ah, well, perhaps you have gotten old and boring. You were great fun."

"If recklessness is what you consider fun, then your failure will be great."

She burst into laughter. "Ever a fitting example of Weston pride. I will forever admire that, despite your lack of humor."

"I find no humor in folly."

She batted her eyes at him. "No, I suppose you do not. I hear you are very serious now. Well, no matter, for the sake of our dear Mr. Walsh, let us not quarrel."

"I have no quarrel with you; my cousin's actions are his own. I cannot claim to be of the same mindset as he."

Weston made her a quick bow, thus excusing himself from further conversation. He kept an eye for Walsh as he returned to Isabelle. A sudden wariness crept over him as the gravity of the situation fell. Having both women whom Walsh had purported to love in attendance at the same event would require discretion. Something Walsh occasionally lacked. Weston made it his personal mission to extract his cousin from the party before he did something stupid. It felt like a lifetime of exchanged greetings before he made it back to Isabelle. And there by her side stood his elusive cousin. Weston had to fight the urge to haul his cousin from the room by the ear like an insolent child. He smiled and approached the group.

"Ah, I see the rest of your party has rejoined, Miss Hampton. Good evening, Miss Millis, Mr. Avery." He nodded as he greeted the others while passing a glass of punch to Isabelle.

She accepted the glass with a bewildered expression and murmured a thank you. Laura looked on in surprise. Weston gave her a small smile. "I trust you are having a pleasant evening?"

She blinked and took a moment before replying: "Yes, it has been rather lovely." She looked uncertainty at Jimmy. He bobbed his head, unaware of the awkwardness with which she spoke.

"Good, good, I hope you will have a splendid evening. Might you excuse us a moment? I just need a word with my cousin." Weston's smile never faltered as he took a firm hold on Walsh's arm, shoving him smoothly away from the group.

"It was a pleasure seeing you. I hope to see you again while you are in London. It is such a unique experience from the quaint countryside, and I would consider it a privilege should you permit me an afternoon to be your guide. Not to say that Miss Millis is not well versed in the finer points of London but know you can rely on me during your visit. We can discuss this further as I feel sure Weston's business will take but a moment." Walsh gave a hurried excuse as Weston hauled him off in a powerful grip.

Laura still looked perplexed. "That was odd."

Isabelle swished the punch around in her glass. "I'm starting to think that Weston is just odd."

CHAPTER 31

Weston ushered Walsh into a hall away from the other guests. Walsh grasped Weston's fingers.

"Weston, you need to let me go. You have cut off the circulation to my hand." Walsh squirmed in an effort to free his arm.

Weston released him and leaned close to him with an accusatory glare. "For the longest time I did not know where you were."

Walsh scowled and adjusted his coat. "Are you my keeper that you must know my whereabouts at every given moment?"

"With your aptitude for romancing young women, I would consider that good reason for having a guardian."

Walsh pulled a face. "Touché. If you really must know, I was dancing with the younger Miss Coombes." He attempted to brush the wrinkles from his coat sleeve. He suddenly grabbed the sleeve and shoved it towards Weston. "See there? Your brutish antics have put a tear in my coat!"

Weston looked unmoved. "If I must, I apologize. However, let us not neglect the case at hand: you have gotten yourself into rather a sensitive predicament with your wonton affections that I fear is about to explode on you here tonight."

"What on earth are you talking about? You speak as though I am about to discredit my good name."

"You may very well be on the brink of that. This could be the end of Edmund Walsh as we know him."

Walsh looked up with a chuckle. "This is a bizarre level of drama from you. Can you be less cryptic?"

"Miss Duke and Miss Hampton are both here this evening. Now do you understand?"

The smirk drained from Walsh's features. "Oh, that is not at all a good joke."

"No, this is not a joke at all. You have made a fine mess and now you've gone and made it worse by offering a London tour to Miss Hampton after you very clearly informed me you love Miss Duke. Have you changed your mind on this matter?"

Walsh shook his head. "No, I have not. Miss Hampton is very dear, but my future lies with Miss Duke."

Weston looked pained. "I hate for others to accuse you of indecent play, but I would advise you to leave immediately. Return to Hanley for the evening and we will sort the rest tomorrow."

"Do I look less guilty if I flee?"

"If anyone were to suspect anything, which I am certain they do not, you look less an arrogant fool if you leave. To toy with two women publicly would be foolishness and very much a discredit to you."

"Of course."

"Leave. Now. I will follow when it appears appropriate to do so."

"Fine," Walsh muttered and summoned a passing servant for his hat and coat.

"Good." Weston turned and was about to leave when the servant arrived with Walsh's things.

"You aren't going to see that I go straight home?" The laugh had returned to his tone. He flashed Weston a teasing smile.

"You're not a child, but if you don't leave, I will escort you out of here like one."

Walsh slipped into his coat ending his laugh when he saw his cousin's serious expression. "Alright, I am going. But Weston," Walsh paused, plopping his hat onto his head, "do try to have a bit of fun." With a quick wink, he departed.

Weston let out a weary sigh. "I should never have brought him to London," he muttered, returning to the drawing room.

"Oh, it's you again. Has Walsh gone?" Isabelle appeared at his side and gave him an appraising look.

Weston froze. "He has." He turned to face her. Her eyes narrowed.

"Oh?"

Weston cleared his throat. "Yes, Walsh has, was, taken ill and wished to return home."

Isabelle raised a skeptical brow. "Home? You mean he's gone back to Lexington?"

Weston shook his head. "No, I mean he went to my house."

"I see." The way she drew out that word made Weston cringe, but she turned back towards the ballroom and Weston could see Laura and James Avery waiting for her. "That doesn't make any sense," she murmured as she walked away from him and drew near her friends.

"What has you looking so perplexed?" Jimmy asked with a puzzled frown.

"Oh, I was talking to Weston. He claims Walsh felt unwell and left the party."

"Is that so difficult to understand?" Jimmy brushed a piece of lint from his sleeve and then proceeded to straighten his jacket.

"I just saw him. He seemed fine then. He also appeared fine when he was talking to Mr. Weston not ten minutes ago. It just feels odd."

Laura smoothed down her hair and regarded Isabelle with a bored expression. "What reason would Mr. Weston have for lying?"

"I don't know what he's up to, but something isn't right. He's always poking into whatever Walsh does."

"Are you perhaps a little conspiracy minded, Miss Hampton?" Jimmy teased with his cheeky grin. Laura swatted him in the chest with her fan.

"If Isabelle feels something is amiss, she probably has good reason. Her future may rely on just how much influence Mr. Weston has over Mr. Walsh."

Jimmy chuckled. "I suspect Weston has quite a bit of pull, what with the whole Billingsley situation a few years back. If I knew either of them better, I would venture to uncover the truth for you."

"Of course! A connection," Isabelle exclaimed.

"What do you mean?" Laura asked.

"You're all so caught up on connections and propriety. I know them both. I see no reason why I shouldn't ask for the truth."

Laura's eyes widened. "I do not support this endeavor. It could go extremely awry."

"I don't see why I can't ask. I wish I'd thought of this sooner."

Jimmy and Laura exchanged a look. "I feel it may be an imprudent approach. If you give me some time, I can certainly find something out for you." Jimmy presented the idea with a less than confident tone.

Isabelle fell silent, fingering the golden tassel on the runner adorning the side table as she plotted her next move.

Weston toured the hall of the large house admiring the large paintings and ornate rugs. He paused before painting of a hunt scene. Cocking his head to the side he studied the picture from a new angle. The painting was blotchy with gobs of paint dabbed about: a charming idea but the artist failed to create a lifelike impression.

"I certainly have more beautiful pieces hung in less prominent places," he muttered slipping into a small sitting room. Bookcases stuffed to maximum capacity lined one wall. A small sofa sat across from the fireplace and a desk and chair stood at the back wall. Weston moved to the fireplace. Leaning on the mantle he stared at the lifeless coals lining the bottom. He took a breath and pondered the latest developments in Walsh's case. A shadow cast over the fireplace outlined the figure of a woman. Weston turned to see who had come upon him.

"Miss Hampton." He made an awkward bow.

"Am I disturbing you?" Isabelle came towards him, twisting her fan in her hands.

He straightened himself and looked down at her. "Not at all. I merely sought some reprieve from the revelry."

"If you wish to be alone, I can go." She said it but made to move to leave.

"If you wish to leave, by all means, but you need not go on my account."

She gave him an inquiring look as she swayed on her feet as if uncertain which way to turn. She opted for stepping forward and running her hand along the back of the couch. "I actually want to talk to you. It's personal and you may think I am out of line." She studied him for a reaction.

He folded his arms across his chest and seemed to be listening. "Continue, provided it is in good taste."

"You may consider me blunt, but I need to know, and I feel I'm in the right to ask."

Weston shrugged. "Then, if that is the case, ask. I shall do my best to answer."

Isabelle was on edge with nerves. Her heart galloped in her chest. She felt uncomfortable making such a bold move, but she could not continue living in uncertainty. She threw out the question before she could retreat. "You are quite close with Walsh, are you not?"

"Hardly a personal question, but yes, that is correct."

She shot him a withering look. "Then you know if he has romantic feelings towards me."

The words made him seethe with envy. Weston leaned back against the mantle and faced her squarely. "Again, that is correct."

Isabelle stopped walking and glared at him. "That is not an answer."

He met her gaze. "You did not ask a question."

She clenched the back of the sofa. "Fine. Does Walsh have romantic feelings towards me?"

Weston gave a curt nod.

Isabelle felt both weak with relief and tense with anger. "If you knew this, then why would you try so hard to keep us apart? That is a question and I demand an answer."

Weston's mouth pinched into a tight line as anger flashed in his features. His stoic expression quickly returned. "I was merely looking out for Walsh's best interest."

"His best interest!" Isabelle sputtered in annoyance. "Do you think I am not in his best interest?"

"I said nothing of the sort," Weston snorted. "Walsh, like any man of reason, seeks council when faced with perplexing circumstances. In this matter, he asked my opinion and I obliged."

"How exactly did you advise him? Did you tell him I was beneath him? Are you the reason he has been distant from me?"

"I merely advised him to exercise some caution. He often acts without restraint and being wonton in a situation such as this would be foolishness."

He distracted himself by toying with the button on his waistcoat. Isabelle spotted his movement, and her cheeks flushed an angry red.

"Why can't you let him make his own decisions? Do you have nothing better to do with your time?"

"By decisions, which do you mean?" His casual tone infuriated Isabelle.

"I mean, what gives you the right to interfere with everything he says or does! You don't own him. He's a grown man capable of making his own decisions without your opinion."

"What makes you think he does not do so?" He appeared unfazed.

"You're insufferable! You speak in riddles and everything about you is a mystery. You're so controlling it seeps onto everyone around you. Not only do you try to control Walsh, but you also tried to control his sister."

At this, Weston started. "Control Irene? Why would I want to do that?"

Isabelle saw a foothold. "I think it's because you enjoy controlling people. You like telling them what to do and deciding who they should get to marry."

A dark scowl captured his features. "That is no business of yours, Miss Hampton. You speak of events of which you know nothing."

Isabelle crossed her arms over her chest. "You can overstep, ask questions, and manipulate others, but when someone else takes the same approach, suddenly the behavior is unacceptable?" She gave a sardonic laugh. "You have a skewed sense of propriety."

"Enough!"

Isabelle jumped when he pounded his fist into the mahogany desk with a resounding crack. His eyes blazed when he stared at her. "You know nothing. You have snippets of information distorted by your weak-minded peers, and yet you stand here with the audacity to accuse me of indecency. You have no validation for your claims against me. You cannot possibly comprehend the weight of the accusation you level against me, despite your complete ignorance on the subject you pretend to understand." His voice thundered off the walls as he spoke. He threw himself into the chair at the desk and ran a hand over his eyes. "I am a gentleman. Blasted woman."

Frightened into silence, Isabelle stood staring at the limp form of the man before her. She could see him struggling with the effort to control his temper.

"You want to hear the story?" His words were so full of venom she bit her lip to keep from crying. She shook her head. His eyes pierced into her soul when they met hers. "You came to me demanding answers now you balk at the tale? You have got much to learn."

Her hands shook as she struggled to regain her composure. "I think I've made a mistake—"

"I will tell you." Weston fixed her with a gaze she dared not counter. He stood and began to pace the room. His size made her feel small and his intensity scared her. She had never seen him so upset.

Taking a bracing breath, his story began: "Several years ago, Walsh's parents died, leaving a young Walsh in charge of his even younger sister, Irene. Some acquaintance of yours certainly told you this portion."

Isabelle sunk down on the sofa to keep her trembling knees from giving way as he continued in a vehement manner.

"My mother offered as much aide as they would accept, but she did not travel much and being that Walsh and Irene remained at Lexington, she saw them rarely. Irene came to stay with us in London for weeks at a time and I would join Walsh on the estate occasionally. I, being a few years older than Walsh, continued to assist in any way possible. With a bit of guidance, they managed well. Walsh has always been outgoing and has no difficulties maintaining connections and Irene is not insensible." Weston rubbed his chin thoughtfully. "We had a suitable arrangement. Until, of course, Irene fell in love," Weston paused and directed his gaze towards Isabelle. She ignored him and stared at the fireplace mantle.

"Walsh knew nothing of this young man intent on winning his sister's affections. Fearing for Irene's interest, he sought my council when this young man's intentions became clear. Swept up in the excitement of it all Irene refused to listen to reason. Walsh begged her to act with prudence, but she wanted romance. When I arrived at Lexington, she accepted an offer from a friend to spend the summer in Bath and was gone. Walsh swore to go after her, but I cautioned him against this as she was already quite angry with him. He pleaded with me to go in his stead. We knew this young man would follow her to Bath and still we knew nothing of him nor his family. I said I would go, but only after we knew something about the risk. Desperate though he was, Walsh agreed to wait until I had discovered something before going after her. I returned to London to make inquiries. During my investigation, I learned that he was of a wealthy family from Liverpool and that he had several broken engagements. He had proposed marriage to three separate ladies and had abandoned them all."

Isabelle gasped. Weston took advantage of the interruption and stood to stretch his lanky body. He stepped over to the sofa and seated himself on the end opposite her. Aware of his movement, she still refused to look at him. She heard him sigh as he leaned back into the sofa.

"The family disinherited the scoundrel on account of his actions. He needed a woman with an inheritance. Irene being young and a bit naïve was the perfect choice. I wrote to Walsh to inform him of this news and then I rode onto Bath myself. Upon my arrival, I crossed paths with a young man of the same name who turned out to be the would-be-suitor's brother. He had been abroad in France for many months and his parents had written him regarding his brother's exploits. Enraged and seeking to clear the family name, he returned to England with the intent to subdue his brother. Together, we sought his brother and Irene. We found them before Walsh arrived in Bath. I tried to convince Irene of her misjudgement, that she needed to return to Lexington. She refused to leave him. When a giant row unfolded between the brothers, Irene heard the stories and her faith in her decision began to weaken. I took advantage of the opportunity to convince Irene to end her relationship with this young man immediately. After deciding to ensure this young man would never again interfere with my family, I turned him over to the charge of his brother. In an effort to clear his family's name, the brother rode with us to Lexington to make peace with Walsh while the scoundrel in question returned to the north."

Weston cleared his throat and adjusted his leg crossed over his knee. "As you can see, Miss Hampton, Walsh asked for my assistance. He values my opinion and seeks it often. I only intervene in his affairs when invited. Your claim that I am controlling him, or Irene is unfounded."

Isabelle still felt confused. Her voice cracked when she spoke: "That story explains some of the mystery. Why don't you get along with her husband? Why do you disagree with Irene's choice in marriage?"

Weston shifted on the sofa. "Your knowledge of my life has many gaps, it seems. The gossip circles do a far worse job disseminating personal details than I would have imagined. The man I chased across the country is Todd Billingsley who is the disinherited brother of Henry Billingsley."

Isabelle started. "I had no idea."

"Yes, I see that. The rumor I assume you heard is that there is bad blood between Henry and myself."

She ruffled a little at this. She raised her chin. "Well, is there?"

"No, there is no reason. No two people always agree, but Billingsley is a good man and has done well by Irene. While I don't go out of my way to associate with him, there is no ill will. Walsh and he get along famously."

"Here I thought you were overbearing in your family yet it seems you are more distant than anything."

"Indeed. If anything, Henry Billingsley is overbearing."

Isabelle cocked her head sideways. "Why do you say that?"

Weston sighed and fussed with the cuff on his waistcoat. "I think he still feels embarrassed over his brother's mistakes. I suspect he still seeks to prove that he is different than his brother. Walsh has never mentioned this, but I noticed the change in his demeanour when I am present. I suspect he fears me. I avoid overstepping my welcome and make him uncomfortable in his own family. So, I leave Walsh to maintain connections with the Billingsleys."

"He's probably afraid of you. You're rather intimidating."

Weston's eyes flickered to her face and for a moment; she met his gaze. "Am I?

Her breath caught in her chest as she returned her stare to the mantle. She felt a slight flush at the base of her neck. "Yes, Mr. Billingsley probably thinks if he makes a mistake, you will run him off the way you did his brother," she remarked with a dry laugh.

A hint of a smile darted across Weston's mouth, before the emotionless stare swept over once again. "I might at that, provided Walsh enlisted my help." When he fell silent, Isabelle became aware of how close he sat to her on that little sofa. She could hear him breathing and feel his warmth on her arm. She drew herself tighter against the arm of the sofa, making herself smaller to occupy as little space as possible.

"That all sounds fine, like you were only being heroic. All your actions sound justified, and I am sure you never act without justification." The sharpness of her words surprised her, and she saw that look of annoyance return to him.

"I wanted to ensure that Irene Billingsley never had to experience more loss than she already had. The pain of love lost, no one should experience that if avoidance is possible."

Isabelle looked into his eyes and saw pain there. Something softened inside her and she felt her anger begin to fade. What he suffered, she did not know, but she knew that he had, and it evoked sympathy towards him. He sighed and glared at the floor.

"I feel certain you've heard the stories of my past." Isabelle flushed. He regarded her for a second. "You may be a newcomer to our midst, but events of the past seem to struggle with remaining in the past."

"Idle gossip, nothing more," Isabelle muttered.

"Not entirely, Miss Hampton. All myth is born of some fact. There was a young woman. I lived a life of recklessness and nearly became a disgrace to the Weston name."

Isabelle shifted in her seat. She was not sure if she wanted to hear this story.

"The things I did were idiotic and brought great harm to others. I will never forget one such incident on the eve I met the young woman. I had involved myself in a midnight horse race. I won at the expense of my opponent. His horse landed badly after a hedge, and it threw the drunken fool."

Isabelle gasped and covered her mouth. Weston looked hard at her. "This is the true story, Miss Hampton. Idle minds have expanded the tale through the years. The boy could have suffered much worse than a broken arm. The tales of my exploits began to circulate the social circles that night as I met the lady that evening."

He leaned towards her, willing her to understand his words. "I wish to rectify that she was not of a failing estate. The other accusations, I will not deign to revoke for the folly they are. Her family was proud. Her father would not permit my attentions, despite the Weston name. I thought I wore my name poorly, that without a father's oversight, I had aged under the hand of dotting mother. My mother, may she rest in peace, had no easy time in my youth. This girl's father seemed intent of reminding me of my past and ensuring he thwart my efforts at redemption. A good marriage and good society will do well to settle young men. A woman can do wonders," he paused. "You do know her fate, do you not?"

Isabelle nodded and averted her gaze.

"Life is so fragile. She thrived on adventure. She thought I was brave and daring. She encouraged my exploits because they got her attention. I rode faster, more wild horses. I took chances. When she wanted to participate, I got a team of horses. We drove every road in the county as fast as those horses would run. Day, night, storm, we made them run. She loved it. And I loved her." He choked on the last words.

Isabelle began to interject. "You don't need to continue..."

He shook his head and ran his hand over his knee. "You asked for the truth. I have meddled in your affairs, and you have asked me why. You deserve to know. We went for a drive one winter evening. It was cold. The wind blew fierce. The horses were spooky. Snow mixed with rain and turned the roads to mud. I was...unwell. I stepped down from the carriage for but a moment. She remained in the carriage. She thought it would be a laugh to run the horses, but they were strong and hard to handle. In the storm, they became unmanageable. They bolted. I could do nothing but watch. The carriage overturned on the riverbank, breaking into pieces, felling the horses, and throwing the driver."

Isabelle felt like her heart might stop in her chest. She looked to Weston. His eyes remained downcast, and he spoke as if in a trance. Isabelle wanted to stop him, but he seemed unreachable.

"She broke through the ice. I dove to save her, but my condition prevented me from doing much good. I pulled us from the frozen river and hauled her trembling body through the broken ice. I carried her to the nearest residence. She never awoke. 3 days later, she was gone." His breathing was shallow. Isabelle felt tears sting her eyes.

"I learned my life's lesson very well. I no longer take risks in life or love. The price is just too great." Hie voice quavered. "I aim to protect others from the same fate. Irene did not need to experience what I had. She did not need to feel that loss and devastation of an ill-fated love. She did not need to live a life bound to a scoundrel." The bitterness in his words caused Isabelle to tremble.

"You suffered quite a lot."

"I received my just reward. The lady suffered a fate far worse because of my actions. Her father failed to stop me and lost his daughter consequently. When I saw Irene heading on the same path with a man like I had been, I grew afraid. Walsh would have acted just as this girl's father had, but Walsh did not have the force required for such a confrontation. I saw this. I had lived that and knew what it would take to release Irene from such a match. It was my duty to spare Irene a similar fate. Perhaps I hoped by taking action I could atone for some of the harm I had caused."

"You alone were not responsible. It was an accident."

"Her role was small. Even in my youth, I had influence. I have always been a respected man within society. I abused that position to live a double life."

"But you've restored yourself. You are a gentleman. Whatever harm you caused lives only in legend. You seem to me like a favourite of society."

He gave a sardonic chuckle. "Yes. But restoration has not come without cost. My life reminds me of Coleridge's ballade."

Isabelle tipped her head to the side. "What do you mean?"

"That I survived a dreadful incident so that I could assume my role in preventing others from similar ill-fated ventures."

"You don't really believe that."

"Irene's happy marriage presents evidence that I do."

"No wonder you hate poetry. You see your life from so bleak a perspective."

He raised a brow. "I would consider myself experienced at life. My attitude mirrors this." He sounded tired. This man started to make more sense to Isabelle now that he had presented the reasons for the things he did.

"You loved her?"

He looked at her in surprise. "Certainly." His gaze met hers. She saw truth reflected there. She could almost feel the pain in his memory. Suddenly, she felt guilty that she had made him dredge up the past.

"You've given me more explanation than I deserve."

He shook his head. "No, Miss Hampton. Like Irene, I desired to save you from such a pain. I barged into your life and was overzealous in my efforts. While not controlling Walsh, I have influenced him. I directed him away from you to prevent harm by his foolishness, but it was not my place to do so. It is I who owes you an apology."

She shook her head in amazement over the fact that Robert Weston, the man who lived in brooding secrecy, had poured out his life's heartache to her because she had been angry with him. Suddenly, her anger seemed foolish. It all seemed so simple now. He responded out of concern for her wellbeing, not malice or spite or whatever else she dreamed was his intent. His appearance now reflected his remorse. He was a good man and she had treated him unfairly. "If you owe me an apology, then I owe you one too. I didn't mean to…"

He raised a hand to silence her. "If apologies are all that remain, then let us settle this thing. I do fear that I have damaged your future happiness. My interference has certainly impacted possibilities."

Isabelle blinked back tears of shame. His expression had softened to one of compassion, but when Isabelle looked deeper, she also saw an intense longing for something she could not imagine. "Did you send me the book?" The words spilled out in a hoarse rush.

Weston paused a moment. He looked about to deny it. "Yes." He lowered his gaze.

As they sat in silence, Isabelle had a realization. She studied the man beside her. He ran his hand over the booted leg resting across his knee. He appeared unaware of her watching him. She fought the urge to reach out and touch him. She wanted to feel the warmth of his skin, the strength of his arms. She now saw all the things she had missed before. The strength of character she knew existed, but the kindness, the tenderness, and the brilliance he had kept hidden. She saw a man she could rely on, someone who could be her companion and friend. All this time, she had been pushing him away when he was the only person who knew what she needed, and he sought to provide those for her. She hid her eyes, overcome with shame. Her thoughts raced. She felt miserable. Images of what life could have been with him crumbled before her eyes and something inside her broke. A choked sob escaped her.

His eyes turned to her face. "Why such sorrow?" His hand stretched towards her.

Isabelle buried her face in her hands.

"I cannot imagine where she has gone. Surely it has just been some sort of mist—" Laura banged open the salon door and stopped in the doorway. She spied the pair seated on the sofa and her brows went up in shock.

Jimmy Avery appeared at her elbow. He gave a wicked grin. "Hey ho, what have we here?"

Laura pinched her mouth closed and flailed her hand at him in an effort to shut him up. She paled when she saw Isabelle hunched over, her hand pressed to her eyes. "Oh, Isabelle, what has happened?" She flew to her friend's side and grasped her hands. Isabelle held her breath to prevent any more sobs. Laura laid a hand to her cheek.

"Jimmy, fetch my mother. Isabelle is ill. We must leave at once."

Weston leapt from the sofa and hurried from the room in search of Mrs. Millis. James Avery stood at the door a moment, looking puzzled, before hurrying after Weston.

Laura continued to stroke Isabelle's cheek. "Oh, my poor dear, we must get you home." Laura stayed on her knees at Isabelle's side until Mrs. Millis arrived and bustled them out of the house. James Avery escorted them to the carriage and Weston followed somewhere in the fray but vanished from view as the carriage rolled towards the house on Barlington Way.

~

Mrs. Millis directed Isabelle to bed immediately upon their return to the house. Laura saw her to her room. Laura helped her dress and get into bed, then laid down next to Isabelle on top of the blankets.

"Oh, Isabelle, won't you talk to me?"

Isabelle sniffled into the pillow as fresh tears flowed.

"Please, dear, I fear something awful. What happened with Mr. Weston?"

"He...did...nothing." Isabelle choked on the words and buried her face into the pillow.

Laura rubbed her hand along Isabelle's back. "Then sleep. Things will look brighter in the morning."

The light went out and Laura removed herself from the room. Isabelle cried softly until she drifted off to sleep.

CHAPTER 32

The next few days passed in a haze for Isabelle. She struggled to rid herself of the feeling of hopelessness that settled upon her. She felt uncertain that Walsh would continue his pursuit of her, especially if Weston told him about their conversation. Then of course she was not entirely sure she wanted him to pursue her since something in her yearned for Weston. Walsh had a lot to offer her, he would make a fine husband, her family already knew and enjoyed him, but her heart just could not accept him.

Her head ached. She withdrew from the Millis family to relive that sitting room conversation in the solitude of her room. She mulled every detail, determined to see Weston as the brute she wanted him to be. But she could not. Every time she went over his tale, he moved further from the role of villain and became alive to her as the hero he had always been. This new understanding of him made the broken connection between them that much more unbearable. How could she admire and respect the man from a distance while feigning love for his closest relation? Her heart would break. Eventually he might choose to marry, and she would stand by and watch, not only participate but expected to be as happy for him as his beloved Walsh. She cringed. She could not do that. She resolved not to do that. She would refuse Walsh if he continued his pursuit of her. She knew there would be criticism of her decision, but she felt that building a life with Walsh would be a lie. It was the life she wanted, but not the person.

She wanted to tell her friend, but she feared Laura would not understand. Laura worried about things like connections and money, but she seemed less interested in love. To her, a good match was all that mattered and loving the person was irrelevant. Laura would surely encourage her to pursue Walsh despite her reservations and interest in Weston. Or worse, Laura would think she was being a fool. Isabelle knew that voicing her concerns to someone would lift her burden, but the risk of being a fool silenced her.

Her tears worried her hosts, but her silence hurt them the worst. Isabelle could see the weight her silence piled upon her friend. Laura's sad eyes watched Isabelle grieve. She begged for an explanation until she drove Isabelle to tears. Once she had evoked tears, she stopped asking for the tale Isabelle longed to share.

Isabelle was not the only person struggling in the wake of that sitting room conversation. A dark cloud hung over Weston, heightening his natural withdraw and creating a moodiness in him. The sulkiness began to worry his lighthearted cousin. Though Weston spoke nothing of his feelings in words, he expressed them through song. His violin filled the house with despondent melodies that haunted the halls and cast a depressive air over the household. The lonesome music flooded the house with sadness.

By the fourth day of this, Walsh had nearly gone mad. The day was cold and dreary, so Walsh sat in the main parlor with the paper. The fire burned low on the hearth offered little comfort or warmth.

Then the music started, and the brooding tones drifted to him. Piercing notes of despair and anguish were too much for Walsh. He jumped to his feet and threw the paper onto the table.

"This must end." His determined stride sent him sweeping through the house towards the upstairs sitting room. He met the maid Bridget in the upstairs hall. She had handkerchiefs stuffed into her ears. She removed them as Walsh halted.

"I couldn't stand to hear anymore of that depressing music," she explained, "I do not know what has gotten into him. There has not been such a darkness in this house since Master Weston died 16 years ago."

Walsh nodded. "Yes, something has gotten to Weston. He is quite disturbed."

The maid looked as if her heart would break in sorrow for her employer's wellbeing.

Walsh offered her a mind smile. "I intend to find out the cause and put an end to all this."

"Oh? Can you, sir?"

Walsh nodded.

The maid flashed a sweet smile. "Aye, that would be wonderful. It seems so long since Mr. Weston was lighthearted."

"We shall see if I can induce some lightness in his heart once again." With a quick jerk at his collar, Walsh shoved on the sitting room door where violin music wafted to him from within. The door flew open with a bang, startling the violinist. The instrument squalled in protest of the bow hauled from its strings.

"Good god, man! Did someone die?" Walsh stood in the doorway, with his hands tucked into his waistcoat pockets, surveying the scene before him.

Weston remained with his back to the door, his fingers rubbing along the violin's neck.

"What is this silence? Have we not come to London to pursue leisure and pleasure? Such a mournful tone for a journey designed to be an adventure." Walsh strolled to his side.

Weston tapped the bow lightly against his leg, pursing his lips.

Walsh tipped his head and leaned forward to inspect Weston. "This madness has gone on long enough: wouldn't you say?"

"Can one put a time limit on grief?"

Walsh's shoulders slumped forward. "No, certainly not. But surely with time the burden becomes easier to bear?"

"Time is relative."

"Not exactly. Time is merely a means to mark the passage of life. It continues despite our emotions or circumstances. Wouldn't you rather continue with it for the journey than stagnating?"

Weston gave a noncommittal grunt and buried the violin under his chin. A singular note stirred sorrow in Walsh's soul. He laid a hand on his cousin's shoulder.

"Does this grief have to do with Miss Hampton?"

"It is a loss I must endure alone." Weston shrugged his shoulder free of Walsh's grasp.

"Is it a loss?"

Weston lowered the violin and eyed Walsh with a cocked brow. "Rejection and loss have the same result: an unresolved desire."

"Ah, so what is it you desire?"

The violin appeared under Weston's chin again and he lifted the bow to the strings, turning his shoulder to Walsh as he did so. Walsh stepped in front of him.

"You cannot dodge me that easy. Tell me. What is it you wanted?"

Weston scowled. "I want nothing."

"Perhaps not now, or at least this is what you pretend. But you had a desire once. I can see it."

Weston gave an exasperated sigh. "It is irrelevant."

"Obviously not or you would not have responded this way."

"It was not meant to be, and it was ordained that from the first meeting."

"You do not believe in predetermination. You think because a meeting did not go well that all future interactions with that person will continue poorly?"

"Perhaps, perhaps not, but the outcome was not solely based on my actions."

"Oh, no?"

"No, someone else got in the middle."

Walsh grew quiet at this revelation. "You *are* referring to Miss Hampton." Weston pursed his lips. "You are. And I got between you and Miss Hampton."

Weston rolled the bow between his fingers.

"You did outright state that you had no interest in Miss Hampton and considered any pursuit of her foolishness."

"I did say that."

"Yes, you did say that. Why then would you hold me in contempt for what you consider ruining your opportunity for pursuit when you had no intent to pursue her?"

Weston's gaze fell full on Walsh who swayed under the intensity. "I had no opportunity for pursuit truly. By the time I realized my mistake, she was quite enamoured with you."

Walsh looked puzzled. "But I have retreated. There is no interference now. You could pursue."

Weston shook his head. "I have already withdrawn my pursuit. You made it clear you intended to pursue her. I saw no reason to maintain any sort of intentions towards her."

"But why? She is free now."

"How foolish are you? How wonton do you think she is with her affections? Surely, she has some feeling for you that will cause her hurt once you reveal your engagement to another woman. I refrained so you could pursue Miss Hampton. That ended poorly for both her and I."

"But I do not understand. If you were interested, you could have pursued."

"Old memories proved challenging to overcome. I felt uncertain she deserved the haunting of my shadowed past. Now, I see that few in London recall or care about what occurred those years ago. The Weston name seems cleared of the folly of my youth."

"Then pursue her now! You no longer have a reason to avoid this." Weston looked at him as if he had grown a third arm. "You desire her. She has no attachments. You could win."

Weston blinked slowly. "You forget one thing, my dear cousin."

Walsh folded his arms across his chest. "And what is this?"

"She loathes me."

"That's absurd."

Weston shrugged.

Walsh chuckled. "Miss Hampton does not loathe anyone."

"Unfortunately, that is no longer the case," Weston replied, lowering himself onto a nearby sofa with a sigh."

"What happened after I left the Coombes party? I know you spoke to her. What did you say?"

"I told her the truth."

Walsh mused his hair in frustration. "The truth about what?"

"Everything."

Walsh looked mortified. "Everything? Does that include my affections for Miss Duke?"

"No, no, your integrity," here Weston gave a derisive snort, "remains intact. I told her the truth pertaining to me."

Walsh sat next to him on the sofa, his gaze intent upon Weston's face. "Really? Why would you? You told no one that tale."

Weston sighed and rubbed his forehead. "She asked for the truth. I felt after all the meddling I have done, that much I owed her."

Walsh took in a sharp breath.

"I also told her about Irene after she confronted me. She accused me of controlling you and Henry Billingsley was her evidence."

"How extraordinary. I have never heard of you being so open."

"It matters not. By the time I had finished speaking, she refused to look at me."

"Was she angry?"

"I am uncertain. She may have been crying, but I cannot say for sure."

"Crying? Whatever for?"

"I do not know. Perhaps she feared I would tell you to end your pursuit of her. She seems to think I have enormous sway in your life and can direct you however I choose."

"Is that not exactly what you were trying to do?" Walsh could not hide the smirk.

"Perhaps at one time. It was in her best interest as well as yours."

"Can you not explain this to her?"

"Are you mad? That would be to admit to the very things she accused me of doing."

"She was correct."

"Only in part." His voice grew quiet. "My aim was to save her and maybe in some way save myself."

"Tell her. She will understand."

"She loves you, remember? She has no reason to listen to me." Weston leapt to his feet. He clutched the violin as he recalled her tenderness at the orphanage, the tears she shed over a child forgotten by the world. He shook his head to rid his mind of the images, reminding himself she did not feel for him what he felt for her. "No, Walsh. The time for conversation has long passed."

CHAPTER 33

"Isabelle, we came to London for fun, yet you are melancholier than ever. London should lift your spirits, not dampen them." Laura propelled Isabelle by the arm along the park path. She had managed to convince Isabelle to leave her room that morning for a brief stroll but was now having difficulty keeping her friend engaged.

"I'm sorry. I don't mean to ruin your fun. Maybe you should have left me at Brooklyn."

"That would defeat the purpose of having a companion on this trip." Isabelle fell silent and her cheeks began to pale despite the warmth from the sunny day. Laura sighed. "Why won't you tell me? Please, dear, it cannot be that bad."

Tears shimmered in Isabelle's eyes. "It's bad."

Laura's brow furrowed. "Oh, Isabelle, do not cry. How I wish you would feel better!" She dug in her bag and offered a handkerchief to Isabelle.

"I'm a horrible person." Isabelle's voice broke as she stopped to dab her eyes.

Laura paused and faced her. "I cannot believe that. Why would you say this?"

"I was so mean." Isabelle's features showed such anguish Laura worried over what her friend might reveal. She led them off the path to a grassy meadow and seated them beneath a tree.

"You have never been cruel. I cannot think of a single situation where you were not lovely."

Isabelle gave a bitter laugh while fighting more tears. "I was mean to him, just awful. I was so rude to him and kept pushing him away. So much contempt against him. The worst part is, I almost enjoyed it. I felt it was my right to treat him that way since he appeared to be intruding in my life."

"Why do you say these things? Everyone loves you. You have been nothing but a picture of charm and grace since I met you."

Isabelle shook her head, her eyes downcast. "You know that isn't true. I've complained about him to you. I've been so frustrated with him, his grating remarks and English pride, I haven't been nice at all."

Laura knew in that instant who was the subject of this conversation. A tender smile tugged on her lips.

"I wouldn't be surprised if he never speaks to me again."

"Why would it matter if he speaks to you? You have no regard for him."

Isabelle sniffed and brushed a lock of hair from her tear-soaked cheek. "If only that were true."

Laura gave a small start. With a quick shake of her head, she asked: "You have feelings for Mr. Weston?"

Isabelle gave a miserable nod. A tiny sob escaped.

Laura was glad no one was in the park that morning as she sat in a stunned curiosity listening to Isabelle's revelation. "But you outright rejected any idea of him. And Mr. Walsh is very intent on you. You seemed happy. What about him?"

"I don't understand it. Walsh is a dear man, but I kept finding myself in situations with Weston that spoke a lot about his character, and I was drawn to him." Isabelle rushed on when she saw the look of confusion on Laura's face. "I didn't mean for this to happen. I often despised our interactions but when I think about them, I realize that Weston was not the monster I thought he was. I misjudged him. He is a good man and London is right to hold him in high regard. I realized this too late." She bit her lip as her voice began to quiver.

"Rumors be true or not, he remains a Weston. They are a fine family, and a Weston will always live up to the name, despite some mistakes along the journey. Our Mr. Weston has always been elegant, if not mysterious. But I do not understand why you feel you so defeated. I knew nothing of your affections until this very moment. I can assure you he has no suspicion of their existence. I see no reason you cannot start afresh and leave what you see as your folly in the past."

Isabelle shook her head. "I doubt that. I demanded information from him. I treated him carelessly, as if his past were something I had a right to know. I know my actions hurt him. I don't know if he can forgive that."

"Mr. Weston is a reasonable man. In time, he will see your change of heart and accept it, I feel certain of this." Isabelle could picture his face now as it had haunted her dreams for the past few nights. A tingle of excitement coursed through her, and she knew that she loved him. She raised her sad eyes to Laura's face. "It may be too late." Her voice was little more than a whisper.

"Nonsense. You are a fine young lady and Mr. Weston knows this. These things take time, but that does not make it impossible."

A flutter of hope stirred inside Isabelle. "Do you really think he could love me?"

Laura reached over and squeezed her hand. "Definitely. You have much to offer. You have connections and would make him a suitable wife. It would be a smart match."

Isabelle smiled a teary smile and pulled Laura into a quick hug.

"Good morning, ladies," a passerby greeted.

Laura looked up with a smile as Isabelle gave a quick swipe along her eyes to rid herself of the remains of tears.

"Miss Millis! I never expected to find you out this morning. What a pleasant surprise."

Isabelle looked up at Laura's response. "Good morning, Mr. Walsh. I didn't think we would see you in London."

He shifted his weight on his feet into a casual lean. "Yes, I usually avoid London this time of year, but I came at the request of my..." His gaze landed on Isabelle and his voice faltered. "Miss Hampton, are you alright?"

Isabelle's hand rose to her cheek. She felt certain she must look like a disaster. "There may be something in the air." She forced a smile.

He looked unconvinced. "I suppose that is a possibility..."

"Are you here to visit Mr. Weston? Has he come to London?" Laura interjected, getting to her feet, and standing a possessive guard over Isabelle.

"Why yes, I am staying with him." Walsh's tone lost its cheery lilt. His mouth tightened. He looked to Isabelle, but she kept her gaze fixed on the handkerchief. She gave little away. He squared his shoulders at her coldness. "I wonder that you did not see him at the Coombes party. He attended with me."

Isabelle flinched. Walsh's quick eye noted it, and he felt a sudden compassion for her plight. His posture softened towards her. Laura noticed this all.

"Ah, yes, perhaps I did see him. The evening was all bustle and noise, I fear I missed him. I do not remember it well." Laura laughed and waved her hand. "Won't you take a turn about the park with me, Mr. Walsh? I fear I have worn out my companion, yet I would love to see the other half of this path."

Walsh could not refuse her invitation as she moved towards him with purpose, and he found himself offering her his arm.

"Miss Hampton you'll be fine?" He threw the question over his shoulder as Laura practically whisked him away.

"Yes, I just need a few minutes to rest. Go on without me." She smiled lovingly at Laura as the pair moved off, and Laura chattered about how charming the duck pond was.

As they drifted away from Isabelle, Laura glanced back to be certain they were out of earshot before she smoothly said: "It seems you have betrayed my dear Miss Hampton."

He gave a physical start and nearly tripped over his own feet. "I beg your pardon?"

Laura turned to Walsh with a sweet smile. "Did you really think I would not know about Miss Duke?"

Walsh stiffened. "Of what are you accusing me?"

"Oh nothing, really," Laura replied with a flippant wave of her hand. "However, it came about, I don't think you meant any harm by it, nor do you have malicious intent towards my friend."

"I can assure you I do not. I care deeply about Miss Hampton and would hate to cause her pain."

Laura cast him an odd look. "Regardless of all that, you have caused her pain. But that matters not for you have done yourself injury by nature of your secretiveness and this to me satisfies my need for retribution." She flashed him a smile.

"Uh, thank you for your understanding," Walsh said haltingly, a slight flush rising in his cheeks.

"Now that's settled, I want to know something," Walsh turned to her expectantly as she paused, "Do you love Miss Hampton?"

His flushed features deepened to a scarlet hue. He lowered his eyes to the path. Laura waited for his response. He took a breath. "I am embarrassed to admit that I do not."

Laura met this confession with silence. They continued walking. Walsh glanced at her, but she gave away nothing. Suddenly, she patted his arm. "Good, I am glad to hear this."

"Why?" Walsh spoke in an injured tone.

"I mean nothing against you by this. You have made your own mistakes, but they are nothing more than the result of immature passion and overall are quite harmless," she sighed. "The truth is, unlike you I believe in speaking the truth on every occasion: Miss Hampton does not love you either."

Walsh stood in a surprised silence. Laura turned to stand square before him. She folded her hands in front of her. After a moment, he spoke: "Miss Millis, I am at a complete and utter loss as to what to do with your bluntness. I have never been so insulted and chided simultaneously by a single person."

"Then I shall tell you what to do. That cousin of yours has Miss Hampton all in a stir."

"Weston? How?"

Laura jerked as if someone had slapped her. "I will not divulge what is personal to her," she took a breath and softened her tone, "but I will tell you she fears she has lost the possibility of engaging Mr. Weston. That he will simply exit her life and have never a thing more to do with her."

"Miss Hampton is a charming young woman. Weston has no reason to reject her."

"You are his nearest relation. If anyone knew anything pertaining to him, it would be you. Do you say this with confidence?"

Walsh paused for a moment. He cared about both parties involved. He spoke after remembering the cursed violin music overwhelming the house. "Yes, I do. I can also add that her fear holds no grounds. I assure you of Weston's affections towards her."

"Oh! Truth I asked from you."

"Truth I gave to you, Miss, Millis. Although at the beginning of this conversation you drew into question my integrity. I hope my honesty now amends for what I tried to keep secret." He made her a quick but humble bow.

Laura clasped her hands under her chin as joy surged within her.

Her smile was radiant. "If what you say is true, this will more than amend your error."

"I have given you what I know to be true. Will you tell Miss Hampton immediately?"

Laura shook her head and fell into step with him as they resumed walking. "No, I want to see how this unfolds. If what you say is true, I may not need to do a thing."

Henley Manor,

"Where the devil have you been?" Weston demanded, bounding down the sweeping stairs towards Walsh upon his return to the house.

Weston's coattails fluttered as he skipped the last step and landed with a flourish in the entryway.

Walsh looked up, handing his hat and gloves to the butler. "Out."

"I've been looking all over for you. You are never going to believe what that horse of yours has done to my stables," Weston paused and scowled. "Why are you snickering?"

Walsh turned and sauntered into the immaculate living room. Weston followed, annoyed but curious. Large, beautiful rugs covered the floors. Rust colored sofas surrounded the fireplace over which hung a mantle dotted with expensive trinkets. Rare and delicate vases peeped out amid the shelves on the stuffed bookcases.

Walsh smiled. "This room is a perfect example of Weston fortune and taste." He flopped onto the sofa nearest the window. "Aunt Phoebe did have a love for fine things. Her collections are immense and quite spectacular." Walsh moved aside a hand embroidered cushion from under his arm.

Weston stood behind the sofa across from Walsh. A large hunt scene painting hung on the wall behind him. "Is there a point to all this?"

Walsh leaned back into the sofa. "Just wanted to be comfortable before I tell you of my morning adventures."

"How amusing. If that is all, I have other things to attend—"

"Oh, wait. You may want to hear this."

Weston leaned forward on his hands on the back of the sofa and stared at Walsh.

"I went for a walk in Madison Park, which really is quite lovely," Walsh halted and crossed one booted ankle over his knee. "The footbridge is quite charming."

"Is this really what you wanted to tell me?"

"You are so impatient, Weston. Perhaps I won't tell you at all."

"As you wish, cousin." Weston straightened and turned to leave.

"No, no, you want to hear this." Walsh spoke quickly. "I met Miss Millis and Miss Hampton in the park."

Weston grew still. After a moment he spoke: "Did you?"

Walsh nodded. "I had the most interesting conversation with Miss Millis."

"I imagine you did."

"Yes, she knows much, and is not afraid to speak her mind," Walsh admitted with some fondness and a dash of shame.

"What exactly does she know?"

"Oh, pretty much everything."

Weston gave a short burst of laughter. "Ah, and she confronted you."

Walsh smirked and averted his gaze. "In a way, yes. But that is not important right now."

"No? I rather enjoy this humbling experience for you."

"I can see that you do. However, you might be more interested in what else she told me."

"I'm listening."

"She informed me that Miss Hampton does not love me."

"You sound oddly calm about that." Weston leaned over the back the sofa, so he was on eye level with Walsh.

"I must admit it was a blow to my pride, but a relief to hear."

"Walsh explain why quickly, or I am leaving this conversation. You tend to get to a point via the long way."

"It seems Miss Hampton has her heart set on someone else." Walsh raised a brow and looked pointedly at Weston.

The clock ticking above the mantel was the only noise to fill the room.

Finally, Weston asked: "Did you speak to Miss Hampton?"

Walsh shook his head.

"You said you saw her. Did she seem well?"

Again, Walsh shook his head. In a flurry of movement and black fabric that startled Walsh, Weston launched himself over the back of the sofa and flew onto the arm of the sofa where Walsh sat. An anxious frown crossed his brow.

"Is she ill?"

"No, Miss Millis said she fears that you have rejected her." Walsh patted his knee with a parental affection.

Weston gave his head a bewildered shake. "That is not the case. I did not pursue her because of you. I know I interfered at first, but it seemed like you were both in love, I wanted it to be. I wanted her to be happy. I never imagined…. this is rather a mess." Weston sighed and his shoulders sagged.

"Yes, well, according to Miss Millis, she never loved me."

Weston turned to his cousin with a new hope shining in his eyes. His pulse quickened. "Does she love me?" He held his breath as he awaited the answer.

"That I do not know."

Weston began to sag again and slid from the arm of the sofa. He hit the floor with a dull thump. "This situation is absurd."

"I suppose you will have to find that answer yourself. I suggest getting it directly from Miss Hampton," Walsh suggested while peering over the edge of the sofa. "Now, stop being dramatic. It doesn't become you."

"This conversation has been rather painful, both physically and metaphorically speaking," Weston griped, hopping to his feet, and brushing off his clothes. "Miss Hampton may not be the only person who does not love you."

Walsh chuckled also getting to his feet. "Where would you be without me?"

"First off, I would not be in this mess with Miss Hampton."

"Ah, but if not for me, you might not have ever met Miss Hampton." Walsh slung an arm about his cousin's shoulders. "You are glad you met her, yes?"

"I am," Weston responded with a grunt.

Walsh smiled his most dashing smile. "Then tell her."

CHAPTER 34

63 Barlington Way,

A morning or two after their fateful walk in the park, Isabelle glided down the stairs in pursuit of Mrs. Millis and Laura. She followed their voices towards the dining room. She could hear the clinking of dishes and spurts of laughter and her pace slowed the closer she got. She felt tired, unhappy, and wondered if she should return to her room. She was uncertain if she was ready for their jovial gossip. But Mrs. Millis spotted her in the door the moment she arrived.

"Good morning, dear! Come, come, the tea is simply perfect this morning and cook has made us some lovely light biscuits." The feather pinned into her tied back hair fluttered as she spoke and gestured.

Isabelle's smile showed her discomfort, but she did not refuse the invitation, instead seating herself next to Laura.

Laura looked up from the newspaper she had been reading, the feather in her own hair flapping in its place. "You are not dressed to go out."

"We're going out?" Isabelle could hear the disdain in her own words. Laura gave her a pitying look and sighed.

"We are in London! This is when we mingle with the socialites. Surely you want to visit the sites?"

Isabelle looked at their outfits: colorful gowns of blue and yellow, strings of pearls, and hair set perfectly in place. She laid a hand on the skirt of her ivory gown and lowered her eyes to the table. "I don't feel well."

Mrs. Millis reached across the table to squeeze her hand. "Quite fine, dear. If you prefer to rest, you can do that."

Laura pulled a face. "No, Mum, she cannot avoid society any longer."

"Laura!" Her mother scolded with an embarrassed edge.

"She cannot. Isabelle, you must stop this. We are young and beautiful, and in London. Let us have adventures. You cannot be this serious already in life. You should have more fun."

"But I don't want to go."

"Nonsense. We have tickets to the theatre this evening. You must come."

"Laura, I'm tired."

"Laura, let her be. Isabelle can make her own decisions," Mrs. Millis interjected firmly.

"No, Mum, Isabelle cannot let London pass her by because she chose to hide in her room with her hurt from the first man to reject her." Laura stood in her passion and bumped the table, knocking over the bouquet centrepiece.

"That is enough, Laura!" Mrs. Millis dropped her cutlery with a clang.

"There's a caller for Miss Hampton."

Everyone in the room stopped. All eyes turned to the maid who stood at the doorway.

"Who is it, Mabel?" Mrs. Millis smoothed her gown and raised her chin, collecting her dignity.

"I have no calling card, ma'am, but Thomas assures me it is someone Miss Hampton knows." The maid stood rigid and folded her hands behind her back. "He is waiting in the garden."

Laura and Mrs. Millis turned to Isabelle. She sat speechless and pale.

"You don't have to go," Mrs. Millis reminded her.

Laura rolled her eyes. "Yes, but if it is *him* you may want to hear what he has to say."

Isabelle nodded. "Yes, I will see the caller." She got to her feet. "If it is him, I want to know why he's here."

The maid dropped a quick curtsey and led the way through the house to the garden. Isabelle's heart began to thump in her chest. She felt warm and nervous as she drew near to the garden. The maid paused at the garden door and held it open for Isabelle.

"If you require anything, please let us know."

Isabelle nodded as the maid curtseyed again. The maid closed the door behind her as Isabelle crossed the cobblestone to the top of the stairs leading to the garden. A man stood on the ground level below her, his back to her and bent over the early blooming flowers. Isabelle halted at the top of the steps. The breeze toyed with her hair and skirt.

"You wanted to see me?" She stood straight, desiring to appear taller.

Weston looked up at her and she felt herself begin to shrink under his scrutinizing stare. She willed herself to the spot.

"Yes, I did, Miss Hampton."

She had hoped for him, but now that he stood before her, images of her foolishness flashed before her, and she felt ashamed to be in his presence. What did she hope he would say to her? Why had she wanted this? Was he here only to torment her? She stood frozen, unable to meet his gaze as her cheeks burned.

He took a step closer to her. When she moved away from him, he paused at the base of the stairs. Biting her lip, she looked down at him as he watched her. She thought she read pain in his expression, but it lasted only a moment.

"I'm sorry, but I have nothing to say to you." Her voice faltered as she spoke. She turned away from him, shaking, towards the house.

"Wait, please." In a single bound, he cleared the steps and appeared at her side. "This is ridiculous!" He took hold of her arm and pulled her gently round to face him.

She stepped back and tried to pull away from him. "Let me go!" Unexpected tears sprang to her eyes, and she blinked against them.

Weston shook his head, the pained expression returning. "I can't." He maintained a gentle but firm grip on her arm.

She looked up at him as a surge of fear rippled through her. The look in his eyes ceased her struggling against him. She could feel his earnestness. She allowed him to draw her into him and stood listening to his quickened breathing. His other hand came up and brushed over her cheek. She pressed into his hand, savoring the warm trail left on her skin. His touch swept across her lips. She shivered. She felt the sharp inhale that trembled through his body.

His breath felt warm over her neck as he leaned close to her ear.

"May I..."

She barely heard his whisper as his lips fell tenderly across hers. His touch was so light it surprised her at first, but in the softness of his kiss she felt his longing, his excitement. Her breath caught in her chest. She rested against his hand pressed to her back. He ended the kiss with a backwards step, but he held her chin cupped in his palm. His eyes reflected fear and his voice belied his trepidation.

"I love you, Isabelle."

He released her. She had no voice. She stared at him, dazed, and confused. He cleared his throat and turned away from her. His shoulders grew rigid. A tear slipped down her cheek.

"Why would you love me?" Her words shook and drew him back to her. His hand extended to her that she felt unworthy to accept. Her heart pounded.

He held his ground. "Why shouldn't I?"

A shiver ran through her as her lips trembled. She bowed her head in shame. "Because I was rude to you. I was ignorant and silly, and you were right about me being childlike. How could you love that?"

His fingertips slipped under her chin and raised her wet eyes to him. "You challenged me. You intrigued me. How could I not love you?"

She looked at his proffered hand. He stood waiting for her answer.

"You're this powerful man with status and whatnot. I don't fit in your world."

"But perhaps it is time for a new world. You brought a fresh perspective into my life, and I would be a fool to lose that."

"I don't deserve you. Every woman I've met would give anything to have your love, better women than me. I'm not what society expects for you. I'm not worthy."

Her words barely landed when he stepped forward and swept her into his arms. His swiftness pulled her into his chest and his strength surrounded her. He laid a gentle kiss on top of her head.

"We would never be humble if we felt worthy of living well. We would never appreciate the gifts of life if we felt we deserved them." He drew a breath and rested his cheek on her forehead. "If you reject my offer, then let your no be no. But if you will accept me, dear lady, I will consider it the greatest honor."

She laid her head against his chest. "I've dreamed you would say these things, but I never imagined I would hear them from you." She sniffed reflexively as tears threatened again.

Weston pulled back enough to see her face. Reaching into his breast pocket, he pulled out a handkerchief to offer her. She spied her initials embroidered onto the corner. Tears rolled down her cheeks as she raised her eyes to his.

"You really do love me."

He nodded and swallowed hard, dabbing away her tears. "I do."

An amazed chuckled escaped her lips amid the tears. "Hearing that is better than I ever thought possible. I've grown comfortable with you in my life and the thought of going on without you just about kills me."

He twisted a lock of her hair round his finger. "I give you my word. You shall never be without me again."

Her smile radiated pure joy and her eyes twinkled with excitement. "I love you."

If Isabelle had anything further to add, Weston never heard it for he pulled her into himself and buried her lips in a kiss that emanated his love and sealed his promise to her.

So lost were they in their revelry that they never noticed the dancing eyes peeking down on them from behind the curtains of the second story window as an approving smile spread through the features of Laura Millis

ABOUT THE AUTHOR

Victoria began writing long before she could actually write, using images rather than words to tell her stories. She developed her craft through telling the tales of characters similar to herself who aged and grew as she did. Relying on her experiences, she adopted a writing style that portrays snippets of real-world adventures and produces a snapshot of daily life. Victoria grew up surrounded by books and read a variety of styles, and genres throughout her childhood. Her love of literature and creative writing prompted her to complete a Bachelor of Arts in English with a focus in creative writing. While honing her skills as a writer, Victoria discovered a passion for short fiction and has presented her short stories at academic conferences and workshops. Victoria finds inspiration everywhere, but she learned the most from Stephen King, C.S Lewis, Jane Austen, and Richard Wagamese about narrative voice and the art of story telling.

Printed in the United States
by Baker & Taylor Publisher Services